Dear Diary,

Daniel Adler's getting m... to Kara Tamaki.

Even though I was the one who persuaded Daniel to talk to Kara about her visa problems, it's my brother, Drew, who's taking all the credit for pushing Daniel into this wedding. The two of them have become best friends over the past few years, and now that Drew's happily married to Julia, he wants to see everyone around him in the same blissful state.

Still…Daniel and Kara? We all know it's a green-card marriage, but that's what makes it even more astounding. Daniel never strays from the straight and narrow. He's a lawyer, for heaven's sake! What would make him risk his career this way? Could love be involved after all?

Kara's beautiful on the outside and the inside, and I'm thrilled that once she marries Daniel, she should be able to work here legally. Kara was a teacher in Japan, and I want to hire her to take over our preschool class at Forrester Square.

Maybe I shouldn't be in such a rush, though. If this is just a marriage of convenience, once Kara has a legal right to be here, she and Daniel might part company. Kara looks like a delicate Japanese butterfly, but she's got the heart and will of a lion. Maybe she's just what Daniel needs to knock his world off its axis!

Till tomorrow,

Katherine

JACQUELINE DIAMOND

began her career as an Associated Press reporter
and television columnist in Los Angeles, and has
interviewed hundreds of celebrities. Now a full-time
fiction writer, she has written over sixty novels, which
span romance, suspense and fantasy. Although
she was born in Texas and raised in Nashville and
Louisville, home is now in Southern California.
She and her husband are the parents of two sons.
Jacqueline has written over twenty-five books for
Harlequin American Romance. She is also a popular
author for Harlequin Intrigue and Harlequin Duets.

E 5A

Forrester Square
LEGACIES . LIES . LOVE .

JACQUELINE DIAMOND
ILLEGALLY YOURS

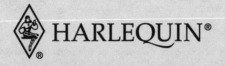

HARLEQUIN®

TORONTO • NEW YORK • LONDON
AMSTERDAM • PARIS • SYDNEY • HAMBURG
STOCKHOLM • ATHENS • TOKYO • MILAN • MADRID
PRAGUE • WARSAW • BUDAPEST • AUCKLAND

A thousand thanks to my friend Jina Bacarr

HARLEQUIN BOOKS
225 Duncan Mill Road, Don Mills,
Ontario, Canada M3B 3K9

ISBN-13: 978-0-373-61276-5
ISBN-10: 0-373-61276-1

ILLEGALLY YOURS

Jacqueline Diamond is acknowledged as the author of this work.

Visit us at www.eHarlequin.com

Printed in U.S.A.

Dear Reader,

Creating a heroine who's three-quarters Japanese proved a challenge, particularly for an author who's never visited Japan.

I relied upon books, articles, the Internet and the help of a friend and fellow author, Jina Bacarr (*How To Work for a Japanese Boss*). In the process, I learned to admire and treasure an ancient culture that's also a dynamic part of the twenty-first century.

Of course, my heroine, Kara, is very much an individual. The real fun was throwing her into a marriage of convenience with a most unlikely partner, Daniel Adler, and watching them fall in love despite vastly different personalities and attitudes.

I also enjoyed interweaving my story with the ongoing mystery of the Forrester Square series and its continuing characters. In addition to relying on our wonderful editors, some of the other authors and I e-mailed one another frequently and exchanged scenes to help make sure our books dovetail.

I'm happy to answer mail sent to me at P.O. Box 1315, Brea, CA, 92822, or e-mail at jdiamondfriends@aol.com. You can keep up with my latest Harlequin books at eHarlequin.com and at jacquelinediamond.com.

I hope you enjoy Kara and Daniel's story!

Best,

Jacqueline Diamond

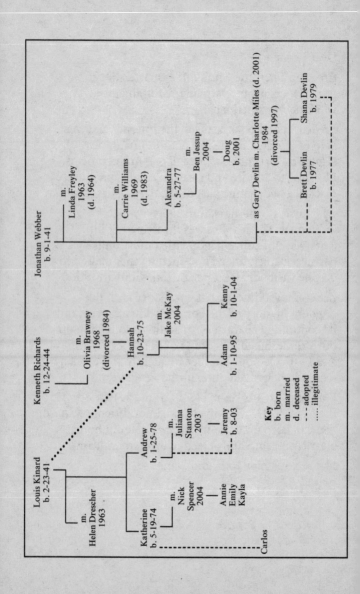

Louis Kinard
b. 2-23-41

m.
Helen Drescher
1963

Kenneth Richards
b. 12-24-44

m.
Olivia Brawney
1968
(divorced 1984)

Hannah
b. 10-23-75

m.
Jake McKay
2004

Adam
b. 1-10-95

Kenny
b. 10-1-04

Katherine
b. 5-19-74

m.
Nick Spencer
2004

Annie
Emily
Kayla

Andrew
b. 1-25-78

m.
Juliana Stanton
2003

Jeremy
b. 8-03

Carlos

Jonathan Webber
b. 9-1-41

m.
Linda Freyley
1963
(d. 1964)

m.
Carrie Williams
1969
(d. 1983)

Alexandra
b. 5-27-77

m.
Ben Jessup
2004

Doug
b. 2001

as Gary Devlin m. Charlotte Miles (d. 2001)
1984
(divorced 1997)

Brett Devlin
b. 1977

Shana Devlin
b. 1979

Key
b. born
m. married
d. deceased
- - - adopted
..... illegitimate

CHAPTER ONE

"YOU WANT MY ADVICE as the attorney for Forrester Square Day Care? Don't get involved in a messy situation that doesn't concern you." Daniel Adler flicked a spot of dust off his dress shoes. Although it was Saturday, he'd worn his best suit to the office because he was leaving shortly to attend a wedding.

Over the phone, he heard his client sigh. "Don't make up your mind until you meet her."

"I'm not planning to meet her." He glanced impatiently through his oversize glass windows. On clear days, he had a spectacular view of Mount Rainier. Today all he could see were a few feeble rays of early-afternoon sunlight struggling to break through the April fog.

"I'm afraid it's too late," said Katherine Kinard, his best friend's sister. She was also a co-owner of Forrester Square, one of Seattle's newest and most highly regarded day-care centers. "She's on her way over."

"I don't suppose she has a cell phone. You could call and stop her." Daniel knew even as he spoke that it was almost impossible to dissuade Katherine once she put her mind to something.

As she'd just explained, she'd been seeking a new teacher for the toddler group and was delighted when the outgoing young Japanese woman who delivered vegetables to the center turned out to have studied child development and taught preschool in Japan. Everything about the applicant clicked with Katherine, and she was on the verge of hiring her, pending a background check.

At the mention of providing fingerprints, the young woman had broken down and confessed that she was using a friend's ID. She lacked a work permit and apparently had some kind of visa problem, as well. Anyone else, including Daniel, would have shown her the door.

Not Katherine. If anything, obstacles only made her dig her heels in harder.

Although Daniel admired his client's tenacity, her refusal to accept his expertise annoyed him. Maybe they were too much alike, he conceded silently: both stubborn and take-charge.

That might be why he'd never felt romantically drawn to Katherine, although she was the sort of woman he ought to go for—accomplished, socially polished, well connected and a good conversationalist. Yet whenever he saw her in social situations, he felt no spark of romantic interest. Something was missing.

Something seemed to be missing in all the women he met, even the lady he'd invited as his guest to the wedding today. But then, Daniel had concluded long ago that he probably wasn't cut out to be a husband.

"You've got to help Tansho," Katherine insisted. "I mean, Chikara. As I told you, she borrowed her ID from someone named Tansho, although she has an international driver's license of her own," Katherine added. "The girl's nine months pregnant, for heaven's sake! She doesn't want to get sent back to Japan. You should hear her story. It'll break your heart."

"I'm a lawyer," Daniel said. "I don't have a heart."

"Was that a joke?" His client chuckled. "I don't believe it! My brother says you're so straitlaced you probably sleep in a button-down shirt. Kara's bringing out the best in you already."

"She needs an immigration lawyer," Daniel said. "Stephenson & Avenida deals with business, not visa issues. Furthermore, if I'm not mistaken, you're only a couple of hours away from becoming a bridesmaid. Aren't you supposed to be sticking flowers in your hair or something?"

"Kara's so upset, I just had to help her," Katherine continued doggedly. "She'll be there any minute. Talk to her." Before he could object further, she concluded, "See you at the wedding," and hung up.

Daniel grimaced. He'd come into the office to review contracts, not to talk to a woman with a visa problem. If what's-her-name—he glanced at his notes—Chikara Tamaki needed an attorney, he'd give her a referral.

He hoped she wasn't going to burst into tears. Displays of emotion made Daniel uncomfortable. His love of order was part of what had drawn him to law in the first place.

He was clicking through a list of immigration attorneys on his computer when the outer doorbell buzzed. Since there was no receptionist on Saturdays and he didn't want to disturb the senior partner working down the hall, Daniel strode through the outer office and opened the door.

The first thing he saw was a butterfly. The gossamer silk creation perched in shiny black hair, picking up the soft-peach color of the woman's jacket and the pale-blue of her flowing dress. She gave a hint of a bow and held up a red carnation, its stem wrapped in pink tissue paper.

"Daniel Adler? This is for you." There was a glimmer of worry in Chikara Tamaki's liquid eyes as she gazed up at him, and then she brightened. "Look! You can wear it in your buttonhole!" Her slender fingers reached out with the flower until he could almost feel them brush his lapel. She stopped short, her lips forming a little O of embarrassment. Quickly, she covered her mouth with her hand. "I'm sorry! Such an important man, and I am wasting your time. Please forgive me."

"Come in. Katherine just called." Taking the flower, he held the door. The woman was so tiny, she walked right under his arm. A light, teasing scent drifted in her wake, and in contrast to the muted hues of the office, her clothing glowed like springtime.

For a moment, Daniel couldn't think what to do next. It was the flower that confused him. He could hardly stick such a dainty thing in a vase, but he wasn't going to leave it on a desktop to wilt. Finally he removed the wrapping, tucked it in his buttonhole as she'd suggested and led the way to his office.

Once there, the woman turned toward him. Daniel had the stimulating sensation that she was looking beyond his trim haircut and tailored suit, taking in the man beneath. There was a directness about her, despite her demure manner, that made him keenly aware of her as a woman.

He blinked, hoping to clear away his odd response as he would a trace of film from his vision. It didn't work.

"You're so kind to see me," his visitor said. "I was surprised that an American lawyer works on a Saturday. I hope I'm not intruding."

"Please sit down." As she obeyed, he noticed that the artful folds of her dress obscured an enlarged abdomen. For nine months pregnant, she was in remarkably good shape. "Miss Tamaki—"

"Kara," she corrected. "I like the way Americans use first names. It's so friendly."

"You speak excellent English," he said.

"My grandfather was American. He was stationed in Japan after World War II and fell in love with my grandmother. He came to live with us after she died."

"So you grew up speaking English?"

"When I was with him, yes." She nodded for emphasis.

Her affable manner wasn't making his job any easier, but Daniel steeled himself. Sitting at his desk, he reached for the computer mouse. "I'm afraid I don't know anything about visas. I can give you a referral, however. I'll have a name for you in just a second."

"I can't talk to anyone else." Kara's chin came up. "Katherine trusts you. So do I."

"I'm the wrong kind of lawyer." He was quite certain her lack of comprehension had nothing to do with cultural differences. Nevertheless, if he repeated the truth often enough, they'd both have to accept it.

"Katherine said to talk to *you,*" the young woman insisted. "You won't turn me in to the police, will you?"

The police? "I'm not in the habit of sending young women off in paddy wagons," Daniel said, adding, "That's slang for police cars."

"I know." Her face brightened. "I love old American movies! *Cat Ballou. Bonnie and Clyde.* Did you see that one? I loved Bonnie Parker!"

"Don't tell me you have aspirations of becoming a bank robber." He couldn't imagine anyone less like the infamous bandit than Kara Tamaki.

With an impish grin, she held out her hands, wrists together. "Lock me up and throw away the key!"

"Nobody's going to get locked up." This playfulness had gone on long enough, Daniel decided. It was distracting him from his responsibilities. "You haven't committed any crime, as far as I know. Well, using someone else's ID isn't exactly legal, but as I understand it, you weren't trying to defraud anybody."

"I was delivering vegetables," Kara said. "Also fruits."

"Don't tell me your employer let you haul crates around in your condition!" He couldn't believe Katherine would have allowed it.

"No, no." The butterfly quivered as her head shook. "My friend Tansho Matsuba lets me make deliveries for her family's company because I need the money and I don't have a work permit. There's a man to carry things inside. I just do the driving."

Although he didn't usually go off on tangents, Daniel couldn't resist saying, "I'm surprised you don't get lost, driving around an unfamiliar city."

"Your addresses are easy to find," she told him. "In Japan, the houses are numbered depending on when they were built, not in order by place. Try finding your way around there!"

"I'd rather not." He returned to the subject at hand. "Since you already have a job, why did you apply to Forrester Square?"

"I love teaching." Kara sighed. "The children are so cute. You should see them playing in the yard like puppies."

"I'm sure they are." Daniel hadn't paid a lot of attention to the children on his visits to the day-care center. He'd always focused strictly on business matters. "How did you think you were going to land a job there without a work permit?"

"I didn't realize it was required. After all, Katherine knew I would take good care of the little ones. My first interview went well. Then this morning, she said they needed my fingerprints." Kara shuddered, as if the experience had been traumatic.

"That's when you broke down and told her the truth?" Receiving a nod, Daniel pressed on. "I don't suppose the father of your baby is American. That might help."

Tears glimmered in her eyes. "My husband was Japanese."

So there was a husband. "What happened to him?"

"He died."

No explanation? Perhaps it was difficult for her to speak about it, or perhaps this young woman was spinning a tale. Her situation might have torn at Katherine's heart, but it was beginning to arouse Daniel's innate skepticism. "Did he die before or after you arrived in the United States?"

"Before," she said promptly.

"Tell me something." Although Kara was gazing at him with enough doelike sweetness to melt an iceberg, he owed it to his client and his professional integrity to set aside his instinctive desire to aid her. "Is it customary in your country for a pregnant widow to apply for a visa and fly to a foreign country to live among strangers?"

"Tansho isn't a stranger. We became friends when she was an exchange student at my high school," Kara said. "Also, I don't have a visa."

Oh, great. This was going from bad to worse. "Are you telling me you were smuggled into this country?" Although local authorities sometimes turned a blind eye to illegal immigration, that didn't change the fact that, as an attorney,

Daniel was an officer of the court and sworn to uphold the law. Katherine had put him in a very awkward position.

The young woman stiffened. "I was not smuggled!"

Daniel waited. When she said nothing more, he prompted, "So how did you get here?"

"I have a visa waiver," Kara said.

"I'm afraid I've never heard of a visa waiver," Daniel admitted. "As I told you, I'm not an immigration attorney. What is it?"

"It's a program that allows tourists from friendly countries to come to the United States for up to three months," she said. "It's faster than getting a visa."

"Let's find someone who knows more than I do." From the computer screen, he selected the name of an immigration attorney he'd met several times at business-related functions. Although rather blunt, Edward Riley was well regarded in the legal community and certainly knew his stuff.

He jotted Ed's name and phone number on the back of one of his business cards. "This is who you should call."

She took the card without glancing at what he'd written. "It expires in two weeks."

"What does?"

"My waiver." She slipped the card into her purse. "I want to have my baby in America. There is no place for her in Japan. We both belong here, but especially her. I try to be strong for her sake, but I am desperate." Her lips trembled.

Daniel held firm. If there was one thing a lawyer should never do, it was allow himself to be manipulated by emotions. "I'm sorry I can't help you." He glanced at his watch. "I'm afraid I have an appointment. Let me see you out."

The color drained from Kara's cheeks as she got to her feet with only a trace of awkwardness. Reminded of her condition, Daniel took her elbow to support her as they exited. Through the soft fabric of her jacket, her arm felt slender, almost fragile.

He expected a torrent of protest or at least some reference to Katherine in an attempt to change his mind. Kara didn't speak at all. She walked so quietly that he looked down to make sure she was all right, but the only thing he saw was the butterfly bobbing atop her head.

When Daniel pushed on the rippled-glass doors to the hallway, Kara slipped past him and swung around. ''Thank you, Mr. Adler,'' she said, her voice scarcely above a whisper, and bowed low.

Large, stricken eyes peered up at him. Her hand flew to her mouth, as if she'd committed some gaffe, and away she fled down the hall. The elevator stood open, as if it had been expecting her.

Daniel started to say something, perhaps ''You're welcome,'' but the doors closed silently. She was already gone.

The hallway echoed with emptiness. And remorse.

She'd trusted him, when all along she must have been terrified. Despite her joking, the possibility of arrest had been very real to her. For the first time, Daniel tried to imagine what it would be like to be a pregnant woman, undocumented in a strange country. He couldn't, but he knew one thing. Coming here today had taken a great deal of courage.

Although he had done what any lawyer would have, perhaps that was the problem. He wasn't any lawyer. And this wasn't any woman.

She'd bowed and thanked him as if he'd done something to deserve her gratitude, when his behavior had been unchivalrous at best. The least he could do was make sure she actually went to see Ed Riley. He should make an appointment and escort her there himself next week.

What if Katherine couldn't reach her by phone? For all Daniel knew, Kara might be sleeping in the back of a warehouse. She might disappear, and he would never see her again.

He definitely needed to make sure she saw Ed, Daniel told himself as he hurried toward the stairs. Halfway there, he broke into a run.

KARA WRAPPED her arms around herself as she stood in the lobby, staring out at the busy street. What a fool she'd made of herself! Perhaps her mother-in-law had been correct: she was a worthless girl who hadn't deserved her husband and couldn't do anything right.

Her mother-in-law had also said that she would no doubt produce a girl child as stupid as she was. The memory of Mrs. Tamaki's cruel taunting stiffened Kara's spine. She could endure the gibes at herself, but not at her daughter.

When a doctor at the clinic she'd visited had performed an ultrasound to help establish her dates and had told her the child appeared to be a girl, Kara had felt only pride. She'd even chosen a name: Dorima, or dreamer.

She was a dreamer, too, but that was no excuse for her behavior upstairs. It was her own fault that things hadn't gone well. She'd talked too much and she'd said the wrong things.

An important man like Daniel Adler couldn't be expected to sit and listen to her chatter about movies and how much she loved children. Then she'd bowed at the end, when she knew that bowing embarrassed Westerners.

She should have acted more American. She should have told Daniel—Mr. Adler—exactly why she wanted to stay, instead of stammering like a bashful child.

She'd been nervous, of course, but that hadn't been the only problem, Kara admitted. The first moment she'd seen the man, she'd had trouble breathing, as if she'd just climbed Mount Fuji.

It wasn't simply his handsome face or the manly contours of his body that had impressed her, although Kara had registered those attributes immediately. More important, behind the confident smile, she sensed a deep wound in need of healing. He aroused in her the same gentleness she felt when children climbed into her lap, or used to climb into her lap when she still had one.

She'd felt something more, too, a sensation she couldn't name. Whatever it was, it belonged to Daniel and only to him.

She inhaled, trying to still her jitters. She must go back. She could not return to Katherine and explain that she'd failed. Summoning her nerve, she pressed the button for the elevator.

The bell sounded and the doors slid apart. Before she could step inside, the sound of someone calling her name froze her to the spot.

"Kara! Wait!" From off to the right, Daniel hurried toward her. His neatly clipped brown hair was ruffled, as if a breeze had danced across it. With his cheeks flushed and his lips parted, he looked like a man ready to claim a woman in his bed. An unfamiliar thrill tingled through Kara.

"I'm glad I caught you," he said. "Let's make an appointment for next week. I'll take you to see the other lawyer myself."

"If he can't help me, he might call the police," Kara protested. "I don't want to have my baby in jail."

Daniel shook his head. "He won't do that. Besides, you said you had two weeks left on your visa waiver."

"I haven't bought a ticket to Japan. They'll know I plan to stay." *They,* as they both knew, meant the immigration authorities.

Impatience twisted Daniel's mouth, and Kara feared she'd offended him with her objections. It was a relief when he smiled. "We're not done yet. Maybe there's something in your background that could help you make a case." He ran his fingers through his hair, further mussing it. "I'll tell you what. I'm on my way to a wedding. How about if I drop you somewhere? We can talk on the way."

"That would be lovely," Kara said. Climbing on and off buses had become increasingly difficult these past few months. "I live in the International District. Is that too far?"

"Not at all." Daniel directed her to a padded bench along one wall. "Wait here while I get my briefcase." He pressed the button to summon the elevator again. As he shifted to glance at her, she noticed how musically he moved, with the strength and flexibility of bamboo. "Don't go anywhere. Promise?"

"I promise." She would wait for hours if necessary.

After he disappeared, her abdomen rippled lightly. Dorima was expressing her opinion. "He makes you quiver, too, doesn't he?" Kara said.

She frowned at herself. It made no sense to think about Daniel this way, as if she were a gooey-eyed girl in a romantic movie. Kara liked strong heroines who had adventures, like Bonnie Parker. She had never had any patience with silly schoolgirl notions of romance.

She folded her hands over her stomach and tried to figure out how she was going to tell Daniel about her background, which must seem strange by American standards. And, most of all, how she was going to persuade him to change his mind about handing her off to another lawyer?

There was one thing about her that Kara didn't intend to let Daniel know, at least not right away. That was how strong-willed she could be.

The first moment she'd seen him, towering in his doorway with a bemused expression on his lean face, she'd known he was meant to be her friend and perhaps something more. If she were wise enough and brave enough, within a short while he would know it, too.

CHAPTER TWO

DANIEL COULD HARDLY concentrate on negotiating through the traffic in Seattle's downtown. He kept glancing at Kara, nestled like a spring blossom against the blue-gray cushions of his sedan.

It was more than ten years since he'd come here on vacation from his home in Chicago and fallen in love with the breezy spirit and international flavor of this city wedged between Puget Sound and Lake Washington. With her enthusiasm and freshness, Kara seemed to embody its most appealing qualities, even though she'd been here only a short time.

The sun was breaking through the fog as they drove beneath scatterings of trees. On the dappled sidewalks, lunch patrons relaxed at outdoor tables.

A leaf blew onto the windshield. Daniel was about to reach for the wiper knob to brush it away when Kara clapped her hands in delight. "How lovely!"

"What is? That thing?" Surely she didn't mean the wrinkled leaf stuck to the glass.

"See how brown and old it is?" she said, leaning forward to examine it.

"It's brown and old, all right."

Her dark eyes sparkled. "It has lasted all winter, holding on to its branch to protect it until a new leaf came to take its place. Now that its duty is done, it has let go at last."

Having raked more than his share of leaves as a boy, Daniel couldn't summon any sympathy for this specimen. "Maybe I should collect some for the bride. I'm sure she's foolishly gone out and bought a bunch of flowers for her bouquet."

"She can't carry old leaves down the aisle!" Kara exclaimed.

"Why not, if they're so gorgeous?"

"A wedding is a time for beginnings." She settled back. "Each thing is perfect in its place. That leaf is like a beautiful old person. Does it matter that the skin is papery when love and understanding shine from the soul?"

"You'd make a good lawyer," Daniel conceded.

"Me?" She blinked in surprise. "Why?"

"Because I haven't won an argument with you yet."

"I'm sorry," she said. "My mother-in-law says I talk too much. I think she is right."

Reminded of Kara's plight, Daniel said, "Surely your mother-in-law would want to help you. At the very least, she must be concerned about her grandchild."

"Mrs. Tamaki hates me," she said. "She hates my little girl, too."

"You're sure it's a girl?"

She nodded. "I'm going to call her Dorima."

"That's a pretty name—unusual, too," he said. "Listen, lots of people have in-law problems. I'm sure if push came to shove, though, she'd do the right thing."

"The only one Mrs. Tamaki pushes and shoves is me." The animation vanished from Kara's face. "She slaps me. She tells me I'm ugly and stupid. She wishes Hiro married a Japanese girl."

"I'm sorry?" He wondered if he'd heard wrong. "You *are* Japanese."

"As I told you, my grandfather was American," Kara said. "I am not pure Japanese."

In Chicago, Daniel had attended school with people from such varied backgrounds that they could have formed a miniature United Nations. No one had cared about or even noticed one another's ethnicity, let alone whether someone had a grandparent of a different race. "Is that important?"

"Back home, people are proud of their pure heritage," she said. "My father is ashamed to be half-foreign. You might say he tries to be more Japanese than the Japanese. Only my grandfather understood me, and he died when I was a teenager. I've tried to find some of his relatives, but no luck so far."

"They might be the answer to your problems, if they were willing to help." It was a far-fetched possibility, he acknowledged, especially since she'd already tried and failed to locate them. "Otherwise, you're better off going home."

"I can't." She left it at that.

The smell of the sea reminded Daniel that they were nearing the port. Downtown skyscrapers had given way to the redbrick buildings of the International District, where apartments rose above the street-level shops and restaurants. Signs bore Asian lettering, although he couldn't tell which ones were Japanese and which Chinese, Vietnamese or Korean. After checking the computer on his dashboard, Daniel headed for the address Kara had given him.

"I can understand that you don't get along with your mother-in-law, but surely your parents would take you in." He eased into a parking space in front of a four-story building. Between the ground-floor pharmacy and a copy shop was a doorway that he presumed led to overhead apartments.

Kara made no move to get out. "As a married woman, I belong to my husband's family."

"Not literally," Daniel corrected. Japan might be more traditional than the United States, but it had modern laws. "You're not their property."

"It would bring shame on my parents if I went back to them."

"And your father is sensitive about such things," Daniel filled in. "I'm beginning to get the picture."

If her family didn't want her, it made sense that Kara had no wish to go back to her own country. In America, she'd found a job, friends and apparently a place to live. Still, how was she going to manage once she had a baby?

Well, he couldn't solve her problems and, in any case, he needed to get moving. He'd promised to pick up his date for the wedding, an aerospace engineer named Brittany with whom he'd gone out several times, and it would take nearly an hour to get to her house and back. "May I have your phone number? I'll call you Monday and we can set something up."

She gave him the number, which he tapped into his pocket organizer. "I work in the mornings, very early," Kara noted.

"I'll call in the afternoon." She shouldn't still be working in her condition, Daniel reflected. Come to think of it, there were a lot of other issues that ought to be addressed. "By the way, are you seeing a doctor?"

"I've been going to a free clinic," she told him. "You are kind to take such an interest."

The tip of her tongue flicked across her lips as she regarded him obliquely. She didn't appear eager to leave, and in spite of his tight schedule, Daniel realized he was in no hurry for her to go, either. There were so many more questions to ask. It was fascinating just to watch the play of emotions on her expressive face.

"You seem remarkably capable," he said. "You've even managed to find an apartment. Do you share with someone?"

"No. I am very fortunate," she said. "My friends the Matsubas own the building. One unit needed repairs and painting. I have done some work, under their direction, and they allow me to live here at low rent."

The ring of his cell phone jolted Daniel. He flipped it open. "Adler here."

"Hi, it's Brittany."

He got a bad feeling. "Hi, Brittany. Is everything all right?"

"Not exactly," said his date. "I've been trying to fight off a nasty cold. A while ago I took some medicine, which cleared up the symptoms but now I can hardly keep my eyes open. I'd be a real drag at the wedding. I'd probably doze off and snore through the ceremony."

Daniel tried to summon a measure of sympathy. After all, it wasn't Brittany's fault she didn't feel well. On the other hand, accepting an invitation to an event, particularly when the bridal couple must have paid for their attendance at the reception, carried a serious obligation. Also, although their relationship had so far only involved seeing a movie and attending a museum opening together, he'd considered this a chance for Brittany to meet his friends.

He reined in his annoyance. "I understand. I hope you feel better."

"Sorry about missing your friend's big day." She didn't sound sorry, though; she sounded almost giddy. Perhaps that was another effect of the cold medicine.

After saying goodbye, Daniel snapped his phone shut. Mentally, he debated whether there was any point in calling the bride, Hannah Richards, who was also one of Katherine's partners in the day-care center. He decided against it. He'd have to make his apologies at the reception.

"What's the matter?" Kara asked. "I hope nothing is wrong with Hannah."

Since he hadn't mentioned whose wedding he was attending, Daniel realized she must have heard about the event at Forrester Square Day Care. Perhaps she even knew Hannah. "Not exactly. The woman who'd agreed to accompany me just begged off. She has a cold."

"Surely much worse." The young woman frowned. "Perhaps it is the flu and she doesn't want to worry you."

"It's just a cold." He heard the edge in his voice. "I suppose I should be more sympathetic, but I was raised to consider it rude to show up alone for a wedding after RSVP-ing for two. It may not be her fault, but she's put me in an awkward position."

"How embarrassing. It is a terrible thing to lose face." Kara's eyes lit up. "I know! I will accompany you. Then there is no rudeness." She bit her lip, as if afraid she was being too pushy. "Would that be helpful?"

"I'm not sure what the etiquette is." Daniel's brain debated the pros and cons. Pro: he'd be showing up with a date, as promised. Con: Kara was a client, or had almost become one, and he never socialized with clients. Pro: she seemed to know the bride and probably knew some of the other guests, as well. Con: being seen with her would inspire gossip, which Daniel hated. Pro: he wanted to spend more time with her. And this time, there was no con. "I don't see how it could hurt."

"In Japan, it is important for everything to look proper at a wedding," Kara said. "If the family is very small, the bride and groom may hire actors to play the part of relatives at the reception."

"You're joking, right?" The woman was constantly amazing him with her information.

"I am most solemn." She maintained a severe expression for a few seconds before her face burst into a smile. "I will love going to the wedding with you! Only a few minutes and I will be changed. Well, perhaps more than a few minutes. I would be happy to serve you tea in my apartment while you wait. American tea, of course! The Japanese ceremony cannot be hurried."

Tea? Her apartment? "Thanks, but I'll wait here," Daniel said, reeling beneath the torrent of words.

Kara thrust open the passenger-side door before he could come around to help her. "I will prepare as quickly as I can. I am very honored by this invitation!" Moving with remarkable lightness considering her condition, she sped into the building.

Daniel killed the motor and sat frowning through the windshield. Had he really agreed for her to accompany him to the wedding? It wasn't like him to act impulsively. Was it possible this sprite of a woman had bulldozed him?

He doubted she'd done so on purpose. As she'd pointed out, he welcomed the chance to avoid offending his hosts. He also had to admit that he was flattered by the implication that she might enjoy his company. Although he doubted the two of them had much in common, he found Kara entertaining.

Rolling down his window for ventilation, Daniel reached into the back seat for his briefcase and set to work reviewing contracts. He lost track of time until he heard footsteps on the sidewalk and looked up to see a vision from another time and place.

What was wrong with him, waxing poetic in the middle of the afternoon on a public thoroughfare? But Kara *was* stunning in a green silk kimono and a pink sash embroidered with yellow and white flowers. With her pale skin and burnished-black hair, which swung midway between her chin and shoulders, she gleamed in the sunlight.

As she slipped into the car, she looked so delicate that Daniel could hardly believe she was real. For the first time, he wondered about the husband who must have loved her very much. How distressed the man would have been to see his exquisite wife left penniless, forced to work late into her pregnancy and to live among strangers. If Daniel ever married, he would make provisions to protect the woman he loved.

A familiar bitterness formed at the back of his throat. His father had loved his mother and given her everything. Yet she'd thrown it in his face. How could Daniel be certain that if he married, he wouldn't end up the same way?

"You don't like it?" Kara smoothed her hands along the flowing cloth. "It is not the American style. Shall I change clothes?"

Ashamed of himself, he shook off the old negative thoughts. "Something else crossed my mind that has nothing to do with you. I love your kimono. You'll put every other woman in the shade."

"I must not do that!" Kara fastened her seat belt as he turned on the ignition. "No one must eclipse the bride."

"I didn't mean her," Daniel said. "Naturally, everyone admires the bride. I think it's a law. If the guests don't ooh and aah enough, they may be prosecuted."

"But you will defend them!" she sang out.

"I'll get them a reduced sentence. A week of smelling flowers at the Arboretum." He grinned. "That ought to make them appreciate beauty."

For a few minutes, he concentrated on making his way through the traffic toward the Harbor Club, where the ceremony and reception were to take place. Although she must have been driving through these streets herself for many weeks, Kara watched the passing scenery in fascination.

Daniel wondered which details caught her attention. His practical bent made him notice a new restaurant suitable for lunching with a client, a roadwork site to avoid in the near future, and a tilted awning that might represent a liability problem for the store owner. He doubted these were the details that sprang to Kara's eye.

He imagined she brought a different sensibility to every aspect of her life. Most likely, judging by her choice of a kimono, her idea of a wedding was very different from his, or from Hannah's.

"Tell me about your wedding," he said. "Did you wear a white dress, or isn't that the Japanese style?"

"Some Japanese women adopt Western fashions, but my family is traditional," she said. "My kimono had a beautiful scene painted on it, with many touches of red. Red is such a happy color."

"Do you mind talking about your husband?" Daniel asked as he drove.

"Of course not," Kara said. "I am pleased to tell you any details."

"I thought it might be painful," he explained.

"I am sad for him." She gazed down at her folded hands. "I am sad that he will never see his child."

"When were you married?" He stopped at a red light.

"A year ago," she said. "That is strange, when I think about it. Only one year ago, yet so much has happened."

Although Daniel knew it might be intrusive, curiosity pushed him to ask, "How did you two meet? Were you high-school sweethearts?"

"High school?" Kara asked in surprise. "Oh, no. Hiro was fifteen years older than me. It is best to marry a man who's established in his career."

"You make it sound so pragmatic. People rarely think of such things when they fall in love."

"Hiro was considerate and good-looking," she said earnestly. "Also, his company planned to send him to the United States for several years. That was one reason why he liked me, because my English is advanced. And I welcomed the chance to come here."

"Wait a minute." He was having trouble understanding her matter-of-fact attitude toward the man with whom she'd planned to spend her life. "You make this sound like it was a business arrangement."

"Every marriage is a business arrangement," she said calmly.

"Perhaps in Japan, but not here." The light changed at last, and he accelerated slowly with the traffic.

"As a lawyer, you must know that marriage is a legal contract in America, too," Kara pointed out.

"Well, yes, but most people don't think of that in advance." At least, he assumed they didn't.

"You mean Americans don't consider finances and children and how they plan to live?"

She had a point. "Some of us do, but a lot of us don't. You're awfully young to be so hardheaded, though." Katherine had given Kara's age as twenty-four.

"My family is more old-fashioned than some Japanese people," she explained. "They live on the northern island of Hokkaido, which is more traditional than Tokyo. I was raised to think of marriage as my job. To my parents, for a woman to be unmarried is the same as for a man to be unemployed."

The self-reliant young woman sitting next to him might be demure compared with American women, but she hardly seemed like the clichéd china doll. "You're obviously a capable person, the way you've landed a job and made yourself at home in Seattle," Daniel pointed out. "You must have gone to school, maybe worked before you got married. Now that I think about it, Katherine said you were a teacher."

"I went to college and I worked in a preschool," Kara said. "When I was twenty-three, my parents became concerned that I was getting too old, so they arranged a marriage for me. In our area, twenty-three is considered old, although in Tokyo the women aren't in such a hurry."

An arranged marriage in the twenty-first century? Daniel nearly asked if Katherine had put her up to playing a joke on him, but he suspected Kara might take offense. "Is this one of those situations where you met for the first time at the altar? Don't tell me the groom didn't see your face until after the vows were said and you lifted your veil!"

"Japanese brides don't wear veils," Kara said. "They wear a hat shaped like a boat."

"I didn't mean that literally!" Following the instructions on his dashboard computer, Daniel made a right turn.

"You're laughing at me." Her cheeks reddened. "I have told no one about how my marriage was arranged because I don't expect most Americans to understand. I thought you, an attorney, would be more open-minded."

She'd made him feel ashamed of himself. "I apologize," Daniel said. "As you mentioned before, marriage is a contract. Maybe we'd all be better off if our parents picked our partners and we evaluated each other as if we were going into business together. It could hardly make our divorce rate any worse."

"You're still not serious." She narrowed her eyes as if daring him to disagree with her.

"I'm fascinated." As they approached the club, Daniel paused in a line of cars waiting for a valet. "How does this arranged-marriage stuff work?"

Kara pressed her lips together, and for a moment he feared she might refuse to answer. At last she said, "It is called *omiai.* The family consults other families for the names of suitable matches."

"They don't go to some sort of marriage broker?"

"There are marriage bureaus, even video dating, but it is more common to go through acquaintances," Kara said. "We exchange photographs and résumés, and then we and our families dine together at a hotel. I met two other men before Hiro, but I didn't like them."

"Too ugly?" Daniel teased.

"Too boring," she said. "I don't have romantic fantasies like Western women. I wanted a man I could talk to."

"Hiro must have been interesting, then." The car edged forward in the slow-moving line.

"We found many things to talk about," she said. "Foreign-trade agreements. International politics. The virtues of Japanese versus American films."

"That's what makes your heart beat faster?" Daniel asked, only half joking.

"I told you, I don't have romantic fantasies," Kara said coolly. "Is this so hard to believe?"

Her story seemed less far-fetched when put into perspective, Daniel decided. Americans in search of mates took out classified ads, went on the Internet and even indulged in something called speed dating. A paralegal at the office had described it as a mass audition in which each couple spent five minutes in conversation before moving on to the next potential partner.

If Daniel had been willing to rely on his father to pick a spouse for him, he supposed he'd have been married by this time. Instead, he'd managed to reach the age of thirty safely single, and he planned to remain so.

He thought about the house he'd bought in Bellevue—a thriving community east of Seattle across Lake Washington—and was currently remodeling. Although he doubted men had the same nesting instinct he'd heard attributed to women, he'd begun to find his condominium confining and had been gratified when it sold quickly. He looked forward to moving next weekend and finally being able to enjoy his new premises.

A man could do just fine by himself. After witnessing his parents' painful divorce, he had no desire to run that kind of risk.

Guiltily, Daniel realized Kara was waiting for his response to her last statement. "I believe you. So you and Hiro weren't madly in love but you liked each other?"

"He was very considerate," she said.

That was hardly rapturous praise. "You became friends?"

"We suited each other," Kara said carefully. "We had only a few months together, but I'm sure our friendship would have grown."

"Do you mind if I ask how he died?"

"One day after work, he went with his friends to a karaoke club," she said. "It is customary to have several drinks and let down your hair, as my grandfather would have said. When they came out, he stepped into the street without looking and was hit by a taxi."

Her straightforward, unemotional manner wasn't what Daniel had expected, but he appreciated her reserve. He'd never enjoyed the way some people, whether on TV talk shows or in the office lunchroom, spilled out their personal angst to anyone who would listen. Just because a person didn't wail and carry on didn't mean he or she lacked deep emotions. No one knew that better than he did.

Another thought occurred to him. "Did Hiro know you were pregnant?"

"Yes," she said. "He was pleased, I think."

"You *think?*" This was carrying self-restraint to the point of rigor mortis. One man at Daniel's office had brought doughnuts and coffee for everyone the day he got the good news, and another had proudly shown off the diamond necklace he'd bought to surprise his newly pregnant wife.

"Hiro gave me flowers the next day," Kara said. "I told you he was considerate."

They finally reached the valets. Even though one of them handed Kara out of the car, Daniel hurried around to take her arm. While she was with him, he considered her under his protection.

In the lobby, they ran into several acquaintances, who regarded his companion with puzzled interest. Daniel returned their greetings and introduced Kara, but made no explanations.

Let them gossip about her pregnancy if they wished. People ought to mind their own business, Daniel thought, and signed their names in the guest book. He'd sent his gift earlier, which saved him the task of seeking out the gift table.

Not until he took Kara's arm did he realize she was trembling. Her vulnerability touched him. This brave little creature wasn't as rock-steady as she appeared.

Slipping his arm around her waist, Daniel tried to let her know without words that she had nothing to fear while she was with him. The message seemed to get across, he gathered, because she straightened and the shivering stopped.

Together they entered the room where a man and a woman were to be joined in holy matrimony. Daniel realized he had a sense of rightness about the fact that Kara and not Brittany had accompanied him today, as if she was meant to be here.

He gave an involuntary shake of the head. He didn't believe in inevitability or fate or any of that nonsense. Things happened at random, or else people made them happen.

Like Kara, he nursed no romantic fantasies. And he wasn't about to start now.

CHAPTER THREE

KARA HAD NEVER understood why some women cried at weddings. What was there to be sad about, unless the bride was marrying a bad man? And if a woman was so foolish as to do that, why had her family and friends allowed the unfortunate relationship to proceed?

To her, a wedding was a beautiful spectacle. It was hard to imagine a setting lovelier than this one, with glass walls giving a spectacular view of the water and the mountains in the distance. Lilting music from a keyboard and clarinet seemed to blend harmoniously with the curving lines of the room set up for the ceremony.

Although she didn't recognize most of the guests, a few were familiar. A smartly dressed woman in her sixties, Helen Kinard, turned and, noticing Daniel sitting beside Kara, gave her a discreet wink. Kara smiled back and offered a slight bow, grateful for the friendliness of Katherine's mother. The retired elementary schoolteacher often assisted at the day-care center.

She tried not to stare at Helen's handsome husband. The center of an old scandal, Louis Kinard had been convicted of embezzlement and stealing software technology from his own firm. His recent release after twenty years in prison had stirred such intense media interest that even a newcomer like Kara had heard about it. Had he been Japanese, he would have been expected to make a public apology, but as far as she knew, Katherine's father had never admitted his guilt.

His stooped shoulders revealed how heavily his terrible

shame must weigh. He was lucky to have the love of a stead-
fast woman.

Watching the elderly couple, whose marriage had weathered such a storm, made her acutely aware of her own escort.
Although he might seem stern, Daniel Adler struck Kara as
the kind of man who, once he dedicated himself to a cause
or a marriage, would not waver.

He was also, evidently, the kind who buried himself in
work, or surely a woman would have claimed him by now.
Perhaps, she recalled, one already had: the absent Brittany. If
the woman hoped to succeed with this man, however, she was
off to a rocky start.

It was hard to imagine what kind of woman might please
him, or how such a woman might do so. Kara suspected that,
unlike with Hiro, keeping a low profile while managing the
home and the children would not be enough. Brittany had
better be careful. She had clearly annoyed her boyfriend today, and he was a man who deserved better than such cavalier
treatment.

To Kara, most people appeared in pale tints, like spring
petals drifting by on a breeze. With his intense silences and
probing gaze, Daniel was a stroke of black ink and a splash
of scarlet so vibrant that she could feel his heat against her
skin.

More and more people filtered into the room. "This is quite
a turnout," Daniel said. "Did you have a big wedding?"

"The ceremony itself was just for family," Kara said. "At
the reception, my father and Hiro's family invited many business associates."

She'd felt like a figurine being shown off. There'd been
little emotional connection with her guests and an acute
awareness of the need to extend every courtesy to the supe-
riors from Hiro's company.

"Was there dancing? Singing? People kicking off their
shoes and making fools of themselves?" he asked lightly.

Kara gave him a startled look. "I believe our guests had a

good time. There was entertainment and singing. No one got very drunk, though.''

"Your parents must have been thrilled. I mean, they'd married you off before you had to join the Elderly Japanese Spinsters Society,'' Daniel joked.

"My mother was happy because my father was happy,'' Kara said. "So was my brother, Enoki. For once, they all approved of me.''

"What about now? They must find it strange that you took off for a foreign country in your condition.''

"They pretend that I am merely visiting my friend Tansho and will soon return,'' she said. "I send them postcards and e-mails describing the beautiful sights of Seattle.''

"How bizarre." Daniel stretched his long legs beneath the empty chair in front of him. A tingle ran through Kara as he accidentally brushed her thigh. Hiro had always held himself politely apart from her in public or private, except when they were in bed. Even then, he had been tidy and efficient.

She didn't want Daniel to keep himself apart; she wanted him to inspire more of these tantalizing sensations. Was this how American women felt with a man? Or was she abnormal in some way?

What foolish ideas! To Daniel, she was simply a friend of a friend whom he had generously offered to help. At most, he might look kindly on her for helping him save face by attending the wedding in place of his ailing lady friend.

"Why do you find it bizarre that I spare my family embarrassment?' she asked. "Wouldn't you do the same?''

"Not if it forced me to lie. My dad hates anything that strays from the straight and narrow.'' He took her hand and traced the back lightly with one finger. Rivulets of longing flowed through Kara to parts of her body very far from her hand.

His words, however, stirred a less-pleasant reaction. "Do you think I'm dishonest?'' Gently, she removed her hand. Daniel blinked, as if unaware that he'd been holding it. "I'm not a liar, I promise you.''

"I didn't mean that. Katherine recommended you, and that's enough for me. I guess we're talking about cultural differences."

"In Japan, people strive for harmony, and too much directness can cause discord or pain," Kara explained. "Besides, Americans tell white lies, too."

"That we do," he agreed. "We call it diplomacy. I guess it's all a matter of perspective."

She nodded, satisfied with his explanation. It had restored the harmony between them.

A couple sat down in front of them, and moments later some new arrivals took the seats to one side. She knew instinctively that Daniel didn't want to continue their discussion within hearing of others.

Some of his traits were almost Japanese, Kara thought. His discretion, for example, and his dismay at the possibility of offending his hosts after his date called to cancel. Also, his hard work, as shown by his presence at his office on a Saturday.

However, she knew better than to assume that she understood him. For Kara, living in a foreign culture often seemed like walking through a minefield, every step a venture into dangerous territory. Then again, she'd sometimes felt that way in her homeland, too.

Giving her full attention to the front of the room, she admired the spray of flowers adorning the altar and the handsome groom standing beside it. Jack McKay looked almost too rugged for his charcoal cutaway coat and gray pinstriped pants. When she'd seen him visiting Hannah at the day-care center, Kara had immediately noticed the scar below his left eye and the slightly crooked nose, signs of a rough early life, or so she'd heard. But he looked tall and commanding as he awaited his bride.

She glanced past the groom's half brother, who was the best man, to the childishly eager figure beside him. Nine-year-old Adam Hawke was, in Kara's opinion, doing a fine job of not fidgeting.

It was Adam who had brought Hannah and Jack together, or rather, *back* together, according to Katherine. She'd explained that while Hannah was attending college in Dallas, she had fallen for Jack, a ranch hand with a reputation for wild living. Although it had thrilled Hannah to defy the strait-laced standards of her family's social circles back in Seattle, neither she nor Jack had believed their relationship was based on anything more than sexual attraction.

When she discovered she was pregnant, reality had hit Hannah hard. She'd been unable to find Jack to tell him, and had relinquished the boy for adoption.

Recently, when she'd tried to find Adam, Hannah had been shocked to discover that Jack had learned of his existence, straightened out his own life and raised the boy himself since infancy. Now the three of them were going to be a real family. In fact, since Hannah was pregnant again, they would soon be a foursome.

Reminded of her own situation, Kara slid her hand across her stomach, touching the hard bulge through the soft kimono. As if in response, her baby wiggled. It was all Kara could do not to laugh out loud.

"What is it?" Daniel ducked his head close enough to keep their conversation private. A hint of aftershave, reminiscent of a fresh sea wind and a cargo of spices, beguiled Kara.

"She poked me with her elbow," she said.

He glanced around. "Who?"

"My baby."

His high-boned face registered amusement. "You can feel her elbow?"

Kara nodded.

"How do you know it's not a knee?"

"Too sharp," Kara said.

"Some people have sharp knees."

"Are you always this difficult?" she shot back, and immediately worried that she'd gone too far. "I'm sorry!"

"No, you're right." Daniel grinned. "I like provoking people by splitting hairs. One of my professors was disappointed when I told him I didn't plan to go into criminal law. He said I ought to, since I'd easily drive the opposing counsel crazy.''

"Is that good?" Kara asked dubiously.

"It's excellent."

"Then you can drive me crazy, too," she said. "I don't mind."

"Be careful what you wish for," Daniel murmured. "You might get it."

At the implication that they were going to spend more time together, Kara's blood quickened. She wished he really meant it. She would love to be Daniel's lady friend and joke with him the way American women did.

It was impossible, of course. She carried Hiro's baby, and she had much more serious problems than a childish longing to be swept away by a man.

The musicians began to play a processional. Kara, along with the other guests, shifted to see better as Katherine and Alexandra, Hannah's two best friends and business partners, strolled side by side down the aisle. Each carried a single white calla lily. In their coral gowns, with shoulders bared, the co-maids of honor resembled princesses from a fairy tale.

"Now, there's a mismatched set." Daniel's voice rumbled close to her ear.

Kara regarded him in surprise. "Why do you say that?"

"Their heights, for one thing. And their coloring."

They *were* quite different, Kara had to agree; Katherine was tall, with shoulder-length chestnut hair, while a feathery red mop crowned Alexandra's shorter frame. As the pair passed, Alexandra performed a quick shuffle to catch up with Katherine's longer stride.

But Americans came in all shapes and sizes, as the saying went. Kara enjoyed their differences. In Japan, people didn't even need to put their eye and hair color on their driver's licenses, because they were the same.

"Don't you have a saying that variety is the spice of life?" she whispered back.

"Touché," came the answer.

There was no more time for talking. The music swelled and, to a collective sigh from the audience, the bride stepped into view on her father's arm.

All the light in the room seemed to emanate from this slender figure. To Kara, Hannah might have been spun of pale gold, she shimmered so brightly. She was softness and grace, from her honey-blond hair to the ivory gown with its beaded empire bodice and satin organza skirt. Her bouquet of calla lilies completed the dazzling portrait.

Escorting her down the aisle, Kenneth Richards cut a dashing figure with his athletic build. What a handsome man, Kara thought. Since Hannah spoke of him as an ideal father, it was hard to imagine why Hannah's mother had divorced him while their daughter was a child.

As Kara followed their progress down the aisle, she was surprised to see Olivia Richards watching from the front row with an almost malicious smugness that appeared aimed at her ex-husband. Kara shivered, reminded of the way her mother-in-law used to shoot her hateful looks while maintaining a polite facade for others.

Quickly, Olivia's features rearranged themselves into a proud smile suitable for the mother of the bride. The calculating manner in which she transformed herself chilled Kara even more than the earlier sneer. It amazed her that such a sweet young woman could descend from such an unlikable mother.

Hannah reached her groom. Jack's joy merged with hers, surrounding them with a radiance that made Kara forget her dark thoughts.

She didn't try to follow the words of the ceremony. Sometimes it became a strain to follow long passages in English, and doubly so when the words were blurred by the acoustics of a large room. Instead of struggling to keep up, she allowed herself to relax and enjoy being in this lovely place with all these happy people.

Nearly three months ago, Kara had flown to Seattle with

little idea of what to expect, even though she'd visited Tansho once before. She'd been eager but also afraid.

In this short time, she'd come to know a new world full of hopes and dreams. Although she missed friends and relatives in Japan, she knew deep in her heart—perhaps had known since she was a little girl listening to her grandfather's stories—that she belonged in a place like this.

Kara peeked at Daniel, who leaned forward, listening raptly. Could he really help her? All he'd promised was to take her to an immigration attorney, but she had no money to pay one. Moreover, in any country, those most likely to conquer bureaucratic systems were those who had both knowledge and a determination to succeed. Despite his initial reluctance, she had known from the moment she first saw Daniel that he was a man she could rely on.

Now all she had to do was convince him of that. But how?

The only way she knew to influence a man was to be as charming and refined as her parents had always exhorted her to be. If she was flawless, she would be irresistible. Unfortunately, Kara had a talent, if it could be called that, for behaving clumsily and blurting the wrong thing.

She had a few hours in which to captivate Daniel Adler. She also had a few hours in which—if she followed her usual course—to spill a drink on him, get food stuck in her teeth or accidentally insult someone close to him.

Taking a deep breath, Kara tried to will herself to be absolutely above reproach for the rest of the day. She would rather have been charged with climbing the Space Needle using a set of suction cups. She'd have had at least as good a chance of reaching her goal, and if she failed, the end would be quicker and more merciful.

To DANIEL, PARTICIPATING in large social gatherings was like attending the symphony. If the orchestra played a piece with which he was familiar, it surged around him comfortably and he never got lost. The minute the players launched into something new, particularly if he didn't recognize the style or the composer, he struggled uneasily to get a handle on what he was hearing and usually had a rotten time.

Similarly, he didn't mind social gatherings if he knew his role. He could play the young lawyer making contacts or the host welcoming guests. However, at a wedding reception, there was no particular part assigned to a friend of the family who also happened to be the attorney for Forrester Square Day Care.

The first step was easy: congratulating the groom and giving the bride his best wishes. Then Daniel exchanged greetings with the people he knew, but not being good at small talk, he couldn't find much to say to them. Kara declined punch and hors d'oeuvres, so he couldn't even busy himself looking after her.

He surveyed the room, which was swirling with animated people, each of whom seemed merrily engaged in conversation. What on earth did they find to talk about once they got past exclaiming over the ceremony? More than ever, he was grateful for Kara's presence, which spared him from total social meltdown.

"I never know what to do at these things," he admitted. There was no point in mentioning the possibility of dancing, although the musicians from the ceremony had been joined by a drummer and were taking requests. For one thing, Kara was in no condition to bounce around. For another, although he knew how to acquit himself respectably on a dance floor, Daniel disliked the awkward sense of being out of his element.

He was in no mood to line up for one of the sailboat rides being offered outdoors, either. Getting a faceful of spray while dressed in a suit wasn't his idea of fun.

"Surely you aren't required to do anything," Kara told him. "People admire you the way you are."

"Standing here like a lamppost?" he scoffed.

"A lamppost shines light on everything around it," she answered.

The lady was gifted. Daniel wished he could come up with

a line like that when he needed it. "Now that's what I called
a tactful response."

"Thank you."

Across the room, a mousy young woman in a loud dress
caught his eye. "Uh-oh." Daniel glanced around for the wedding planner, Dana Ulrich, who'd been instructed to keep
members of the media at bay. The last thing Hannah and Jack
wanted was anyone harassing Louis Kinard at their reception.

"What's wrong?" Kara asked.

He pointed. "See that woman in red? She's not supposed
to be here, although it has nothing to do with her being a
walking fashion disaster. And please, don't find something
nice to say about her, because even you have to admit it's a
hideous outfit."

"It could be improved on," Kara conceded. "Why isn't
she welcome?"

"Debbie North is a newspaper reporter. I suppose she's
good at it, because she never gives up, but this event is closed
to the media. She has a lot of nerve, crashing a wedding!"

Debbie had written a number of in-depth stories about
Louis when he was first released. She'd tried to pry information out of anyone even remotely connected to the family,
including Daniel, who'd been forced to issue a series of *No
comment*s before she gave up. During recent months, he'd
seen her byline on an article rehashing the death of Alexandra's father in a house fire.

On the point of nominating himself to escort the reporter
out of the room, Daniel saw Katherine stop to talk to her.
Surprisingly, their conversation appeared friendly.

"What do you know? It looks as if she was invited." He
shook his head in disbelief.

"Katherine must have taken a liking to her," Kara said. "I
imagine she sympathizes with a woman who works so hard
at her job."

"Let's hope that North woman understands the difference
between people talking on the record and people carrying on
private conversations she might overhear." At last Daniel put

his finger on why the woman's presence disturbed him so much. "Don't mention your legal situation within her hearing. She might sense a human-interest story and write you up. I can assure you as a lawyer that the last thing you need is publicity."

Kara's eyes grew large. "Why?"

Before he could answer, he saw Katherine bearing down on them. "Daniel! Kara!" As always, Daniel felt the force of her hard-driving personality, softened by an equally powerful warmth. "I'm not going to say one word about the fact that you're here together! Well, all right, I already did, but I won't do it again. What a gorgeous kimono, Kara! I love that shade of green."

"Thank you." Kara gave a small bow. "The bridesmaid dress is very flattering to you. What perfect shoulders! I could never wear anything so daring."

"Thank you."

Daniel considered asking about Debbie North's presence and decided it was none of his business. Instead, he said, "I'm going to arrange for Kara to see an immigration attorney next week. I'm afraid I don't know anything about visa waivers."

"I know you'll do your best," the tall woman replied cheerfully.

Daniel tried to think of a suitably innocuous response, but it was hopeless. He didn't have the right personality for chit-chat. With relief, he spotted Katherine's brother across the room, temporarily adrift from his new wife, Julia.

"I'm going to go say hello to Drew," he told them. "If you ladies will excuse me?"

"Of course." Kara started to bow and stopped in confusion.

"It's all right," he told her. "You're free to follow whatever customs appeal to you."

"I like this!" Katherine said. "You actually talk to her. Words flow from your lips."

"I'm sorry?"

"You're normally a man of deep thoughts and few words,"

Katherine replied. "There's something different about you with Kara. But I wasn't going to mention that!"

"I can't tell you how profoundly I appreciate it," he murmured ironically. The odd part was that, as he left them to greet his friend, he had to suppress a sudden impulse to bow to the ladies. He almost wished his own society included more formalities. They might make social occasions easier on people like him.

But Katherine was wrong about one thing. Daniel didn't believe there was anything different about him when he was around Kara. He simply wanted to make a foreign visitor feel comfortable in an alien culture, because on occasions like this, he knew exactly how she felt.

"Spill the beans!" Katherine demanded.

"I'm sorry?" Although she'd spoken English since early childhood, Kara didn't always grasp idioms.

"That means, tell me everything," her friend explained. "How did you get our notoriously gun-shy friend to bring you? At least, I'm assuming you came with him."

"Yes. He had invited a lady friend, but she became ill." Kara's gaze followed Daniel's progress as he approached Drew Kinard, who shook back his longish hair and clapped Daniel on the shoulder.

"Daniel has a lady friend? That's news to me." Katherine waited with obvious curiosity.

Hope fluttered inside Kara. "Perhaps she is only a casual acquaintance. I would be sad if he was already taken." What was she saying? "I mean, he deserves a woman who makes a greater effort to keep her social engagements."

"Do I detect a romantic interest?" teased her tall companion. "Go for it! If he has a relationship, it isn't of long standing. Daniel went to a dinner-dance with Hannah, Alexandra and me in January, and there was no mention of any girlfriend. Frankly, I think he's a great catch."

Kara hoped she wasn't missing some subtle signal from her

friend. "I know he's a close acquaintance and you are both single. Perhaps you are the one with a romantic interest."

"In Daniel?" Katherine laughed. "He's a great guy, but we strike about as many sparks as a wet blanket."

"I'm sorry?"

"We don't turn each other on," her friend clarified.

"I think I understand. You dream of someone with more…" Kara paused as she searched for the right word.

"Oomph," Katherine filled in. "I want to be swept off my feet."

"You might fall and hurt yourself!"

"No. I might fall in love!" came the response. "My idea of Mr. Right is a guy so crazy about me, I'm his reason for getting up in the morning and, definitely, for going to bed at night! Is that asking too much?"

"I've never seen a man act like that with a woman," Kara admitted.

"Certainly not Daniel," Katherine said.

Kara wondered if it was possible for him to lose himself so completely in emotion. She doubted it.

Across the room, something Drew said must have made Daniel uneasy, Kara noticed, studying him surreptitiously. Beneath the tailored suit, she could see his muscles stiffening and read tension in his jaw. "I agree. He has a conservative nature."

"Truthfully, it doesn't sound like anyone I'm likely to meet in this lifetime." Katherine's mouth pursed. "I don't mean to sound like I'm feeling sorry for myself, even though I am."

"Why?" Kara could see no reason for the founder of Forrester Square Day Care to be downhearted. "Many people cherish and need you."

"What a sweetheart you are!" The tall woman gave her a hug, careful not to squeeze her too tightly. "No wonder everyone likes you!"

"Do they?" The compliment made Kara blush.

"You bet!" A determined smile replaced the wistful expression. "I haven't given up on hiring you to work with the toddlers, you know, once Daniel gets your immigration status sorted out.''

''I would love that!''

''Me, too. I like happy endings.'' Katherine gazed around the busy room. ''What a great day!''

''It certainly is.'' Kara became aware of gentle movements inside her womb. They came so frequently these days that she didn't always notice them right away, as if they were a part of her.

It must be agonizing to give up a child, as Hannah had done. These past months, Kara had tried very hard not to think about the possibility that adoption might be the best course for Dorima, and the closer she came to her delivery date, the less she was willing to consider it. Surely Daniel would help her sort things out so there would be a happy ending for her and her daughter, too.

''Look at my parents.'' Katherine indicated the couple circling the dance floor, their faces suffused with tenderness. ''Despite everything they've been through, their love has triumphed. They've set the example I'd like to follow, if I could just find the right man.''

The slow music was replaced by a rock beat that made Dorima kick harder. As Kara watched, Alexandra surged onto the dance floor, pulling her date with her. The man, who dwarfed his petite companion, had a trim mustache and sideburns.

''Do you think those two will find such happiness?'' she asked, and realized she already knew the answer. Alexandra seemed more interested in smiling and waving at friends than in flirting with the man. She was far from being in love.

''Who can tell? That's Griffin Frazier, by the way,'' Katherine said. ''I don't know if you've met him.''

Kara shook her head.

''He's a police officer,'' she said. ''Nice fellow, but I don't think Alexandra's as smitten with him as he is with her. Well, she's one up on me. I can't even find Mr. Maybe.''

''You seem troubled.'' It wasn't like Katherine to feel sorry for herself. "What is the American expression? Ah, yes. 'Something's eating you.'"

"So it is," her friend said. "I'm glad you brought it up, because I need a good listener."

"I am pleased to listen." Kara was honored to be chosen as a confidante.

"Next month, I'll celebrate my thirtieth birthday. I always imagined I'd be married and have children by now."

"You do have a child." Kara indicated Carlos, Katherine's thirteen-year-old foster son. In one corner, he and Adam were striking silly poses and snapping photos of each other with disposable cameras.

"He's a wonderful kid, isn't he?" her friend said. "There's a wise old soul inside that gangly teenage body. He made me sit in the Wishing Chair at the Smith Tower, not that it will do any good. There's nothing mystical about true love."

Kara had also visited the historic building, once the tallest in the West, with Tansho. They'd both giggled when they saw the old Chinese chair, which was said to possess a special magic: any unmarried woman who sat in it would be married within a year.

Tansho had insisted Kara perch on it for a photograph to send to her parents. Afterward, they'd both dissolved in fits of giggles. "Old legends can be charming, but I agree, they're not very reliable. I sat in it, too, and there is no chance I will marry soon!"

"We can't trust luck to put our lives on track." Katherine squared her shoulders. "So I'm going to take fate into my own hands. You've got to promise not to tell anyone what I'm about to say. Not even Daniel."

"I promise." Kara would never divulge a friend's secret. Grateful that Katherine trusted her, she waited eagerly to hear what plan her friend had made.

CHAPTER FOUR

KATHERINE LOWERED her voice. Kara leaned forward to hear over the music. "I've decided to have a baby on my own. I'm going to call a sperm bank and make an appointment."

One of Katherine's American friends would probably have answered, "Good for you!" Although Kara wanted to be supportive, too, she wasn't sure how to react to the idea of a woman deliberately seeking motherhood without a mate.

She sought a tactful response. "You're lucky to be part of a loving family. Having them to turn to should make it easier to raise your child."

Katherine, as usual, took a more direct approach. "Do you think I'm out of my mind?"

This time, Kara didn't hesitate. "I think you're brave. I also think the men you know are missing their chance. Any man who has a chance to marry you is foolish not to fall in love with you, and then you could have a child together."

A sigh greeted this comment. "If only it were that simple. Love isn't something that strikes just because you like someone."

"Surely you can arrange for it to happen, if you really want to," Kara said.

"I wish that were true, but it's not. Love catches you off guard and throws you into the arms of someone when you least expect it. That's how I've always dreamed it would be."

Kara frowned. "I don't want to be caught off guard and thrown into someone's arms."

"Haven't you ever dreamed of meeting your soulmate?" Katherine asked.

"I don't dream about men," Kara replied. "My goals were always to become independent and travel to America."

"I have goals, too," Katherine said. "I've worked hard to start the day-care center and I took the risk of accepting an open-ended loan that I have no way of paying back. Love is different. You don't have to earn it."

Kara struggled to grasp what she meant, but couldn't. "I'm afraid I don't understand. I have to work at everything I do."

"What about your husband?" her friend asked. "When you met him, didn't the earth move?"

"An earthquake?" Kara shuddered. Such events were dangerous in Japan, and elsewhere, she presumed.

"I mean, didn't your heart beat faster?" Katherine pressed. "Maybe you found it hard to breathe. And he seemed, oh, somehow more real than anyone else you'd ever met. Wasn't it like that?"

Hiro had been a sturdily built man, pleasant and intelligent, not unlike many of her parents' friends. His death had shocked Kara, and she would always remember him in her prayers. He certainly wasn't more real than anyone else, though. "No. But he was nice."

"Nice! Love shouldn't be nice, it should be…unnerving." Katherine stared off into space. "It should push you outside your comfort zone."

For some reason, Kara thought of Daniel. Right now, with half a room and dozens of people between them, she could pick out the tone of his voice over the music even though she couldn't understand the words. And she'd certainly been nervous when she met him this morning. "That isn't love, it's anxiety," she blurted.

"You do know what I mean! Come on, tell the truth, Kara. Whose arms do you wish you could fall into right now?"

"My heart beat fast and it was hard to breathe when I met Daniel," she admitted. "I'd be embarrassed if I fell into his arms, though!"

"Are you sure?" came the teasing response.

Kara felt her cheeks grow red. Quickly, she covered them

with her hands. The idea of being held by Daniel, of being caressed and kissed by him made her go hot all over. Why was she responding this way? It was very awkward. "I hope I don't fall into his arms. It would be improper."

"Impropriety is only the first step," Katherine said. "You don't want to stop there, or you'll never have any fun."

"Is love supposed to be fun? It sounds painful."

"It can be both, I guess." Her friend patted her shoulder reassuringly. "You're such an innocent, Kara. If Daniel's capable of falling for anybody, it ought to be you."

"He's much too dignified to fall for anyone." A distinguished man like him would never lose control the way Katherine had described. Kara was sure of it.

"You may be right, unfortunately."

Leaving his camera on a table, Carlos ambled toward them. "Hi. I was wondering if you'd like to dance." His hopeful smile was fixed on his foster mother until he noticed Kara. "Oh, I don't mean to be rude, Mrs….uh…"

"Tamaki." She smiled.

"Would you mind?" Katherine asked her.

"Of course not." Kara wanted her friend to have a good time. "You should enjoy yourselves."

"Yeah." Carlos nodded. "It's a shame to waste the music."

"Waste the music?" She didn't understand what he meant. "It isn't wasted while people are listening to it. But please, go and dance!"

They needed no further urging. With a quick farewell, Katherine swiveled and went to rock 'n' roll with her enthusiastic ward.

Kara admired the woman for being a mentor to so many people, including Kara herself. How sad that Katherine's dream of romantic love remained unfulfilled, although if it was really so inconvenient and disconcerting, surely in time she would be glad she'd escaped it.

Her eyes found Daniel in the crowd. He faced away from her, deep in conversation with his friend. The tension had eased from his shoulders and he stood with his head cocked, absorbing whatever Drew was saying. It was best not to interrupt such an earnest conversation, Kara decided.

From the buffet table drifted the scents of Swedish meatballs and teriyaki chicken wings. Those were too messy, but surely she could find something spillproof. She felt *peko peko*—so hungry her stomach was smacking its lips. After all, she was eating for Dorima, as well as herself.

As gracefully as she could manage in her hungry state, she glided toward the food table, trying to keep her eyes averted from Daniel. Although she would never have admitted it to Katherine, when she looked at him, she got that hot, anxious feeling all over again.

It wasn't love, though. At least, Kara profoundly hoped not.

As HE TALKED to his friend, Daniel kept catching hints of floating green-and-pink silk from the corner of his eye. He liked the way Kara's hands fluttered, covering her cheeks one minute, resting lightly atop her kimono the next. She transformed the smallest gesture into an art form.

"I never knew we had so much in common," Drew joked.

"Excuse me?" Sometimes it was hard to follow his pal's mischievous turns of thought. Although they'd hit it off immediately when they met at a networking session for young professionals several years ago, their friendship had been cemented as much by their contrasts as by their similarities.

"Pregnant women," Drew prompted.

That didn't help. "Let's start over," Daniel said. "We have something in common. We both like your sister and we're both attending Hannah's wedding. Now what's this about pregnant women?"

"You're forgetting how Julia and I met."

"Oh, right." It had been one of those crazy adventures that could only happen to Drew. Julia, in labor and pursued by a killer, had landed on his doorstep in a rainstorm.

After she gave birth practically in his arms, he'd let her stay with him and helped protect her from her greedy uncle, who'd been after the trust fund she was about to inherit. A few months later, she and Drew had married and were now parenting her baby son by her former fiancé, whose murder had been arranged by her uncle.

"I always wondered what kind of woman would turn you on," Drew continued. "Now I get it—demure, exotic and ready to deliver a baby any day."

Daniel wasn't keen on being the target of other people's romantic speculation, even his close friend's. He wished Drew would confine his imagination to designing buildings, which was what he did for a living. "Getting turned on had nothing to do with it. I invited her because my date canceled at the last minute. Besides, I figured she'd enjoy it since she knows Hannah."

"Are you denying you like her?" A raised eyebrow accompanied the question

"Kara's a sweet young woman."

"'A sweet young woman'? Spare me!" The man clapped a fist to his chest for emphasis. "Loosen up, pal!"

"I don't deny that I'm attracted to her." It was more than Daniel would have revealed to anyone else and probably more than he should have revealed to Drew, who, like his sister, had a well-meaning tendency to poke his nose into other people's business. "But she's got immigration problems. I'm going to put her in touch with an attorney who might be able to help. That's all I can do. As far as her accompanying me today, it's nothing personal."

"Nothing personal? Who are you kidding? You can't take your eyes off her."

That was nonsense. He'd simply checked a couple of times to make sure his escort was having a good time. "You've been hitting the champagne too hard."

"They haven't served the champagne yet," Drew pointed out. "Listen, I've never seen you exchange more than half-a-dozen words of conversation with a woman before. And rarely that much."

"That's not true." Daniel bristled. "Brittany and I had an interesting discussion the last time we went out."

"You mean *she* had an interesting discussion," responded his friend, who'd met Daniel's date at the museum opening. "She did most of the gabbing while you nodded and stood there looking like you'd rather be somewhere else."

"Postmodern art isn't my thing," Daniel said.

"Neither are postmodern women, I'm guessing," Drew said. "Take a leaf from my book and rescue the girl."

"Do I look like some sort of superman to you?"

"Maybe a little around the jaw." His friend shrugged. "Besides, what's that got to do with getting married?"

Daniel couldn't believe he'd heard correctly. "How did we get onto the subject of marriage?"

"We didn't. I just brought it up because it's the obvious solution. Katherine told me about Kara's visa problem. Did you see the movie *Green Card*? Marry her and her troubles go poof!" Drew grinned, pleased with himself.

"Is that so?" It was the most outrageous idea Daniel had ever heard, even from his unflappable friend. "More likely, I marry her and my career goes poof!"

"It's the gentlemanly thing to do." From a passing waiter, Drew snagged a stuffed mushroom.

"It's also illegal."

"That depends on your point of view." Drew downed the mushroom in one bite.

"Let's assume for one minute that you're serious."

"Absolutely."

"It's illegal to marry someone for the purpose of defrauding the U.S. immigration authorities," Daniel said. "Lawyers who break the law lose their licenses. Even if they don't go to jail, that's the end of their careers."

"There's nothing wrong with marrying the woman you love," Drew said. "If anyone questions your short engagement, I'll testify. 'Your Honor, the first time I saw them together, I knew they were meant for each other.'"

"Sure, you'd be a great witness," Daniel scoffed. "You can't keep a straight face."

"Give me another reason."

"Another reason for what?"

"Another reason why you won't marry her, when it would be a huge favor to her and might bring a little color to your sepia-toned existence." Another waiter, induced to pause in midstride, was relieved of an assortment of puff pastries.

"As I said, it's unethical," Daniel reminded him.

"What's unethical about it?" Drew hammered his point as if he meant what he was proposing. More likely, Daniel thought, he simply enjoyed the debate. "You have no financial motives and nothing to gain. Except love, of course, which is the reason for marrying someone in the first place."

"I'm not in love, so you haven't resolved my ethical dilemma," Daniel retorted. "This whole idea of being meant for each other is pure wishful thinking. Just because you fell head over heels for Julia is no reason to ascribe the same sentiments to me."

"Spoken like a lawyer!" Drew declared. "Well, here's a good argument, if you aren't persuaded by your own heart or by that young lady's state of distress. If you marry her fast, you might get a discount on Hannah and Jack's leftover flowers."

"You didn't mean a word of what you were saying, did you." Daniel hoped they'd reached the end of this absurd argument. It was disconcerting enough that his attraction to Kara had come to his friend's attention in the first place.

"Sure I did," Drew said. "Sort of. Don't dismiss the idea too quickly. Sometimes you have to go with your gut feeling."

"There's a lot of people behind bars who went with their gut feeling about doing all sorts of illegal things," Daniel grumbled. "Besides, the idea of a green-card marriage never even occurred to me." Although the cards that indicated a person had permanent resident status in the U.S were no longer green, they were still referred to that way, as far as he knew.

"But now that I've mentioned it…" The words trailed off suggestively.

"Now that you've mentioned it, my gut feeling tells me to forget the whole idea."

Drew grimaced. "Your problem is, you don't have gut feelings, or if you do, you refuse to acknowledge them."

It amazed Daniel how differently two men could view the world. "I prefer to be ruled by logic, not emotion."

"You're more emotional than you give yourself credit for," his friend said. "Right now, I'd guess your ruling emotion is denial. Inside you, there's a knight in shining armor struggling to get out. How long do you think you can keep him locked away?"

"Should I wear that shining armor over or under my three-piece suit?" Daniel shot back.

"I know you better than most people," Drew said. "I've always suspected you had your heroic side. Not that anyone else would notice."

"I don't know whether to be flattered or offended."

"Try a little of each."

A small shriek startled them both. By the buffet, Kara was twisting her hands together while Debbie North dabbed ineffectively at her kimono with a paper napkin. A plate lay on the floor, its contents scattered.

"Looks like somebody ran into your date," Drew said. "Or vice versa."

Although he normally had a hard time tuning in to other people's emotions, Daniel read Kara's reaction instantly. What might strike most people as a minor incident had clearly upset her. "I'd better go see if I can help."

"Watch out! Somebody might think you're riding to the rescue."

"I'll be sure to buff my armor and sharpen my lance," Daniel said. "See you later."

"You bet."

Daniel hurried away, aware of Drew's smug expression. Trying to make matches for friends must be a side effect of being a newlywed, Daniel figured.

As he approached, Kara's stricken face made him miss his stride. Anyone would think she was distressed for his sake. Surely she didn't expect him to get angry about a silly accident. "Are you all right?"

"It was my fault," Debbie said. "I'm really sorry. You can send me the dry-cleaning bill."

"No, no—I'm the clumsy one," Kara protested.

"You were just standing there!" the reporter said.

"I was in the way." Kara stared down at her soiled garment in dismay.

"Honestly, you should let me pay for that." Receiving a determined shake of the head, Debbie insisted, "At least let me help you clean up the worst of it. Let's go to the ladies' room."

"She'll be fine." Daniel was more concerned with putting distance between Kara and the reporter than in resolving the pointless question of who was at fault. No way was he letting the town snoop get close enough to sniff out a story.

Debbie extended her business card. "I wasn't looking where I was going. Really, I insist on paying."

"Forget it." He waved the card away. The one thing guaranteed to draw the unwanted attention of the authorities was for a reporter to turn Kara into a cause célèbre.

Debbie didn't look dissuaded. Known for her doggedness as a reporter, she apparently applied the same tactic to her social life. The only solution was to whisk Kara away himself.

"Come on, let's get you cleaned up," Daniel said, and on that pretext, hurried her across the room and out of Debbie's sight.

WHAT A DISASTER! If only she hadn't shrieked, Kara thought. At least she could have avoided alerting everyone in the room to her predicament. Now she'd created an awkward situation for Daniel, the last thing she'd meant to do.

The hurry with which he removed her from the situation showed how uncomfortable she'd made him. Stricken, Kara stood silent in a secluded corner of the hallway as he dampened his handkerchief in a water fountain and began removing the remnants of Debbie's chicken and meatballs.

"She really did a number on you," he said.

"I'm sorry." The words came out in a whisper.

"These things happen."

Not to other people. I'm the one who always gets things wrong.

It wasn't only Mrs. Tamaki who had scolded Kara for her awkwardness. Although her father had been less harsh, she'd felt his disapproval keenly from the early years, when she ran eagerly to hear her grandfather's stories, and later, when she became friends with Tansho. He'd rarely been satisfied with anything, from the books she read to her demeanor in company. Now she'd shamed herself in front of Daniel, as well.

He didn't speak as he scrubbed the kimono. Thank goodness it was made of a light nylon, instead of silk, which might have stained, since Kara hadn't had the presence of mind to forestall Daniel before he applied water to it.

Slowly, as he worked, her initial humiliation faded. She found herself distracted by his dark head bent over her, by the leashed strength in his hands and by the way each movement made the fabric swish lightly against her skin.

As the cloth caressed her body, Kara became aware of a tightening in her breasts. Her whole body grew warm and heavy. She didn't think she should feel this way, yet she wanted it to go on and on.

Tendrils of desire curled through her. Where had this strange ache come from? She'd never experienced such sensations before, not even on her wedding night. That evening, she'd been frightened and ill at ease. Thank goodness, when it came time to get under the covers together, Hiro hadn't expected anything beyond compliance, because she didn't know what else she could have done.

When her husband had held her, there'd been no sparkles

glimmering across her skin. Her breath hadn't caught in her throat, and she certainly hadn't been gripped by an impulse to run her hands through his thick hair. But she was feeling all those things now.

Was this what Katherine meant by falling in love? Surely not. Any woman would experience a powerful response to being handled by such a distinguished, attractive man. It meant nothing and it could lead nowhere, particularly for one so unworthy of him, Kara told herself.

"I'm afraid that's the best I can do." Daniel released her and stepped back.

She inspected her kimono. Under the water blot, she could make out a large greasy stain. "I should have worn a jacket. Then I could hide it."

"Yes, too bad you didn't consult a fortune cookie so you'd have known Debbie North was going to dump food all over you," he said ironically. "No, wait. Fortune cookies are Chinese, not Japanese."

"I believe they're American," Kara said.

"Really?"

"My friend Tansho told me they were invented in California," she said.

"I learn something new every day." A pucker formed between his eyebrows as he regarded his wet handkerchief. If he put it into one of his pockets, it would make a mess, she realized.

"Please, I will take care of it." Lifting the wet cloth gingerly between thumb and forefinger, Kara tucked it into her pocket. She suspected the sodden lump was creating yet another blotch, but she preferred to mar her own garments rather than Daniel's. "I will launder it and return it to you."

"You don't have to do that."

"It's my pleasure."

"Well, thank you."

She felt as if she'd won a small victory. At least she could compensate him a little for the trouble she'd caused. Also, deep inside, a flicker of happiness reminded Kara that she now had a reason to see Daniel again.

As they took their leave of the bride and groom and went out to Daniel's car, she reminded herself that the most she could ask of him was to help her stay in Seattle long enough to have her baby. She couldn't think any farther ahead than that.

Yet simply laying her hand on Daniel's arm to get into the car, and catching the scent of his leather briefcase inside, heightened Kara's sense of herself as a woman. She didn't want to give up this magical awakening, even though she had no idea where it might lead.

She glanced wonderingly at the man sliding into place beside her. Did she arouse any of the same reactions in him? She could scarcely breathe, waiting to hear what he might say next.

He said nothing. He simply put the car into gear and eased away from the curb.

All the way home, topics for conversation eluded Kara. She couldn't repeat what Katherine had mentioned about planning to have a baby, since it had been told to her in confidence. It seemed impertinent to inquire what he and Drew had discussed.

Besides, Daniel was frowning and avoided looking directly at her. Kara's confidence, always uncertain, shrank like a quivering leaf. She should have stayed away from the refreshment table. She'd known better, but as usual, she'd yielded to impulse. Now she was dirty and still hungry.

The traffic that had dogged their trip to the wedding had vanished along with the morning fog. April sunshine, all the more precious because it was likely to be brief, glimmered off the panes of office buildings. When she lowered her lashes, she could make out rainbow hints in the dazzle.

Kara wished she could dare point out their beauty to the man beside her. However, it was best not to break into his thoughts, especially when he was in an unsettled mood.

Daniel halted in front of her building. "I'll call Edward

Riley on Monday and set up an appointment for you. If you need help with transportation, I'll make sure you get there."

"That's very kind of you." Kara hoped the other attorney's office was located on a convenient bus route, assuming he was willing to see her at all. She didn't want to impose on Daniel, even though earlier he had offered to take her himself. It would be presumptuous to ask for anything more, after all he'd done. "I will return your handkerchief in a few days."

"Keep it as a souvenir. I've got plenty."

She didn't want to keep it. She wanted to launder it and iron it and fold it neatly. She intended to wrap it in a square of silvery paper she'd saved in a drawer, top it off with a red cord and present it to Daniel with a flourish. "It will be an honor to return it to you personally."

"Please don't bother." He exited and came around to the passenger side.

It was plain he didn't plan to see her again. In Kara's mind, a cloud came over the sun, and the city seemed to sink into shadow. She'd been kidding herself to imagine she could ever be gracious enough to appeal to a man like Daniel Adler.

"Thank you," she said as he opened her door. She tried to lift herself smoothly from the seat, but the pregnancy threw off her sense of balance and she stumbled against him. With his usual steadiness and courtesy, he righted her. "I'm sorry." How many times had she said that today? Hurriedly, she added, "I enjoyed attending the wedding. I hope your lady friend recovers quickly."

"Brittany? I'm sure she'll be all right." He escorted her to the apartment entrance, made sure she could mount the stairs safely and left.

Kara paused on the second-floor landing to catch her breath before climbing to her third-story apartment. She didn't understand what she wanted from Daniel. Just to see him again and hear the deep timbre of his voice, she supposed. Perhaps to have him touch her gently, the way he had today. Yet she wanted those things so intensely that she could hardly bear not to have them.

It was alarming and confusing. She had never doubted that she could adjust to life in America if only she could solve her immediate, practical problems, but this was different.

For once, Kara had no idea what was going on or how to begin to resolve it.

CHAPTER FIVE

ALTHOUGH HE USUALLY ENJOYED Drew's teasing, Daniel gritted his teeth with annoyance as he wove his way across town after dropping Kara off. He wished his friend hadn't brought up the idea of a marriage of convenience, because it had lodged itself in his brain and refused to let go.

As a lawyer, Daniel could ill afford to flout the law, but it might not be illegal for an American to marry a foreign woman if he received no advantage or compensation. If things got sticky, the couple would simply have to stay married for a few years to make it look good.

Not him, of course. Also, he wasn't certain such a marriage would really enable Kara to stay in America long-term, although it would obviously allow her enough time to have her baby here. The child would automatically be an American citizen, improving Kara's chances of gaining a visa to return with the baby later.

For heaven's sake, why was he contemplating the idea, even in the abstract? Daniel's upright father, Vernon, would hit the ceiling if he heard of his son getting involved in something like that.

He'd also taught Daniel to be generous and socially conscious. In a way, Daniel could see how marrying Kara would demonstrate both those qualities.

"What are you, crazy?" he asked aloud. His brain, however, kept buzzing with annoying images of Kara in a red-printed wedding kimono, smiling up at him.

It didn't improve Daniel's mood to discover a strange van parked in one of the two garage spaces reserved for his condo.

Even though there was still room for his car, he didn't like it when people presumed on his turf. Worse, several times he'd come home to find both his spaces occupied.

It would be a relief not to have to deal with parking hassles when he moved into his house next weekend. Although escrow on the condo he was selling didn't close until next Saturday, Daniel had already taken possession of his thirty-year-old house in Bellevue.

He'd hired a contractor to do much-needed remodeling during the overlap period. The painters had finished their work yesterday, and the old carpet and linoleum were to be replaced next week.

This past year, Daniel had felt a strong drive to buy a house and fix it up. He supposed most men would want a wife to go with it, and perhaps a couple like Hannah and Jack, who clearly loved each other, might be able to make a go of marriage. Given the divorce rate, however, he remained skeptical.

After witnessing the mismatch between his upright father and unreliable mother, Daniel was convinced that a good marriage required compatibility of temperament, goals and attitudes. Despite a few involvements over the years, he'd never really clicked with anyone, and given his family history, he believed he was best off staying single.

After taking the elevator to the tenth floor, he let himself into his unit. It seemed a bit bare, since he'd given some of his furniture to charity a few days ago rather than bother moving it. He'd meant to replace the secondhand pieces long ago, and this would force him to do it.

The answering machine was beeping. He listened to the message, and by the time it finished, had begun cursing under his breath. It was a good thing he'd turned off his cell phone during the wedding, because this call would have spoiled his enjoyment.

Barely taking time to change from his good suit into slacks and a polo shirt, he headed down to his car. There was only one advantage to receiving this bad news: it drove all speculation about a green-card marriage out of his mind.

DANIEL WAS STILL SEETHING late Sunday morning as he set out for a jog. Although he exercised at a gym several times a week, he needed to get outdoors and pound the pavement.

How could the contractor have waited until this late in the game to discover dry rot under the flooring? The kitchen and bathrooms had to be torn up and repaired, forcing a delay before the new carpet and tile could be installed. The house would be unlivable for at least a week past his move-in date.

He'd tried to put in a call to the real-estate agent who'd handled the sale of his condo, hoping to delay the close of escrow to allow him to stay where he was. When her voice mail instructed him to leave a message, Daniel had obeyed with as much cool professionalism as he could muster, but he felt his blood pressure soaring.

It was frustrating and annoying to have his schedule disrupted after he'd planned so carefully. But this was only a temporary setback, he reminded himself, trying to put the situation in perspective as he jogged along a cobblestone street near the harbor.

Even on a Sunday morning, the Pike Place Market exploded with life. People flocked to enjoy the restaurants, boutiques and fish market at the rambling center. The scent of baked goods reminded Daniel that he'd skipped breakfast.

Although he wanted to stop, he hurried onward. The pounding of his legs and the stretch of muscles was only beginning to thwart his agitation.

Seattle was a feast for the ears, as well as the other senses, this morning, from the call of gulls to the rumble of a trolley car. The rhythmic slap of Daniel's running shoes added to the jumble of noises as he headed south toward Pioneer Square.

Against the sky fanned the lacy branches of trees verdant with springtime. Daniel remembered how Kara had exclaimed over a dry old leaf. Anyone could find beauty in what was fresh and new, but she'd awakened him to the exquisiteness of something he would otherwise have brushed aside.

There was a calmness about Kara that soothed him, even just thinking about her, he reflected as the hilly course forced him to slow to a walk. She'd radiated a quiet charm at the wedding reception that made people smile when they spotted her.

Despite her reticence, he'd noticed that she opened up with Katherine, laughing and talking with a spontaneity that Daniel wished he could master. That was the point, he supposed. You didn't master spontaneity. You had to let it master you, and that went against his nature.

His head was starting to buzz from lack of caffeine. He was tempted to go on defying that particular need out of simple stubbornness until he caught the rich fragrance of coffee wafting from a sidewalk café ahead of him. It was time to ease up, he decided.

He crossed the street toward the café, glancing at a petite, dark-haired woman pushing a baby carriage in his direction. Idly, he took in her pretty Japanese features and the gentle swell of her abdomen beneath a long-sleeved cotton top. Although she reminded him of Kara, there had to be hundreds of women who resembled her in a city with such a large Asian population. Besides, this woman obviously had a child already.

Even so, Daniel's gaze fixed on her, willing her to look up. When she did, she beamed with delight.

"Daniel!" Her enthusiasm swept away any awkwardness at the unexpected meeting. "I am happy to see you."

"I'm glad to see you, too." Was it possible that, subliminally, she was the reason he'd been drawn toward the International District? Daniel had to concede that it might be. "I'm afraid I'm not at my best." He indicated his dark-blue sweatsuit, which clung damply to his chest.

"Exercise is good for the body and the spirit," she said. "I combine my exercise with baby-sitting, as you can see."

So that explained the carriage. Coming alongside, Daniel examined an alert infant with black, tufted hair. He wore a thick blue sleeper. "Who's the little guy?"

"His name is Brian," Kara said. "I watch him for my

neighbor, who's from Taiwan. She and her husband like to go shopping on Sundays and the baby gets restless.''

"You're very industrious." Apparently she took every opportunity to augment her income from the delivery job. It was an admirable quality.

"I baby-sit several children. It's fun for me. They like to learn things all the time, and I like to teach." She paused, and Daniel hoped she wasn't going to excuse herself so soon.

He wished he dared cup her elfin chin in one hand or trace the edge of her full lips with his thumb. To reinforce his self-control, he thrust his hands into his pockets.

"I was going to stop for a cup of coffee and a muffin.'' Daniel's voice came out thick. He cleared his throat. "Would you care to join me? My treat, of course.''

To his relief, she made no pretense of thinking it over. "I'd love to." Quickly, she added, "Is it all right if I have tea, instead of coffee?''

"Certainly."

They found an outdoor table with a heat lamp to ward off the morning chill. In the pram, Brian worked his way to a sitting position and studied his surroundings with interest. When a waitress appeared, Daniel ordered a selection of muffins along with their drinks.

"I thought the baby might want to eat, too," he said.

Kara smiled. "It's educational for him to try different flavors. All of the senses should be stimulated, although not too much.''

"Definitely not too much." Daniel's own senses were stimulated more than enough already.

Their order, when it arrived, proved colorful and aromatic, the muffins tucked into a basket and accompanied by a ceramic tray filled with a variety of teabags. Brian seized on a bite-size piece of muffin that Kara cut for him and stuffed it into his mouth.

"I've written to my parents about Hannah's wedding, to tell them how splendid it was," she said as she poured hot water over a lemon-flavored bag.

"I hate writing letters," Daniel admitted. "I've never been good at describing things."

"I tried to create a lovely scene for them, like a poem," Kara said. "That way, a special moment may be treasured by others who were not present. Beauty reflected in a pool may be a little blurred, but it can be as beautiful in its own way as the original."

"Do you write them by e-mail?" Daniel occasionally updated his father electronically. The brevity and speed suited them both.

She shook her head. "My friend Tansho gave me some pretty paper. My calligraphy with Japanese characters isn't as elegant as hers, but I do my best. It makes my parents happy when I make something attractive."

"I'm fascinated by this mutual pretense that you're here on vacation," he admitted. "Surely they know you're pregnant."

"Oh, yes." Kara reached into the baby carriage and dangled a toy, which Brian seized upon. "We don't speak about it. It would be rude to bother them with my problems."

"You mean your mother doesn't worry about you?"

"If she does, she never says so." Carefully, Kara removed her used teabag and set it aside.

"My secretary says her mom pesters her for details of every date and keeps asking when she's going to get married," Daniel said. "She'd envy you."

"She should not envy me." Kara's eyes brimmed with moisture. Embarrassed, she blinked to clear them. "I wish I could talk to my mother, but it makes her angry to hear my problems."

"Why? Everybody has problems." Daniel took a deep swallow of coffee. The caffeine percolated into his bloodstream with a welcome jolt.

"My mother is eager to please my father and my brother," Kara said. "To her, I am an extension of her unworthy self. She wants me to be perfect, as she wants to make herself perfect."

"Nobody's perfect." Daniel stopped himself in midargument. "You'll have to excuse me. I know you come from a different culture. I shouldn't make judgments about how people act."

"I'm grateful for your comments." Kara cut a slice from her muffin and slid it carefully into her mouth, spilling not a single crumb. When she'd finished chewing, she said, "Your mother must be very proud of you."

"My mom's hardly even aware of me. Even if your mom isn't the warmest person in the world, she looks like a saint compared to my mother." Daniel washed down a bite of muffin with more coffee. The waitress stopped by to refill his cup and provide more hot water for tea.

When she was gone, Kara asked, "How is that possible? It appears your mother did a good job of raising you."

"Only until I was fourteen. That's when she left my father and me." He was amazed at how easily the words slipped out. Usually, he considered his personal history nobody else's business.

"I don't understand how she could do that."

"She wanted to go her own way and she didn't care who got hurt in the process," Daniel said. "Don't Japanese women ever leave their husbands?"

"Yes, but divorce is less common there," Kara said. "Most couples stay together for the sake of the family. If a woman does leave, these days she usually takes her children with her."

"Mostly it happens that way in America, too, but not with my mother. As far as I can tell, she was as eager to get away from me as from my father."

Although he'd tried to outgrow the old bitterness, it rose afresh in Daniel's throat. Renée Adler, now Renée Leroy, had wasted no time in acquiring a new man, a new career and, a few years later, a new baby. Although she claimed to love Daniel, she'd rarely visited and made no attempt to gain custody.

"I can't imagine a woman who would leave her son!" Kara said. "Did she ever explain?"

"No," Daniel said. "Not that we talk much, although she does write me once in a while." Trying to be fair, he added, "I don't think she wants to stir up trouble. She seems to want to leave the past alone."

"There must be some reason she left." Kara frowned as if trying to solve a puzzle. "I apologize if I am being too personal, but it perplexes me."

"Me, too. She never claimed my father abused her or cheated on her." Those would be understandable reasons for leaving, although they didn't fit Vernon Adler. "My father's stern, but he's also deeply loving. I was fourteen then, going through my own upheavals, and he's the one who held things together. He didn't deserve the way she treated him."

At first, Daniel had blamed himself, at least partly, for his mother's abrupt departure. Like most kids, he'd had his grumpy moods during junior high school, and there'd been times when he knew he'd tried his mother's patience. After she left, he'd withdrawn. He'd been too angry and afraid to try to send word about how much he missed her, because it would have hurt too much if she'd rejected him again. In time, he'd grown to accept that she was no longer part of his life.

He'd tried to persuade himself to forgive his mother when, during his college years, she'd begun inviting him to visit her new family. Once, he'd flown to her home in Denver, but he'd felt so awkward that he couldn't wait to leave. Now, each year, he politely declined her invitation to join her and her family for the holidays. His only regret was that he scarcely knew his teenage half sister.

Reaching across the table, Kara touched his wrist. "If your father is anything like you, she made a big mistake."

Gently, Daniel took her hand. It was so small it could have disappeared inside his.

"My hands are puffy!" she said, trying to pull it back. "It's because of the baby."

He held on teasingly. "Aren't you going to let me read your palm?" Daniel had no idea where that idea came from, since he was the last person on earth to put stock in fortune-telling, but he enjoyed the startled look she gave him.

"You can read palms?" Kara asked.

"It's an ancient regional skill," Daniel fabricated. "Very common among people in Chicago." He struggled to keep a straight face.

Her mouth quirked. "You're joking with me!"

"Try me and see," he challenged.

She pressed her lips into a thin line as she struggled to decide. After a quick glance at Brian, who had dozed off cradling a toy, she nodded. "All right. You can tell my fortune, Mr. Lawyer from Chicago. But don't expect me to believe any far-fetched stories. I already know most of the American legends."

"Name three," he said.

"Davy Crockett, Johnny Appleseed and Al Capone," she replied.

"That's quite a trio. Okay, forget the nonsense about Chicago. But I'm going to tell your fortune, anyway." Daniel pried open her fingers and stroked her palm lightly. Her eyes grew large as she watched him. He lifted her palm to his cheek and brushed it across the slight roughness, a telltale sign that he hadn't shaved this morning. "Does this scratch?"

She shook her head. "No. Does that tell you something about my future?"

"It tells me you'd get along great with a hairy man," he joked. Lowering her hand and pretending to inspect it, he said, "Also, you have a bountiful nature."

"Bountiful means I'm going to have children." Kara clicked her tongue. "I know that already. What about my future?"

"You will make the people around you very happy." That much was certain.

"I would like to do that," she said. "Anything else?"

Without thinking, Daniel said, "You will fall in love with a tall, dark man."

Her sharp intake of breath warned that he'd strayed from

the realm of silly playfulness. When he looked up, he discovered Kara's gaze fixed on him with a kind of stunned fascination.

As their eyes met, tenderness and longing shone from her unguarded heart. It was as if, with his offhand comment about falling in love, he'd tapped into an emotion she hadn't even acknowledged to herself. He had the sensation of staring directly into her soul.

Maybe she *was* growing to love him, Daniel realized with a start. The frightening part was that, in a way, he wanted her to.

What was wrong with him? He had no business falling for a woman he'd just met, a woman with whom he had almost nothing in common and whose problems included being nine months pregnant with another man's child. He didn't want or need that kind of involvement.

Being brutally honest with himself, he admitted the possibility that he was toying with her. Sure, it felt good, being on the receiving end of her innocent sweetness, but where would it lead?

A chill crept through Daniel. He knew the answer to that question. He'd seen the torment in his father's face and lived with the sense of loss that had haunted their house like an evil spirit. It was a cruel game he was playing, luring Kara into trusting him. He didn't want her to go through life devastated, the way his father had, by loving someone who couldn't return the same measure of devotion.

"I meant a tall, dark Japanese man," he amended.

"I don't know any tall Japanese men," Kara said.

"Maybe he's Chinese." When she didn't respond, he shifted her hand as if to get a clearer view of the lines. "Or he might be blond. My reading is a little foggy this morning. That's probably because we're in Seattle. My skills worked fine in Chicago."

"Your reading is foggy?" Kara repeated. "That sounds more like San Francisco." She managed to smile, with an effort.

"You're right. In any case, I have to go." After scanning the check the waitress had placed on the table, Daniel topped it with a generous payment. "Take your time. Enjoy some more tea. I'm afraid duty calls."

Kara blinked, caught off guard. "You haven't finished telling my fortune."

"It was a silly idea," he said. "People can't read the future. Certainly not me." The problems with the new house, temporarily forgotten, rushed back. "The only thing I can predict is that I've got one devil of a week ahead. Don't worry. I won't forget about the immigration attorney."

"I know." Kara couldn't quite muster another smile. "Thank you for the tea and muffins."

"My pleasure." With the sense of making his escape, Daniel strode away. His mind raced ahead, trying to figure out where to catch a bus so he wouldn't waste any more time getting home.

He didn't want to look back. He knew he'd been abrupt, but in the long run, it was kinder than staying.

What on earth had clouded his judgment back there? Whatever it was, he'd make sure it didn't happen again.

STUPID, STUPID GIRL. Kara shook her head as she pushed the stroller toward her building. Every time Daniel saw her, she made another mistake. He must think her the clumsiest woman he'd ever met. No wonder he'd been so eager to depart!

This time, her error hadn't been as simple as knocking into Debbie North and smearing herself with food. Instead, she'd made a display of her private emotions in public. From getting weepy when she talked about her family to gazing at Daniel with schoolgirl adoration, she'd behaved without dignity. Where was her self-control? Why did she show such weakness around the man she most wanted to charm?

As she walked, Kara became aware of the breeze caressing her heated skin. When Daniel held her hand to his cheek, a silver liquid had coursed through her. She hoped she would dream about him tonight, so she could enjoy his touch again.

Although these feelings were new, Kara recognized them from the movies. The next step was to kiss the man. If she did, would it offend him? If only she knew whether he had experienced this same sense of magical longing.

It was a question she would never dare ask Daniel. But she might dare to ask Tansho. The more she thought about it, the more determined Kara became to learn about these feelings before she saw Daniel again and risked making an even bigger fool of herself.

CHAPTER SIX

EGGPLANTS. BEANS. Chinese cabbage, winter melons, herbs, kale, decorative serpent gourds. Kara checked the computer. "The order is ready to go."

"Thanks for helping in the office. I know you've got your own route to handle." Leaning over her shoulder to see the screen, Tansho clicked the print button.

Slightly taller than Kara and stockier of build, Tansho could face down men twice her size and make them repack a crate until it met with her approval. Yet she looked completely feminine with her short layered hair and fuzzy yellow sweater over designer jeans.

"I hope your arm feels better soon." Kara indicated the flexible cast that encased her friend's wrist. Although she was only twenty-five, a year older than Kara, Tansho had developed carpal tunnel syndrome after spending many hours book-keeping for her family's business. That was why Kara had come in early on a Monday morning to help.

"I hope so, too," Tansho said. "My parents can't figure out this computer stuff and my brothers are too impatient."

The small room, cluttered with desks, computers and paperwork, overlooked the loading dock. Through its tiny window, Kara could see men stowing crates onto trucks in the predawn hour. The Matsuba Asian-American Fruit and Vegetable Market specialized in providing fresh Washington state produce to restaurants, hotels and other businesses.

"I had better go make sure my truck is ready." Kara moved her chair back.

"Whoa. You came in so early, you've got plenty of time."

Tansho planted her hands on her hips. "Remember what we were talking about on the phone yesterday?"

Kara felt her cheeks heating. "I asked about kissing."

"And I told you people don't stop at kissing anymore. You watch too many old movies." Tansho clicked off the program and collected her printout. "I know you've been married, but in some ways you don't seem to know much."

Kara patted her abdomen. "I know plenty. Here's the proof."

"Yeah. Here's the proof that Hiro knew how to leap from Step One, Shaking Hands, to Step Ten, Getting It On." Reaching into a drawer, Tansho removed a book. "I picked this up at a bookstore last night. It ought to help you fill in the blanks."

Although she'd grown up speaking English with her grandfather, Kara frowned in perplexity at the title, *Sexual Frolicking*. Used together, the words didn't make sense. Sex was a matter of procreation and a duty to one's husband. Frolicking meant playing. "I don't understand," she said.

Tansho held it out. "Read the first page."

Hesitantly, Kara took the book, almost afraid it might give her an electric shock. As she skimmed the introduction, she found herself instinctively moving away from the window. She would feel humiliated if one of Tansho's brothers spotted her reading this suggestive volume.

Sex, the author proclaimed, was central to life. It ought to be fun, and it ought to be frequent. She—the author was a woman, which reassured Kara a little—advocated having sex at various times of day and in different locales. She also advocated using parts of the body that Kara had never considered relevant to sex. Although Kara had heard of "pillow books," erotic Japanese tales that featured drawings of men and women making love, this was the closest she'd ever come to seeing anything like that.

She handed the book back. "Thank you, but this has nothing to do with the way I feel about Daniel Adler."

"Look at these." Tansho flipped to some pictures so suggestive that Kara shaded her eyes. "Take it home with you."

"I can't! What if one of my neighbors saw it?"

"You've got to get over this maidenly-blushing business if
you're going to land an American male," Tansho told her.
"I'll admit that when I was staying in your village, I saw
advantages to the way the girls were growing up. It must be
great to think of your body simply as a healthy part of you
and not to worry about how your dimensions compare to some
model in a magazine."

"I would never pose for a magazine, so why should I
care?" Kara asked. Nudity itself seemed natural to her—at
one time men and women had shared public baths in Japan—
but she didn't understand the fixation some women had, even
at home, with trying to shape themselves into some fashion-
able ideal.

"I care." Pages ruffled as Tansho spoke. "Half the time I
don't like my body because I'm too small on top and not
small enough in the hips."

"Do men mind about that?" It had never occurred to Kara
that Daniel might not like her body, except possibly for the
fact that she had a baby in the middle of it. But that was only
temporary. As for the rest of her, there was nothing she could
do about it.

"I'm not sure whether they mind or not," Tansho admitted.
"Mostly they want to have sex, or at least, that's what my
brothers say. I don't mean you have to jump into bed with
the guy, especially at your stage of pregnancy, but you can't
sit there like Miss Priss, expecting a peck on the lips. Oh,
here's my favorite chapter, 'Sensual Eating.'"

"Of course eating uses the senses," Kara said. "You taste
food and you smell it."

"That's not what they mean by 'sensual.' Did you ever see
an old movie called *Tom Jones*?" Tansho asked. "It's got a
scene that illustrates the point. Here. What does this remind
you of?" She thrust out a photograph of a cucumber gripped
upright in a woman's fist.

"It reminds me of a vegetable," Kara said.

"What else?"

"It looks like a ...baby bottle." She deliberately chose the least-offensive object she could think of.

"A baby bottle?" Her friend shook her head. "You have got to be kidding! Try a *matsuke*." The word, which meant mushroom, was a common euphemism for a certain portion of the male anatomy.

Kara clapped her hands over her cheeks. "Tansho! I never saw one, so why would I think of that?"

"You mean Hiro just slipped it to you?"

"We were under the covers!"

"You just sort of did it without looking? I always figured..." Her friend stopped in midsentence.

Her embarrassed grin gave Kara a clue. "Wait a minute. Have you ever seen one?"

"A cucumber? Sure."

"You know what I mean," Kara said. "You're just pretending to be an expert about sex, aren't you?"

Tansho sighed. "Okay, you got me. But if I ever do get my hands on a *matsuke*, I'll make sure I get a good look at it."

Kara remembered that they'd begun this conversation because of her feelings for Daniel. "I don't want to look at it. I'm only thinking of kissing him. Thank you for showing me the book, but I don't think I care to learn any more."

"Well, it's a start. I can't expect you to learn sexual frolicking in one easy lesson." To Kara's relief, Tansho stuck the book into the drawer. "I know how far you've come. When I met you, you hardly dared look anybody in the face. Now you've become much more Westernized."

"I'm glad I met you," Kara said. "I am especially grateful that you invited me here when I had nowhere to turn."

"Hey, I owed you a big debt," Tansho said. "You saved my life."

Accustomed to her friend's exaggerations, Kara merely smiled. "It was good timing for us both."

As an exchange student at Kara's high school, Tansho had been a social disaster, unwittingly moving from blunder to blunder because of her awkwardness with the language and customs. Since the other students considered her Japanese, they refused to make the allowances that they did for other foreign students. Every breach of etiquette—and in Tansho's case they'd been almost non-stop—had made her more of an outsider.

Kara had been drawn to her first out of curiosity and later from a sense of kinship, since they were both out of sync with their surroundings. Having lost her grandfather only a short time before, she'd found it a joy to meet someone who understood the sense of individuality and the irreverent humor she'd learned from him.

With Tansho, she'd visited Tokyo for the first time and seen the growing independence and sophistication of more urbanized Japanese women. During college, the two of them had kept in touch, and once she was working, Kara had bought an airline ticket and visited Seattle as a tourist. She'd fallen in love with the city and the country, as she'd always suspected she would.

In her desperation after Hiro's death, one of the first people she'd turned to was Tansho. With Mrs. Tamaki making her life miserable, the Matsubas' offer of a job had come as a godsend, even though it wasn't in Kara's preferred field of childhood education.

"You know what?" Tansho said. "I've got an idea."

"I hope it doesn't involve vegetables, unless I'm delivering them," Kara said.

"No cucumbers, I promise." The lilt in her voice promised mischief, however.

"Is this about Daniel?" Kara asked suspiciously.

"Sure. He's the topic of the day, right?" Tansho said. "The way I see it, he ought to help you. I mean, as a lawyer, it's no big deal for him to give you a hand. And he must like you or he'd never have invited you to that wedding."

"I told you, he would have lost face to arrive alone."

"It's more than that." A little humming noise indicated she was thinking. This could be dangerous, because Tansho was even more impulsive than Kara, with fewer internal restraints. "Men are suckers for the poor little crushed lotus blossom, which is probably how he sees you. And who knows what some other lawyer will do? Probably charge you a bundle and get you deported."

"That's what I'm afraid of," Kara admitted.

"I'm going to give Daniel a nudge."

"Please don't bother him," Kara said, distressed. "I wouldn't want to make him uncomfortable."

"I won't do anything that would lose face for either of us," Tansho promised. "There's nothing wrong with a little guilt manipulation, though. Heck, my mom's a champion."

"Guilt manipulation?" Kara had heard the term, but she didn't know how it worked. "What's that, exactly?"

"Reminding him that he's got a conscience. Kind of like Jiminy Cricket. I'll go see him later today. What was the name of that law firm again?"

Reluctantly, Kara gave it to her. "I don't know if this is a good idea. It might make him angry."

"I just want to see what he looks like," Tansho said. "It'll be fine. I'll give you a full progress report. Now let me think. I've got to plan what I'm going to say."

It occurred to Kara that a woman who compared men to cucumbers might not be an ideal advocate under the circumstances. She couldn't stay and argue, however, or she'd be late with her deliveries.

Wondering what sort of catastrophe she'd unloosed, she trudged out to the loading dock. The floor was wet with drizzle tracked in from outside, and the lowering clouds visible through the open doors intensified her sense of foreboding.

NOTHING WENT WELL for Daniel on Monday. The buyers' real-estate agent returned his call to say that her clients, who were moving West due to a job transfer, would arrive in town Sunday with their two toddlers and a moving van full of furniture. Although they agreed to let him stay over Saturday night, under no circumstances could they delay the close of escrow.

Performing a few mental calculations, Daniel decided to move what remained of his furniture into the garage of his Bellevue house, but he couldn't sleep at a place that torn up. He'd have to stay at a hotel.

As for Ed Riley, when the immigration attorney came on the line and heard about Kara's situation, he wasn't encouraging. "A visa waiver is intended strictly for tourists," he said. "There's no way to extend it or apply for a visa while she's here. She'll have to leave the country and submit her application from a foreign country."

"She's nine months pregnant," Daniel said. "I can't send her off on a trip by herself. What if she runs into problems?" The prospect alarmed him. "Do you really think she's likely to be deported?"

"That depends on whether they catch her," Ed said. "I'd advise her to lie low for a while."

"You mean hide? She has to make a living."

"She's working? With a visa waiver?" The lawyer whistled. "I'll cut to the chase. This woman sounds like trouble."

"She's a friend," Daniel said.

"Take my advice. Forget about being friends with this lady. Believe me, she's just using you."

Did the man have to be so abrasive? "Thanks." Gritting his teeth, Daniel said, "I appreciate your time."

"No problem."

He hung up with a sense of angry helplessness. There was no way he could leave Kara's fate in the hands of a man like Ed Riley.

A short time later, his secretary buzzed him. "There's a young woman here to see you," she said. "She declined to give her name."

"What's it about?" Law offices sometimes attracted oddballs, such as a homeless woman who'd wandered in one day wanting to sue the manufacturer of her favorite park bench because the legs were uneven. Daniel had arranged for shelter and an evaluation for mental illness.

His secretary gave a polite cough. "She says it's personal."

Kara! "I'll be right there."

In the waiting room, the first thing he saw was shiny black hair and smooth Asian features. Daniel's heart leaped. Almost at once, however, he registered the fact that this short-haired, round-faced woman bore only a superficial resemblance to Kara.

"I'm Daniel Adler," he said. "How can I help you?"

From her bright-yellow rain slicker to her red jogging shoes, his visitor looked thoroughly American. When she spoke, her unaccented voice confirmed the impression. "I'm Tansho Matsuba. May I speak to you about Chikara Tamaki?"

"Of course." So this was the friend Kara had mentioned, the one who'd done so much for Kara. "Come in."

"Great!" Instead of entering hesitantly and waiting to be asked to sit, Tansho marched into the office and plopped onto a chair. To his suggestion that she remove her coat, she declined politely but firmly.

As Daniel crossed to his desk, Tansho's frank scrutiny gave him the impression he was being sized up. When he regarded her directly, however, she assumed an expression of polite blandness.

"I assume you're here about the visa situation. I'm afraid I don't have good news." He outlined what Ed Riley had told him.

"If it's a question of money, my family and I will be happy to pay," Tansho said. "We're very fond of Kara. She's like the sister I never had."

"It's not about money," Daniel told her. "I wish she'd obtained a visa in the first place, instead of a waiver. Then we'd have something to work with."

"She was distraught." The young woman gestured dramatically. He noticed that her wrist was wrapped, but decided that, under the circumstances, her injury wasn't any of his business. "And it's getting worse. You should have seen her this morning! She was practically a basket case."

"She seemed calm enough yesterday."

"That's the front she shows the world," Tansho said. "It's this Japanese thing. Everything's supposed to look smooth and harmonious, no matter what's going on inside. But she's different with a close friend like me. I'm telling you, she's up against the ropes."

Daniel wondered if Kara's passionate friend might be exaggerating. On the other hand, his strength was logic and analysis, not intuition, so perhaps his skepticism was out of line. "She feels that desperate?"

"Frankly, I'm worried. My family and I don't know what else we can do for her. You've seen how fragile she is, or maybe it's not as obvious to you as it is to me. She's so worried that she hardly eats anymore."

It was true that at the wedding reception, Kara hadn't taken a bite. She'd nibbled at a muffin yesterday, but Daniel would hardly call that eating. "That can't be good for the baby."

"My point exactly." Tansho leaned forward and propped her elbows on his desk. "She has this nightmare where the authorities swoop down while she's in the hospital and take the baby away as soon as it's born. They don't really do that, do they?"

"Not that I know of." Daniel didn't believe the system was that harsh, even if Kara was removed to a detention center. After his talk with Ed, however, he knew she had reason to be concerned.

"That's what I tried to tell her, but she's a stranger in a strange land, and everything scares her." The young woman scarcely paused for breath before rushing on, "I'm afraid she might give birth outside a hospital. I mean, she doesn't have medical insurance, and I can't talk her into applying for a state program because she doesn't want the authorities to notice her."

"She may have to leave the country until she can secure a visa. I don't know how long that takes."

"Is that the best you can do?" Tansho demanded.

Daniel bit back a sharp retort. Her critical tone annoyed him, since he was indeed doing his best. What this woman needed most, however, was some good advice. "By the way, you should never let another person borrow your ID. You could get in a lot of trouble."

Tansho jumped up. "I'm sorry I wasted your time."

"Wait a minute!" He got to his feet, too. "I only pointed that out because I'd be remiss if I didn't."

"I guess I should have known you'd act like part of the establishment, being an attorney and all. No offense. I'm sure it's nothing personal to you. But don't worry. I won't tell Kara what you said about leaving the country. The last thing she needs is more grief." Her features tight with disapproval, she whisked out of the office.

Accustomed to showing his visitors every courtesy, Daniel followed, although he had no intention of making a scene in front of his secretary. It was a moot point, anyway, because by the time he reached the outer office, his visitor was halfway to the elevator.

He clenched his fists as he stared down the hall at the retreating figure that, even from a distance, bristled with outrage. Tansho ought to understand that he couldn't change the law any more than she could.

However, he wasn't about to chase her. Especially since there was nothing he could say even if he caught her.

He walked over to his secretary's desk.

"Yes, Mr. Adler?" she asked.

"I'm going to lunch." Although normally he ate a sandwich at his desk, Daniel needed to let off steam. "When's my next appointment?"

"Three o'clock," she said.

He checked his watch. It was after one now. "I'll be back in plenty of time," he assured her, and went to get his raincoat.

Tansho's comments haunted him all the way to his car.

Beneath her cheerful exterior, Kara must be tied up in knots. If only he could reassure her. But how?

Marry her and her troubles go poof!

Why was he thinking about Drew's ridiculous suggestion? He wasn't going to enter into some crazy marriage of convenience. Real people didn't do that, especially not lawyers. And that went double for this one.

Drew's comment hadn't been entirely true, anyway, Daniel reflected as he drove through the light rain with no particular destination in mind. The government didn't automatically allow the spouse of a U.S. citizen to stay in the country, although such a marriage should make it easier for her to return.

One thing marriage definitely would provide, though, was medical coverage, since Stephenson & Avenida had an excellent insurance package for its employees. Also, being married to a U.S. citizen should allay Kara's fears of having her baby snatched away.

He wondered how she would react to a proposal for a temporary marriage. Since she'd married the first time for practical reasons, it was possible she'd be open to the idea. On the other hand, Daniel might be compromising his own future if he entered into such an arrangement.

The problem wasn't the distant future, it was right now. The possibility that Kara might try to give birth outside a hospital, perhaps with the aid of some medical charlatan, worried him deeply.

When he realized he was heading toward the International District, he decided there was nothing wrong with stopping by Kara's apartment to make sure she was all right. He'd leave her a note if she wasn't home yet from her delivery rounds. At the very least, he wanted to talk to her and make sure she gave birth safely under a doctor's care.

After a couple of wrong turns, he spotted the pharmacy and copy shop on the ground floor of her building. He was pulling into a parking space half a block away when, in the rearview mirror, he saw Kara's familiar figure in a blue smock, approaching, alongside an elderly man who leaned on a cane.

Her umbrella, held in such a way as to shelter both of them, made a cheery splash of poppy-red against the gray afternoon.

She hadn't seen him yet. He could drive off unnoticed and do what any sensible man in his situation would have done: phone and regretfully inform her that he'd been unable to find a way to help with the visa problem. Kara wasn't his responsibility. She had other friends, and he'd only agreed to see her as a favor to Katherine.

Of course, he could also give her the bad news in person and offer some assistance. Help with medical bills, perhaps. A promise to come to her aid if the feds did catch up with her. Or maybe something else, something still tickling the back of his mind.

Daniel got out of the car and turned up his coat collar. As he caught Kara's eye from down the block, he still had no idea what he was going to say.

CHAPTER SEVEN

THE MOMENT SHE SAW Daniel, Kara knew that Tansho must have gone to see him. Judging by his severe expression, her friend had irritated him.

Despite her misgivings, her pulse sped up at the sight of him, just as it had when his hands had moved across her abdomen at the wedding reception, scrubbing the stain from her kimono. With his broad shoulders beneath a tailored raincoat, he cut an imposing figure.

Daniel wasn't someone to toy with. Why had she agreed to let Tansho go to his office? An important man like him deserved respect at all times, as did the elderly minister at her side, whom she'd offered to escort home after spotting him outside the Matsubas' market.

"It's good to see you," she told Daniel. "May I present my esteemed neighbor, Mr. Sakioka?" In Japanese, she explained to the minister who Daniel was.

He bowed. She was pleased when Daniel bowed in return.

In English, Mr. Sakioka said, "It is an honor to meet someone who is assisting our dear Miss Tamaki. She is very well liked in our building."

"I can understand why," Daniel said. "It's an honor to meet you, too."

"Mr. Sakioka is the pastor of a church a few blocks from here." Kara wondered if she should suggest they get out of the rain, but Daniel didn't seem to mind the mist falling around him. He was probably accustomed to the wet weather in Seattle, just as she'd been accustomed to the frequent rainfalls in Hokkaido.

"We have a small congregation of immigrants," her neighbor explained. "It is a storefront church of little importance."

"I'm sure it means a great deal to your members," Daniel said. "May I help you on the stairs?"

"I would be grateful." Although Mr. Sakioka never complained, on days when his arthritis acted up, he sometimes sat on the steps and waited until someone came along to assist him. Kara was always glad to help, but Daniel had stronger arms.

His gentleness and patience as he assisted Mr. Sakioka to the second floor impressed her, especially since she knew he must be on a tight schedule. She was glad that he respected his elders, just as she did.

After making sure the minister was safely inside his unit, Kara hesitated. Was it a breach of etiquette to invite a man to her flat? But there was no lobby or other public place for them to sit.

Uncertainly, she glanced toward Daniel. With his dark hair dampened and water beading his face, he had a raw, masculine look. "If you like, we could go to my apartment," she said. "It's one floor up."

"Is that all right with you?" he asked.

She nodded. "I would be pleased if you would accept my humble hospitality. Perhaps some refreshments?"

"I just want to talk to you."

"Of course." Was he going to scold her about Tansho's imposition? Or perhaps he had some news regarding a visa.

Trying to disguise how her hands trembled, Kara gripped the railing on her way up the next flight. Her pregnancy made her less stable than usual, and it was a relief when Daniel caught her arm.

As they ascended side by side, his solid physical presence intrigued her. Her mind flashed back to Tansho's book with its photographs of couples entwined in each other's embrace.

The thought of holding Daniel that way, of feeling his skin against hers and burying her face in his chest, filled Kara with an unfamiliar glow. She imagined Daniel's long legs enclosing her and his hands stroking up her back to the sensitive nape. Even when she averted her face, the images persisted.

"Are you winded from the climb?" he asked. "You're breathing hard."

Kara could hardly swallow. "I'm…fine."

"You're not fine. These stairs are exhausting you." He kept his grip on her elbow as they reached the landing.

"I'm not accustomed to being so close to a man," she blurted.

He snatched his hand away. "I didn't mean to be improper."

"There was nothing wrong with what you did." Her impulsive comment had made everything worse! "I'm a silly girl, that's all." She started down the narrow hallway. When he didn't immediately follow, Kara reached out and tugged his hand.

She must be out of her mind. She'd just admitted that it flustered her to be around him, yet here she was, hauling him to her apartment. The problem was, she couldn't think straight. His large, strong hand felt so good that she simply wanted to hold it, and she craved more of his nearness. Without him, her little home would seem very empty.

To her delight, a smile softened the stern contours of Daniel's face. "I never know what to make of you. One minute you're the picture of shyness, and the next you don't hesitate to let me know what you want."

"Sometimes I confuse myself," Kara admitted. "Come, come."

When she opened her door, light flooded around them. Even on the grayest days, the yellow-flowered wallpaper and posters of outdoor scenes magnified any hint of sunshine. Two pots of flowers, which she rotated to keep them flourishing, made bright splashes against the simple couch, low table and rattan bureau.

Daniel's presence made the room seem smaller and yet more vibrant. Kara could feel the air molecules stirring, or perhaps that was her lonely spirit, welcoming his arrival.

"You've done quite a job here." He surveyed the room, as much as he could see of it, since a translucent screen obscured the kitchenette. "It looks great, considering you must have been working with the smallest budget in history."

"The Matsubas let me choose from items that were left behind." She had been surprised to learn that tenants who sneaked out owing rent sometimes departed so hastily they didn't take all their belongings. A large stock of furniture and knickknacks in the basement was made available to current tenants.

He checked around the airy room as if seeking something. She discovered what it was when he said, "Do you mind my asking where you sleep?"

Kara indicated the couch, with its wooden frame and blue cover. This was where she took refuge at night, dreaming of Dorima's happy future. And, these past two nights, of Daniel's dark eyes and deep voice. "It's an American-style futon, the convertible kind. It's a couch during the day, and then it pulls flat like a regular futon to sleep on. Please, have a seat."

"No, thanks. I can't stay long." He walked over and glanced behind the screen. Kara was glad she'd washed and dried her breakfast dishes, despite leaving extra early this morning. "This is cozy."

"It suits me very well." Kara knew from Katherine's statements how unusual it was for Daniel to make polite conversation. Despite a tug of impatience to find out why he'd come here today, she was pleased that he chose to share his thoughts with her.

"I don't know if I mentioned that I've bought a house in Bellevue." He paced back restlessly. "People suggested I hire an interior designer, but I'm trying to learn about decorating so I can make my own choices. Once that's done, I'll move on to landscaping."

Kara was glad to hear he took such matters seriously. "I hope you'll have good *feng shui.*"

"*Feng shui?* I've heard that term, but I'm not sure what it means," Daniel said. "Does it have something to do with good luck?"

"It's a matter of harmony," Kara explained. "Good *feng shui* requires light and openness, as well as plants and flowers. It's more complicated than that, though. For example, an expert would make sure the doorways and windows face in the right direction for your personality."

"What happens if I get it wrong? Forty years' bad luck?"

"People whose houses have bad *feng shui* can suffer from headaches, family quarrels, even money problems," Kara said earnestly. "You're fortunate you have an opportunity to get it right from the start."

"Maybe you can refer me to an expert," he said.

"There's a lady in our building, Mrs. Yamamoto, who knows something about it," Kara said. "I'd be happy to introduce you."

"Thanks." He cleared his throat. "I'm afraid I need to get to the point of my visit."

Kara didn't really want him to get to the point. She wanted to help him plan his decor, or simply stand here talking about any subject in the world except how foolish she had been to send her friend to plead her case. "First, I have something to give you." From atop her rattan bureau, she took the bright package that contained his laundered and ironed handkerchief.

"A present?" Daniel asked in surprise.

"It's your handkerchief," she said. "There's no need to open it now."

A mixture of emotions, so complex that she couldn't read them, flashed across his face. "Thank you," he said. "I, uh…" He gave a small cough before continuing.

"I'm afraid I have bad news."

Outside, a gust of rain hit the window. Kara wished she dared stop him right there. She wanted to freeze this moment so that she never had to hear anything negative. Politeness forced her to speak, however. "Yes?"

"I talked to Ed Riley. I'm afraid there's nothing he can do about getting you a visa." Daniel folded his arms, as if he wished he could hold the unpleasant words inside. "You'll need to leave the country and apply from abroad."

"I have to go back?"

"Not right away, and you might be able to get a visa from a consulate in Canada. In the meantime, he suggested you avoid attracting the attention of the authorities."

Despite Daniel's warnings, she'd believed that he would find a way to help her. What would happen to her and Dorima now? If she left the country, even to go to Canada, the authorities might not let her back in, especially if they began to suspect that she'd been working illegally. She was too close to her due date to take that chance. Dorima deserved to be born in her grandfather's country.

Perhaps Kara would have to hide in one of Seattle's many underground passages like a criminal. Or her worst fear would be realized: giving birth in prison. How could she subject her daughter to such shame?

The room faded and Kara's mind seemed to float above her. She grabbed the arm of the futon couch to steady herself.

"Are you all right?" Daniel asked.

She must not show weakness. After everything he'd done for her, it would shame her to crumble in front of him. Even worse than her concern for herself was the sense that she'd failed Daniel. She'd put him in a position where he had to suffer the unpleasantness of bringing her bad news. To weep or faint would only make things worse.

"I will manage," she said. "It is you who concerns me."

"I'm sorry?"

"This is an awkward situation for you," Kara said. "You should not have to take time from your busy day to deal with this unhappy chore. And what about your house? Mrs. Yamamoto has gone to San Francisco to visit her daughter. If I have to leave the country, how will I introduce you? I don't want your home to have bad *feng shui*."

"I don't believe this." Gently, he eased her onto the couch. "You've just taken a blow, and you're worrying about me?"

"I have been selfish." Much as she hated to admit that her

mother-in-law was right, Kara could see that, to suit herself, she'd created a great deal of trouble for many people. "You and Katherine and the Matsubas have been so kind. How can I repay all these favors?"

"No one expects to be repaid." Leaning down, Daniel tucked a loose strand of hair behind her ear. "We like you, Kara. We want to keep you around."

"For myself, I can make a life in Japan if I must," she said, although now that she'd lived here and made friends, she dreaded going back to a land where she felt as if she had no place. "It's my baby who worries me. What if I have to give her up, the way Hannah gave up her son?" She couldn't bear to do that. "But this is not your problem. Forgive me, Daniel. I am interfering with your schedule."

"That's not a problem."

"I must make plans." But she couldn't think with Daniel standing so close. His masculine scent, touched with spices, captivated Kara. He was like a vast continent filled with new sensory experiences. She wanted to lose herself in him.

He began to pace. "I hate feeling so helpless! I went into law because I was idealistic. I wanted to right wrongs, to help people who couldn't help themselves. Unfortunately, I ended up with college loans to pay off and the reality that a person can't live on air."

"Everyone must compromise," Kara said sympathetically. "That is the only way to achieve balance."

"Maybe I've compromised too much," Daniel told her. "The system is too rigid. You came here legally and you only want to work and contribute. I can offer you a place to live and medical insurance. Why shouldn't I?"

How could he offer her those things? "I don't understand," Kara said.

"If we got married…" He broke off in midsentence, as if he'd caught himself by surprise.

A small candle lit inside her, shedding light into darkness. For the tiniest moment, she allowed herself to imagine that it was possible for her and Daniel to get married. But it was not possible. She must have misunderstood. "I'm sorry. What did you say?"

"I didn't phrase that very well." He fiddled with the small package that held his handkerchief. "Let me explain it another way. You had an arranged marriage in Japan, so you understand that sometimes people marry for practical reasons."

Confused, she said, "That isn't the custom in America."

"That's true." His jaw worked. "However, if you and I were to get married—I'm speaking theoretically here—it would offer you and the baby a measure of protection. My medical insurance would cover you, for one thing, so you wouldn't have to consider delivering outside a hospital. Also, the feds aren't likely to lock up the wife of a U.S. citizen."

"But as you said, you're speaking theoretically." Kara struggled to keep her hopes from soaring and then being dashed.

"We'd have to stay married long enough to convince the authorities that it's a real marriage, or until we find another way around the visa problem." Daniel seemed to be talking to himself. "I'm not sure how long that would take."

"You're talking about a temporary wife?" Had her circumstances not been so desperate, Kara might have taken offense. "Thank you, but I am not Madame Butterfly!" She'd watched the opera on video with Tansho, and although she'd loved the music, she'd groaned at the melodramatic ending.

"Kara, look, I know this is crazy." He strode back and forth like a caged tiger. "But I have to do something. I can't stand by and watch you get railroaded. I'm not sure I understand it myself, but my gut tells me we should get married."

"For how long?" she asked. "A week? A month?" Her head was whirling again. This couldn't be real.

"I have no idea." He took a deep breath. "Technically, it isn't legal for me to marry you simply to help you gain residency. We'd have to stay married long enough to convince the authorities it's real. This is a spur-of-the-moment idea. I haven't researched it."

"And you might regret it," she felt compelled to point out.

"If it is illegal, you'll bring trouble on yourself. I've caused enough difficulties already."

He shook his head, throwing off her objections. "Let's do this, Kara. Let me help you by giving you my name."

"My mother-in-law said I was an unlucky bride," she blurted.

"It's not your fault your husband got hit by a car," Daniel said. "I don't believe in luck. I believe people make their own destinies."

Kara swallowed hard, trying to find her voice. If only she knew what she wanted to say!

Her heart filled with joy when she imagined herself helping Daniel settle into his new house. What fun it would be to shop for furniture together, to cook for him, to see him every evening. Best of all, baby Dorima would spend her first months safe and happy. But it would only be temporary. And when it was over, how could she give up such a kind, handsome man?

"May I think about it?" she asked. "You need a chance to reconsider, also."

"I won't go back on my word."

"You haven't given your word," Kara said. "You've only spoken theoretically."

"I asked you to marry me," Daniel said. "I meant it."

It would be rude to refuse him outright, even if she could bring herself to do it. Most likely it would not be necessary. He would soon regret his impulsive offer.

"We will talk again tomorrow, and you must be frank with me if you change your mind," she said. "Remember, you have a money-back guarantee."

"Once I make a commitment, I keep it," he said. "In the meantime, I'll check out what's involved in getting a marriage license. I want to make sure your immigration status won't present any problems."

"That is sensible." Perhaps he'd find that they couldn't marry, after all. "We will talk again tomorrow."

"You're very strong," Daniel said. "I'm offering you a safety hatch. Most women would leap at it."

"I don't wish to leap and then come crashing down," Kara said. She had a feeling the crash would be harder than he could imagine.

Daniel smiled almost in spite of himself. "I love the way you phrase things." A glance at his watch banished the smile. "I'm afraid I have to get back."

"I understand. You were kind to come here."

He moved toward the door. "Don't get up."

Ignoring the command, Kara tried to glide to her feet. Unfortunately, gravity and the baby had other ideas. She managed to lift herself a few inches before sinking down again.

"Let me show you out," she teased, although obviously she could do no such thing. "There. That way is out." She blinked up at him. "I hope you don't get lost in this enormous apartment."

"No fear." He smiled again. "If it suits you, I'll pick you up tomorrow around six-thirty."

"I'll cook dinner for you here," Kara said. "We can talk more comfortably over food." She wanted to show how much she appreciated his generosity, even though she doubted anything would come of it.

"You're not getting anywhere near a stove," he said. "I mean that. In your condition, you can't stand close enough to a stove to cook on it."

"I can turn sideways," she said. "Besides, I'm not that big."

"I'll cook dinner in my condo to show you that I haven't changed my mind." Daniel paused in the doorway. "The more I think about it…"

"We must take time to consider," she reminded him.

"It's funny," he said. "This time, I'm acting on impulse and you're looking at all the angles."

"Perhaps that is a sign." Kara leaned her head back. "Now I must figure out if it's a good sign or a bad one."

"Let's hope it's a good one," he said. "I'll see you to-morrow."

"Yes. And thank you, Daniel."

With a last nod, he went out. Kara sat motionless, trying to clear her mind. She could feel his presence all around. How was she ever going to make a sensible decision when she already missed him so much?

THE WEIGHT ROOM at the gym had the steaminess of a rainy day. Thickened by the stink of sweat and the aroma of suspiciously underwashed gym clothes, the odor was enough to knock a man flat if he wasn't already exercising in that position, Daniel mused as he and Drew lay side by side doing bench presses.

Although the two of them met here only occasionally, Daniel was glad tonight was one of those nights. His natural reluctance to share private information even with a close buddy had yielded to the need to gather information about marriage.

He hadn't been able to think clearly about the ramifications of getting married. It had been a busy afternoon, and when he had a free moment, he'd spent it researching the facts, rather than considering what lay ahead.

Daniel still could hardly believe he'd proposed to Kara. Entering into marriage as a subterfuge went against everything he believed, or at least everything he'd thought he believed. Yet he felt such an overwhelming urge to protect her that he could never withdraw his offer.

Despite the ribbing he knew was inevitable, he'd just told Drew the whole story. "I can't believe you really did it," was the first reaction. "I know I suggested a marriage of convenience, but...wow!"

"Uh," was all Daniel managed to reply, because he was pushing the barbell to arm's length. The strain rippled along his arm and chest muscles.

"Man, when Katherine finds out, she'll be dancing on the ceiling," Drew said.

Slowly, Daniel lowered the barbell. Although he ought to

continue lifting, he couldn't talk and work out at the same time, and right now, talking had the higher priority. "You're not going to tell her!"

"I won't have to. You can't keep this secret for long." Drew didn't even make a pretense of lifting his weights. "Are you sure it's possible? This marriage, I mean?"

"Possible in what sense?" Daniel asked.

"Don't people need to be residents to get married here? Or at least take a blood test and wait two weeks?" Then Drew held up one hand. "Come to think of it, I guess Julia and I didn't do that."

"There's no blood test," Daniel agreed. It had been a relief this afternoon when he looked up the facts. "We don't have to show ID, either. We just apply and wait three days, and then any minister or judge can perform the ceremony."

Dealing with the federal government was going to be harder, although he decided not to mention that. Sometime within the next year and a half, he and Kara would have to undergo intensive interviews. Even once they convinced the authorities that their marriage was genuine, she would only be issued a temporary green card and would have to wait two more years for a permanent one.

When he'd first considered a marriage of convenience, Daniel had thought in terms of months, not years. On the other hand, the point was to keep Kara safe until after she had her baby. With the immediate pressure relieved, they might be able to find a quicker way to secure her a work permit.

"It's amazingly easy to get married, from a legal standpoint," Drew said. "Not that I'm objecting."

"It's harder to get a divorce," Daniel said. "If it weren't so complicated, a lot of lawyers would be out of business."

"That's a twisted way of looking at it!"

"Just dealing in reality here."

"Hard-hearted is the way some people would look at it," his friend joked. "I hope Kara knows what she's letting herself in for."

"I don't think either of us has a clue, to tell the truth.

Besides, she hasn't said yes yet.'' Daniel made a halfhearted attempt to resume exercising, but soon gave up. "Maybe we should free up these stations for someone else."

"Can't we just lie here? I don't see anyone lining up." Drew grinned. "That's what I've mostly been doing, anyway, lying here. I wouldn't want to wear myself out, after all."

"There are people waiting. You're just not looking very hard." Daniel signaled to an attendant to take the barbell so he could rise. "If we're not going to finish our weight training, the least we can do is head for the treadmills."

"I only came here tonight because Julia said I was getting a little pudgy," Drew complained. "I figured I'd use the pool and maybe the sauna."

"Aren't you glad you have a friend who's such a good influence?"

"You're not a good influence. You're a pain in the neck." Seeing that his good-natured insult had no effect, Drew gestured to the attendant to relieve him, as well. "Okay, but I'm not working up any more of a sweat than I have to."

"Suit yourself."

They claimed treadmills and set the dials for resistance and speed. When they began walking, Drew picked up the thread of conversation. "Exactly how married do you plan to be, assuming she says yes?"

"We're only doing this for the sake of the baby and for Kara's well-being," Daniel said stiffly.

"No nooky?"

"In her condition?"

"I mean afterward."

Although he hadn't allowed himself to think about it, Daniel knew the answer instantly. "It wouldn't be fair to Kara." He was determined to prevent either of them from forming an emotional attachment.

"How about what's fair to you?" Drew shot back. "You're a guy, after all, and she's a cutie. Don't tell me you're going to lie there in an adjacent bedroom night after night thinking about what kind of shelving to put in the garage."

"Let's talk about something else."

"You tell me you're getting married and then you want to talk about something else? Get real!"

"I meant, let's talk about something other than sex." Daniel was beginning to wish he'd gone a little easier on his treadmill settings. He was breathing hard while his friend, true to his word, strolled at a leisurely pace and barely broke a sweat.

"Okay, let's talk about what you're going to wear to the wedding," Drew said. "I've got it! A tuxedo. Can we can get back to sex now?"

Daniel wondered, not for the first time, why he'd struck up a friendship with a guy who was so different from him. Still, even at his most provoking, Drew always kept him entertained.

"Speaking of sex, I wanted to ask you about babies," he said.

"You mean where they come from?" Drew asked. "I can explain that. First, the bird picks up the bee in a bar and offers to buy her a drink. After she's had two or three, she says, 'Your hive or mine?'"

Daniel hated to laugh, but he couldn't help it. "I didn't mean how you make them. I mean, what's it like having one around? Especially one who isn't exactly yours."

"Jeremy *is* mine." Drew was in the process of adopting his infant stepson, which Daniel knew, since he'd drawn up the papers as a favor. "Some people make a big deal about having a genetic attachment, but the fact is, you bond with a baby the minute you gaze into his little face and see the love shining back. You realize that he's utterly dependent on you and thinks you're the greatest thing in the universe. It doesn't matter if you're his biological father or not, you couldn't love him any more."

"That's quite a speech."

"I can be serious…sometimes. Not for too long at a stretch, though."

"Isn't he noisy?" Daniel asked. "Does he keep you up at night?"

"Sometimes," Drew said. "I don't mind, because I love him so much. In your case, Kara will probably keep the whole situation under control."

"I hope so."

There were a lot of other things Daniel wanted to ask, but he found it difficult. They were either too trivial, such as how you divided up the household chores, or too personal, such as how you figured out a woman's moods. Marriage of convenience or not, they were going to be sharing quarters for who knew how long.

In silence, the men concentrated on their exercise. It was amazing that Drew, despite his professed disdain for working up a sweat, appeared to be in great shape. Well, he was only twenty-six. By thirty, he'd have to work harder, Daniel told himself.

"Julia's going to be thrilled when she hears about this." Drew's wife worked in infant care at Forrester Square. "She thinks Kara's perfect to take over the toddler class."

Despite his sore lungs, Daniel upped the resistance on his dial. He wanted a good burn in his muscles tonight. "I don't see why Kara would need to work while we're married. She's due for a break."

"She might want to," said his friend.

"I've heard that being a mom is a tough job. Especially at first."

"Some women like to work," Drew said. Drew's mother had given up teaching elementary school after her children were born, although she had returned to work when her husband was sent to jail.

"Doesn't her husband get any say, assuming he has her best interests at heart?"

His friend stopped his treadmill. "Hey, pal, I thought you were bucking for the title of knight in shining armor, not dictator."

"I'm only trying to do what's right." Daniel slowed his

pace, but he didn't want to stop cold turkey. "Temporary or not, as long as she's my wife, she'll be under my protection."

"Under your protection or under your rule?"

"That's putting it a bit strongly!"

"I doubt most women would think so."

Daniel didn't want to argue what seemed to him an obvious point. Pregnancy and childbearing were physically hard on a woman. Kara was going to need time to recover and to adjust to her new situation. And from everything he'd read, the bond that formed between the infant and mother during the first year was critical to the child's well-being.

"I guess I was brought up in an old-fashioned way," he said. "Besides, I hardly think Kara wants to go on driving a delivery truck."

"From what Katherine says, she's always wanted to work in child care." Drew wiped his neck with a towel, although he scarcely needed to. "Besides, you said yourself you're not going to stay married forever. Forrester Square is the perfect opportunity for her."

That was true. Daniel didn't understand why the discussion left him so dissatisfied. "We're putting the cart before the horse. She hasn't agreed to marry me yet. We can work out the details later."

"You sound grumpy," Drew said. "You're not changing your mind, are you?"

"Absolutely not!" It was true. Not once since he'd left Kara's apartment had he regretted his offer.

By the time he got home that night, Daniel was weary from the exercise and the long day. His mood didn't improve when he stumbled over a box of books.

When he finally got to bed, he kept picturing Kara in her cheerful room, floating on a futon suspended in its wooden frame. If she said yes, she would be installing her futon in his new house and making tea in his kitchen.

It sounded like fun. The two of them got along so well, he expected they'd have a good time for as long as it lasted.

Just before falling asleep, Daniel thought, *Please let her say yes.* He was surprised at how much he meant it.

CHAPTER EIGHT

KARA DECIDED not to explain to Tansho why she was borrowing the *Sexual Frolicking* book. She had to make her own decision about Daniel's proposal. Although her friend's advice was often useful, in this case Kara was reminded of the old Japanese saying: Too many captains will sail a boat up a mountain.

That was why she slipped into the Matsubas' office during the dinner hour on Monday, when she knew her friend was dining with her parents, and was pleased to find the book still in the drawer. Judging by the smudged fingerprints on the jacket, it had been thumbed thoroughly, probably by Tansho's brothers. Kara left a note promising to return it the following morning.

She didn't open it until she was home. Even then, she found herself embarrassed to look at the pictures.

Daniel hadn't specified whether this temporary marriage involved sexual consummation, but she had to assume that it might, and as an American, he would surely be disappointed if she failed to respond with enough ardor. Her passive acceptance might have satisfied Hiro, but she suspected Daniel was very different.

She'd been keenly aware of the differences the whole time he'd been in this room. When she was near Daniel, her skin rippled like a silk scarf and she could hear his breathing as clearly as if he were whispering in her ear.

Shyly, she peeked at one of the photos. The model had a sleek body with large breasts, not like anyone Kara knew, and she wasn't afraid to display them for the camera. She seemed very Western. Although Kara had read that Japanese men attended strip shows and watched movies about sex, in her circles everyone had dressed and behaved modestly.

How could she possibly entwine herself around Daniel that way? Turning a page, Kara gasped at an even more erotic pose. What kind of woman would let a man touch her like that?

She didn't know why she grew hot between her legs, thinking about what he might look like without clothing. Yes, it would be a pleasure to stroke his cheek and kiss him, perhaps to be held in those strong arms. But she would be much too embarrassed to see his powerful body unclothed, let alone behave like the woman in this book!

If she wasn't going to accept his proposal, Kara thought, she must find another option. Her grandfather had once told her that whenever a door closed, somewhere a window opened. The trick was to find that window and find it quickly.

Setting the book aside, Kara went down the hall to Mrs. Yamamoto's apartment. She had a key, since she'd promised to water the plants while her friend was in San Francisco, and she also had permission to use the computer.

She kept hoping one of the search engines would turn up the name of her grandfather's brother, Franklin Loesser, whose last-known residence had been in Cincinnati, Ohio. Perhaps if she could afford to subscribe to one of the databases that helped families reunite, she might have more luck. Still, her great-uncle might have died long ago, and without knowing the names of any of his descendants, Kara was at a loss. Her best hope was that, like Mrs. Yamamoto, he'd recently gone online or joined a club with an online newsletter in which his name might appear.

She knew only a little about her paternal relatives. Her grandfather, Albert Loesser, had grown up in Cincinnati, where his parents had owned and operated a small grocery store. While serving in Japan after the Second World War, he'd fallen in love with Kara's grandmother, Umeko, and married her.

In those long-ago times, the marriage across racial and cultural lines had shocked her American great-grandparents, who'd refused to have anything further to do with their elder son. Franklin had sided with his parents, a choice for which Bert had never forgiven him.

After leaving the military, her grandfather had opened his own small shop, specializing in imported American goods. Bert and Umeko's only daughter had died of polio. Their son, Kara's father, was so distressed at being of mixed race that, as an adult, he'd taken his mother's Japanese surname.

It was Kara who'd attended to her grandfather when he came to live with them after her grandmother died. Unlike her brother, who was busy with sports and didn't like speaking English, she'd loved listening to tales of long-ago days during the Great Depression in America. She could still see Grandpa, his long legs stretched out in front of the heater, pulling on the beard that had embarrassed her clean-shaven father.

Although he addressed other family members in heavily accented Japanese, Grandpa seemed much freer and livelier when he spoke English to Kara. He'd shown nostalgia for the country of his birth, and yet he'd never suggested moving back. "There's nothing left for me there," he'd said. "I wish I knew what happened to Franklin, though."

Kara will still trying to find out. Unfortunately, after nearly an hour of searching, the Internet once again turned up no trace of her great-uncle. Her chances of finding him were growing fainter every day.

Giving up for the moment, she checked her e-mail for messages from her family. Her brother, Enoki, had sent digital pictures of himself and his wife on a recent trip to Mount Fuji. "You're not the only one who knows how to take a vacation!" he'd written.

As Kara typed in a thank-you, tears burned in her eyes. How she missed her brother and parents. Sometimes, like now, she wished she could go back, but then she remembered that going home meant living with Mrs. Tamaki. It was unthinkable.

Besides, she had dreamed since childhood of coming to her grandfather's homeland. It was as wonderful as she'd imagined, full of excitement and opportunities. For her baby's sake, she must be brave. She must find a way to stay here.

After logging off and locking up, Kara returned to her room. Her gaze flew to the shelf where she kept a photograph of her grandfather.

"What shall I do?" she asked him. "Would this temporary marriage shame you? What if I do the things with Daniel that are shown in that book? How will I feel when he is no longer my husband?"

She could almost hear her grandfather saying, "Follow your dream," as he often had when he was alive. Kara wanted to obey, but right now she was afraid of where her dream might take her.

A wave of exhaustion washed over her. She'd arisen extra early this morning to help Tansho in the office, and she must arise at her usual early hour tomorrow to make deliveries. She was in no frame of mind to make an important decision.

By tomorrow night, she must choose her future and that of her child. She hoped she would make the right choice.

ON HIS LUNCH BREAK Tuesday, Daniel went to check out a centrally located hotel with rates advertised as budget. They certainly didn't suit the budget of a man who also had to make house payments, he reflected ruefully. On the other hand, the room looked comfortable and there was a data port, a sports lounge, a café and free parking.

He made a week's reservation beginning Sunday. Whether his Bellevue house really would be ready for occupancy by the end of that period remained to be seen.

At least the rain had ended. Emerging into patchy sunlight, Daniel strolled to the nearby Pike Place Market to grab a sandwich. He ate it while window-shopping in the North Arcade, enjoying the array of artisan-made jewelry, clothing, ceramics, leather goods and other crafts. He had to remind himself not to buy anything, because it would have to be trucked over to the hotel or stored in his garage.

As he was leaving, a tinkling noise caught his attention. In an open booth, he spotted a basket arrangement of feather flowers and sparkly balloons. In the center, miniature glass wind chimes dangled from a fan-shaped support. The breeze stirred by his passing had set the chimes jingling.

Onto his mental screen flashed an image of Kara examining the arrangement in his condo tonight, her mouth curving at its fancifulness. It was exactly what he needed to brighten the half-empty place during dinner, and it would make a lovely gift for her to take home afterward, he decided, reaching for his wallet.

Outside, he balanced the basket in his arms as he inhaled moist air and briny sea tang. In a rare impulsive gesture, he threw back his head and let the spring sunshine warm his face and shoulders.

Brakes rasped on the street. Glancing toward the curb, Daniel saw a panel truck labeled Matsuba Market double-parking.

A young man sitting in the passenger seat turned to the driver and said something. Although Daniel couldn't understand the words drifting through the open window, he recognized the scolding tone. A moment later, Kara appeared around the back of the truck.

"Is something wrong?" Daniel called.

"No!" Her face shone with excitement. "I saw you in the sunshine. Your spirit was dancing! There's music all around you."

"You must have heard the wind chimes."

Beneath her flowing top and loose pants, Kara's movements suggested a dance of her own as she touched the feathery flowers and stirred the chimes lightly with her forefinger. Daniel stood there beaming back at her, feeling utterly unlike his usual self.

From the van, her passenger called, "Come on, Kara! We're due back."

"So what?" she responded. "The produce is all gone. Nothing will spoil!"

"I want my lunch," the young man grumbled.

"Never mind Akio," she told Daniel. "He's very immature."

"He's also hungry," Daniel said, although he had no desire for her to leave.

"He has no soul," Kara declared. "He has no sense of *wa*, or harmony. How could I not stop?"

"You'll see the wind chimes tonight," Daniel promised. "In fact, you'll be taking them home with you. They're a gift."

"Thank you, and I will enjoy them, but you must understand," Kara said. "that this moment is a work of art. It is a perfect form that requires sunshine and surprise to make it complete, and it will never happen again exactly this way." As she spoke, her fingers fluttered as if to mime the scattering rays of sunshine. "I could not pass by without stopping to appreciate you."

"Is the element of surprise part of *feng shui?*" Fascinated by Kara's enthusiasm, he found himself wanting to keep her here longer. If he'd had a way to surreptitiously send out for pizza to stop Akio from complaining, he'd have done it.

"This is not the same thing," Kara said. *Feng shui* requires careful attention and planning. But to me, sponta…" She stumbled over the word and tried again. "Spontaneity can lead to great beauty, also."

"I'm afraid I'm not known for my spontaneity," Daniel admitted.

"Then you have made a great leap today," she told him. "I will match you. Until I saw you, I had no idea what I was going to tell you tonight. Now I know. Yes, I'll be very happy to marry you! We can enjoy each moment. So what if it's temporary? Life is temporary, also."

It took him a moment to realize that she was serious. She'd made an important decision based on nothing more than sunshine and instinct. Yet what better reason was there to make such a choice? In some situations, logic seemed woefully inadequate. "That's excellent. I mean, I'm glad."

"Yes." A sheen of moisture formed in her eyes. "Yes, me, too."

"I haven't filled you in on the details." Despite a strong urge to simply take her up on her decision, Daniel knew he had an obligation to inform her fully. "Dealing with the government isn't going to be easy. We might have to stay married for a couple of years unless we can find a quicker way to get you a green card. But I'll get to work on that."

Kara shook her head playfully. "You must not talk like a lawyer at such a romantic moment."

"I'm afraid I am a lawyer."

"I think you're a magician. You appeared at exactly the right moment to cast a spell on me." She brushed a crumb from his lapel. "You can be many things, Daniel Adler. All of them amazing!"

"Only with you." There was no flattery in his words, just truth.

"Kara!" called the man in the truck. "Do you hear the rumbling? Is it an earthquake? No, it's my stomach!"

"He's going to drive me crazy," Kara said. "Wait until he finds a girlfriend—then he'll understand. Or perhaps he'll tell her, 'I'm sorry. I can't speak poetry to you. I have to go stuff my tummy!'"

Daniel started laughing and didn't want to stop. He felt like a bird that has just learned how to fly. This woman had the strangest effect on him.

Kara touched his arm lightly. "I have to go. I will buy some food for us to cook tonight."

He had to admit, he hadn't shopped yet or even planned a menu. "That would be great."

"See you!" With a wave, she darted back to the truck.

Daniel stood planted on the sidewalk, watching her drive off. It took a while for him to realize what had just happened. She'd said yes. He, Daniel Adler, was engaged, and in a few days he was going to be married, at least for a while.

Kara had called him a magician. There was definitely magic in the air, he thought, but she was the one who'd created it.

KARA COULD HARDLY believe she'd made her decision about marrying Daniel so easily after struggling all night. It had been the right choice under the right circumstances. Her spirits had soared when she spotted him strolling along the street with that whimsical basket in his arms. He was irresistible.

Of course it wasn't a real marriage. She didn't care. She chose to relish each moment for its own beauty. Let this be a special time of her life, for her sake and for Dorima's.

Now that she'd accepted, she wanted to make everything perfect, starting with the menu for tonight. After parking her truck and turning in her receipts, she went through the aisles of the Matsubas' market picking out the best produce. She started with broccoli to go with fried rice. What else should she serve? she wondered.

Tansho, who hadn't been in view when Kara parked by the loading dock, walked up behind her. "Why are you rushing around?"

"I have to go to the meat market. I think Daniel would like a pork cutlet, don't you?" she said. "We're cooking dinner tonight."

"Oh, you're seeing Daniel! Is that why you borrowed my book last night? Thanks for returning it, but you could have kept it as long as you liked."

Kara blushed. "I only wanted to prepare myself."

"That's what I figured," her friend teased. "You must be expecting an exciting dinner party."

"I didn't need the book for tonight," Kara said. "It's because we're getting married."

For once, Tansho had nothing to say. She simply stood there staring. At last she said, "You're going to marry Daniel?"

"No—Akio." Kara made a face. "What do you think?"

"About Akio?"

"I was joking!"

"Seriously? Daniel Adler asked you to marry him and you said yes?"

She nodded. "Maybe chicken would be better. Not everyone likes pork."

"Kara! This is so sudden!" Tansho's eyes narrowed. "It's a green-card marriage, isn't it."

Kara was glad she'd heard that term before, so she didn't have to appear ignorant. "Well, of course. But please don't tell anyone else that. I don't want him to get in trouble."

"You're not going to stay married? That could be tricky."

"I refuse to worry about it."

Her friend trailed her along the aisle as Kara picked up and rejected half-a-dozen other vegetables. "When did he ask you?"

"Yesterday afternoon."

"You mean, right after I went to visit him?"

"I suppose so," she conceded.

"Boy, when I work a guilt trip, I really work a guilt trip, don't I?" Tansho grinned with satisfaction.

Kara wanted to argue that Daniel had proposed on his own initiative, not because of anything he'd been told. But it obviously made her friend happy to think she had played a role. Besides, how could anyone be sure what had spurred him to take such an unexpected step?

The one thing Kara knew was that he hadn't fallen in love. That took time, and also, he'd made it clear his goal was to protect her from the authorities, for which she was grateful.

"You're a master matchmaker," she told her friend. "Perhaps you could hire yourself out."

"No one wants a matchmaker who makes temporary marriages." Tansho handed her a bottle of Ton-Katu sauce. "You should take this in case you need it. Don't substitute Worcestershire sauce! It's not the same."

"I know that," Kara said. "And I'm not going to worry about it being temporary. I expected to stay married to Hiro forever, and five months later he was gone."

"You never know what will happen," her friend agreed.

"It would be better if I could leave sooner," Kara said. "I don't want to be unfair to Daniel. He might meet an American woman he wants to marry." Her heart squeezed at the thought. Yet if it happened, she would have to accept it.

"If you don't have papers, you can't leave sooner." Tansho accompanied her to the cash register. Since the clerk was helping another customer, Tansho went behind the counter to ring up Kara's purchases.

"I still might find my grandfather's relatives." Kara refused to give up hope. "Surely they could help me stay in this country. After all, I'm one-quarter American."

"That reminds me. What about your parents?" Her friend swiped the scanner across the universal product code on the sauce bottle. "Are you going to invite them?"

"I don't know," she said. "I'll have to think about it."

"What sort of wedding will you have?" Tansho asked. "Are you going to do the whole bit with the special kimono and the *uchikake* gown over it and that funny-looking hat?"

Kara's wedding to Hiro had been a modest production, but she'd worn the traditional elaborate clothing. "I don't see how I can. There's no time and I have no money." She made a face. "Besides, Daniel would think it was silly for me to wear a boat-shaped hat. That's such a funny idea, that I have to cover up my horns of jealousy!"

"It's more fun to do it American-style, anyway, since you've already had a traditional Japanese wedding," Tansho said. "You can rent a big white gown. In your case, a *really* big white gown."

Kara laughed. "I don't even know if I'm going to have a big wedding, but if I do, maybe I should mix the traditions. Can't you see me wearing a white maternity dress with the *tsuno* horns on my head, sailing down the aisle like a ship? I'd need a rudder!"

"Instead of a bridesmaid's dress, I'll wear a sailor's uniform," Tansho said. "I'll lash a rope around your waist, if I can find it, and tug you back into the aisle when you veer off course." They both laughed.

A clucking sound alerted them to Mrs. Matsuba's presence. A sprinkling of gray hair and a thickening waistline only added to her authority as she folded her arms and demanded, "What are you girls making such noise about?"

"Kara's getting married, Mom!" Tansho said. "To her friend the lawyer."

"Is it true?" Mrs. Matsuba asked in astonishment.

Kara nodded. "It's what they call a green-card marriage." She explained the arrangement to Tansho's mother, who listened thoughtfully. "We don't want other people to know about this. We might not even need a ceremony. As a lawyer, Daniel can arrange for a judge to sign our marriage papers."

"No ceremony?" the older woman cried. "Of course you must have a ceremony! You will get married at our house." The family owned a lovely home with a garden. "That is, if your new mother-in-law agrees."

"My mother-in-law!" Kara hadn't considered how Daniel's parents might react to the news. "He isn't close to his mother. He said she left him and his father when he was a teenager."

"You mean you won't have a mother-in-law?" Tansho said. "This man sounds perfect."

Mrs. Matsuba took a playful swat at her daughter. "What if your brothers' girlfriends talk about me that way?"

Tansho threw her arms around her mother. "They will never talk that way, because everyone knows what a wonderful mother-in-law you would be."

Her mother gave a snort. "You're a tricky girl! I don't believe you." But she smiled.

"Thank you for your generous offer to have our wedding at your home," Kara said. "I'll ask Daniel."

"It will be a pleasure to host a wedding," Mrs. Matsuba said, "since my own clumsy daughter can't even find herself a boyfriend."

Undaunted, Tansho waved a hand dismissively. "The men I meet are too ugly, and they all have dragons for mothers."

She turned to Kara. "Come on, let's go shopping. We should look for a pretty dress on sale so you won't have to rent one."

"I'm not finished buying food for tonight," Kara protested.

"We'll get the rest on the way home from our shopping." Tansho winked at her mother. "You can spare me for a few hours, can't you?"

"Okay," said Mrs. Matsuba. "Since you don't have a boyfriend to cook dinner for, you can work this evening to make up for it."

Tansho made a face, then gave her mother another hug. As the two young women sauntered out together, Kara wished she had such a close relationship with her own mother. More than ever, she was grateful for having found the Matsubas.

THE BASKET with the wind chimes didn't seem like enough decoration, so Daniel stopped on the way to Kara's apartment to buy a flower arrangement. He'd already stocked up on ice cream and apple pie, in case she didn't think of dessert.

He was still trying to absorb the fact that he'd offered Kara a green-card marriage. What would it be like being a temporary husband? This was going to be strange.

Then there was the issue of what life would be like once the infant arrived. He knew as little about taking care of a baby as he knew about raising iguanas. Maybe less, because iguanas didn't wear diapers.

Kara was waiting on the sidewalk with a sackful of groceries. After double-parking, Daniel hurried to help her.

She exclaimed over the flowers, taking time to admire each blossom. On the way to his condo, she told him about her friend's offer of her home for a wedding. Daniel was dubious at first, until it occurred to him that when it came time to "prove" their marriage was real, the wedding pictures could be essential.

They agreed to get their marriage license the next day, which, because of the required three-day wait, meant they could get married on Sunday. Daniel hoped that having the ceremony so soon wasn't going to inconvenience the Matsubas.

Another possible problem occurred to him. "Are you still in official mourning?" he asked. "I don't know the Japanese customs. People in this country used to stay in mourning for a year."

"Such a long time!" Kara said. "For us, mourning lasts until the fiftieth day. By then, the soul has left for eternity."

Daniel was glad that remarrying didn't violate her customs. The subject reminded him, however, that she had a family to consider. "Do you think your parents will come? Or do you plan to keep them in the dark about the whole thing?"

"I've decided not to tell them yet," Kara said.

"That's wise."

She regarded him obliquely. "What about your parents? Are you going to tell them?"

He'd thought long and hard about that. It went against the grain to keep secrets from his father, even though Daniel wasn't looking forward to Vernon Adler's reaction when informed about the reason for their union. "I'll invite Dad, of course. It's unlikely he'll come."

"What about your mother?" Kara ventured.

"I'm not going to ask her." That was all he cared to say. "Now, tell me what we're eating tonight."

With obvious enjoyment, she launched into a description. The menu consisted of fried rice with fresh vegetables, miso soup, pork cutlets and pickled vegetables. It didn't sound complicated, which was a relief, given that Daniel stocked only the basic pots and pans. As for the unfamiliar soup and vegetables, he was more than willing to try them.

Once they arrived at his condo, Kara took over the kitchen. Despite her girth, she was a diminutive whirlwind, emptying her shopping bags in record time and setting up the counter to her liking. By the time Daniel had removed his jacket, tossed his tie over the back of a chair and washed up, she'd put the rice on to cook and was heating water for the instant soup.

"You've got to let me help," he said as she washed a head of broccoli. "I promised I was going to cook."

"You can fix dessert," Kara said.

"That's too easy! I bought pie and ice cream."

"Next time, I will do the easy part." She gave him a sideways glance that was both assertive and playful.

"Are all Japanese women as bossy as you?"

"In the home, yes," she said, taking no offense. "To a Japanese woman, her home is her kingdom. She takes charge of the finances, the house and the children's education."

"The finances, too?" Daniel tried to reconcile this information with his image of Japanese women as shy and compliant. Evidently the stereotype omitted a few important details. "What does the husband do?"

"He works." She whipped out a cutting board and began mincing the vegetables into tiny bits.

"All the time?"

Her dark hair swung as she nodded. "Long hours. Then he goes to a club with his friends to hang out."

"I want to hang out with you," Daniel said.

She turned, her eyes widening. "Even though we're only getting married so I can stay in your country?"

"Sure," he said. "I go to the gym sometimes, but mostly I want to spend time around the house."

She swallowed. "What do you want to spend your time doing?"

He hadn't meant to make her nervous. "Oh, nothing special," Daniel said. "The place needs some fixing up. And when the baby's asleep, I hope you and I can relax together."

"What do you mean by 'relax'?" She watched him as if his answer carried some deep meaning. What on earth was she worried about?

"I whirl through the house with flaming swords," he told her. "Think you can handle that?"

"You do not!"

"Okay. I like to watch science-fiction shows on television,

and one of these days I might put in a hot tub," he said. "What did you think I meant?"

"You're funny." Kara returned to her cooking. "You make jokes just like my friends do." He wasn't sure what she'd been afraid he might say, but apparently his answer had reassured her.

"I hope I am one of your friends," Daniel said. "Didn't Hiro make jokes?"

She mulled his question before answering, "Not to me."

"How boring."

"Entertaining me wasn't part of our arrangement." She opened a lower cabinet and bent to reach inside.

"Whoa! I'll get out whatever you need." A Japanese woman might run the house, but no way was Daniel going to let her dig through the cupboards at this late stage of pregnancy. As he caught her shoulders to move her gently aside, he found that she fit perfectly against the protective length of his body. Quickly, he shifted away.

Kara folded her arms. "If you won't let me go through your cabinets myself, please take out all your skillets."

"All of them?"

"I need several sizes. I want to see what you've got."

Embarrassed by his instinctive excitement at her nearness, Daniel busied himself pulling out his pans, all three of them. "It's lucky I didn't pack these yet. I have to move out by Sunday."

"To your new house?" Kara set the pots on the burners.

"It won't be ready for occupancy until next week at the earliest," Daniel said. "I've reserved a room at a hotel."

"A hotel?" Kara asked. "But you will be my husband. You must stay with me."

He hadn't given the practical aspects of their marriage much thought, he realized. "I don't see how we're going to manage that. I mean, you only have one bed."

Kara turned to face him. He must have been standing closer than she'd realized, because her uptilted face was only inches below his own. "You think I'm afraid to be alone with you. But I'm not."

"We're alone now," he pointed out. His instincts, barely tamped down from a few minutes ago, revved into high gear again.

"Yes, and I'm not afraid at all." She gazed up, lips parted. "See? I'm not a silly girl. Nothing you can do will frighten me."

Daniel couldn't resist the challenge, not when he was aching to hold her. As he lowered his head, he knew, only an instant before it happened, what he was going to do. "Not even this?" he asked, and touched his mouth to hers.

CHAPTER NINE

KARA LIFTED HERSELF on tiptoe as Daniel's lips grazed hers. A wonderful weakness trembled into her knees when he kissed her again more firmly. Impulsively, she flicked her tongue against his teeth.

Daniel's low moan sent sparkles glimmering across her skin. She hoped he was experiencing sensations like hers, in which case they definitely should do more of this. Much more.

With a spurt of boldness, Kara slipped her hands up his arms, enjoying the smoothness of his shirt. His clean scent made her want to press her nose into his chest, but she was enjoying the kiss too much to break it off.

Daniel drew her close, angling her so the baby posed no obstacle. Kara loved the way his eyelids drifted down, as if he were blocking out everything but her. She wanted to linger in this private world for a long time.

When he shifted his grasp, her breasts grazed Daniel's hard chest. Heat flared into her core, and abruptly Kara understood why the woman in the book had twined herself around the man as if to meld the two of them together.

Shocked, she tried to draw back. Daniel held on a moment longer, breathing hard, before releasing her.

"I'm sorry," he said. "I'm not sure where that came from."

"Where it came from?" The expression baffled Kara.

"I didn't intend to put you in an awkward situation." Daniel shook his head. "I assure you, I have no intention of making you uncomfortable during this marriage. I'm trying to help, that's all."

His remark snapped Kara back to reality. "Of course. I understand." She reached for the nearest pan. "We both behaved foolishly. We will pretend it did not happen."

She tried to ignore the residual traces of desire sparking through her body. How unexpected to discover that she was capable of responding sexually to Daniel. Why had she never experienced such sensations with Hiro? Kara wondered as she returned to work. How awkward to feel this way now with a man who could never be more than a friend.

She wondered if excitement still raced through him, too. If so, he gave no sign of it as he swung a chair backward and sat astride it, watching her. "As we discussed, I'll stay at the hotel next week. Once we move into my house, we can have separate rooms. I assure you, you'll have complete privacy."

Kara wasn't ready to relinquish the possibility of exploring these new sensations a little further. "What if the authorities find out we slept apart during our honeymoon?"

"Why should they find out?"

"I'll bet they're very good at snooping."

"You've got a point," he admitted. "I'll have to think about it."

Kara wanted to share her little room with him, because being around him made her feel more alive. Yet if she told him so outright, he might worry that she was trying to lure him into a permanent marriage. She hit on a compromise. "We can buy an inflatable mattress. If you sleep on my floor, it will be almost like having two rooms."

"I promised you'd have your privacy." He shifted his position on the chair.

"Yes, but you need to be there." Kara searched for a practical reason and, to her delight, found one. "I could go into labor at any time. Just think how it would look to the immigration people if my husband wasn't around to take me to the hospital."

He gave her a crooked grin. "You're a persuasive woman."

"We can buy the mattress tomorrow when we go to get

our marriage license," she said, trying to look as if it were a matter of no importance. Although she yearned to awaken in the first light and feel the room pulse with his presence, she must not say so.

"You're efficient, too."

Was he agreeing? To keep the tone light, she quoted a line she'd heard on television: "You ain't seen nothin' yet!"

Daniel laughed. "Here I thought you were a poor lost soul."

"We can buy the mattress at a store down the street from my apartment," Kara went on. "Now I'd better pay attention to what I'm doing, or I might stir-fry the soup by mistake."

Inside, her spirit exulted. He was going to stay with her!

Cheerfully, she finished fixing the food. During her marriage to Hiro, preparing a meal had been a chore, not a pleasure. The first few weeks, she'd often overcooked an item or had to serve dinner in courses because nothing was ready at the same time. To her shame, her mother-in-law had dropped by several times and commented on her lack of domestic talents.

Around Daniel, everything was easy, as if mistakes didn't matter. Kara even enjoyed the way he watched her, as if he found her fascinating. She would have hated letting Hiro hang around the kitchen, not that it would ever have occurred to him to do so.

She was transferring the soup into bowls when the baby began to kick. As usual, Kara placed a hand over her abdomen so she could stroke Dorima.

"What's wrong?" Daniel jumped to his feet. "Is that a labor pain?"

"No, it's just the baby." She drew his large, gentle hand toward the place where hers had lingered a moment before. "Do you want to feel her?"

When his wrist tensed, she stopped just short of her bulge. "I might hurt her."

"You won't," she said.

"It's better if you tell me about her." He withdrew his hand gently and sat down. "I'm a bit awkward with the whole pregnancy thing. Remember, you've been going through this for nine months, but it's new to me."

Kara tried not to mind. After all, she doubted Hiro would have enjoyed caressing her big stomach. For some reason, however, Daniel's response disappointed her.

She hoped he would get over his reticence by the time the baby came. Since they were going to spend so much time together, it was important that he care about Dorima.

He *had* asked her to talk about the baby. That was a start, at least. "You should have felt her a few months ago," she said. "When she was smaller and had more space, she used to perform somersaults. Perhaps she's going to be a gymnast."

"It's hard to think of a baby that hasn't been born yet as a complete person." Daniel got up again and carried the plates to the table. "Not that I have much experience with children. Practically none, in fact."

Anxiety quivered inside Kara. Some men, she knew, got annoyed when they heard crying or were inconvenienced while the wife took care of the baby. And this one didn't even belong to Daniel. Surely, though, he would accept Dorima once he held her in his arms.

"I love children." Kara balanced the bowls of soup carefully en route to the table. "I love seeing them at the day-care center. Each one shines in a special way."

"Speaking of the day-care center, I have a request." Daniel held her chair for her. Unsure how this custom worked, Kara lowered herself slowly. He pushed the chair forward until she fitted beneath the table as well as she could with her stomach in the way.

"Thank you," she said. "What's the request?"

He sat down, his long legs bumping hers before he shifted them to one side. "Since you won't need money while you're married to me, and in view of your condition, I'd like you to quit driving the produce truck. Surely the Matsubas can find someone else to do it. I don't think it's safe when you're this close to childbirth.''

''Akio has a learner's permit,'' Kara told him. ''He's planning to take his driver's test this week, but the Matsubas aren't sure they trust him to drive. I will ask them.''

''They're going to have to replace you sooner or later. I'd rather it was sooner.''

Although she knew he was right, Kara hesitated. Yes, it was hard to reach the pedals these days, and she knew the Matsubas could find a substitute even if Akio didn't work out. Quitting work, however, would mean an end to her daily visits to Forrester Square.

She and Tansho would see each other regardless of whether they worked together, but what about Katherine and Alexandra and Hannah? During the past few months, she'd come to consider them good friends.

''This food is delicious,'' Daniel said. ''You did a great job.''

Kara beamed. ''Thank you.''

''Was I supposed to eat the soup first?'' he asked. ''I just went ahead and dug in.''

''That's okay,'' she said. ''You can take a bite of the pork, then a little rice, then some soup, except that if we were eating the real Japanese way, we would sip from the bowl, instead of using a spoon. And of course we'd have chopsticks.''

''I think that might take a while for me to get used to,'' Daniel said. ''You should eat whatever way you want.''

''I'm pretty good with a fork, although I do spill food sometimes,'' Kara admitted. ''It's a problem, because napkins don't stay on my lap anymore.'' She hadn't realized she was still thinking about his request that she quit work until a solution hit her. ''I know! Is it all right if I volunteer at the day-care center?''

''Would it involve heavy lifting or long hours?'' Daniel asked.

She shook her head. ''I helped make lunch while Millie

was away. She used to work part-time in the kitchen. Now she's left to get married, and they're shorthanded again.''

"I don't suppose it can hurt, as long as you're not on your feet too much," Daniel said. "It's just until the baby's born, right?"

"I'm sure Katherine will find someone permanent for the kitchen by then." Kara wondered if she should mention that she still wanted to take the teaching job, but decided not to pursue the issue right now. Besides, she had to wait until she was able to secure a work permit.

They had a great many things to handle, with the wedding and moving in together and her pregnancy. After that, who could predict what might happen? It would take only one lucky break to find her father's family.

During her teen years and since Hiro died, she'd fantasized about them a great deal. In her daydreams, they welcomed her with open arms, urging her to live with them. She'd imagined the scene so often that it seemed almost inevitable.

Perhaps it was. If so, that was all the more reason to avoid conflict now and simply enjoy herself.

Studying Daniel's dark head as he bent over his meal, Kara knew she didn't want to lose one moment with him. She had read once about a woman who was saving precious memories to cherish in later years. Kara didn't want memories. She just wanted to live right here and now with Daniel.

ON THURSDAY, Kara told Akio he could take a break after he unloaded the produce at Forrester Square. "Go have a coffee when you're done," she told him, indicating Caffeine Hy's next door. "I'll pay for it."

"Really?" His eyebrows shot up. "Even a double mocha latte with hot sauce?"

"You made that up!" she said. "Anything over three dollars, you pay for yourself."

"Okay," he said, and shouldered a crate of apples with renewed enthusiasm.

As always, Kara paused to enjoy the sight and sound of

children playing in the grassy rear yard. Closely supervised, the youngsters were busy digging in the sandbox, climbing on the equipment and riding tricycles.

The beautifully maintained playground was only one of the touches that enhanced the three-story sandstone building. Kara loved the arched windows, the flowers in window boxes and the scent of burnished wood when she stepped inside. Every detail reflected the love poured into the place by its three owners, as well as their appreciation of children.

Hannah was still away on her honeymoon in Southern California, but Kara hoped Katherine and Alexandra would be here. They were going to be very, very surprised when she broke her news.

Yesterday afternoon, Kara and Daniel had gotten the marriage license. Her hands had trembled when they arrived at the downtown county office, until Daniel's arm around her waist calmed her. She'd had no trouble filling out the application, and no one had asked for identification or a blood test, neither of which was required in Seattle. Only a few more days now until she became Mrs. Daniel Adler!

She found the two women in the kitchen. Alexandra, her short red hair mussed, directed Akio to put the apples on the counter for the day's snack. Katherine, her long dark hair secured at the nape, was making sandwiches for lunch. How typical of them to pitch in and share the work, Kara thought.

"Shoo, shoo!" she said to Akio when he was relieved of his burden. In Japanese, she added, "Take your time drinking the coffee!"

"You bet," he said in English, and strolled out jauntily.

"You look radiant," Katherine said. "Tell me Daniel found a solution to your visa problem."

"Well, yes," Kara said.

"Good for him." Alexandra rinsed an apple, cut it into quarters and reached into the cabinet for a jar of peanut butter.

"I can't believe she eats them that way," Katherine said. "You'd think she was a little kid."

"What can I say? They taste better this way," said her

friend as she spread the goo on an apple slice. "I'm just glad we have no peanut allergies here." She glanced up at Kara. "Come on, what did Daniel come up with?"

Kara took a deep breath. "We're getting married."

In the silence that followed, she could hear children shouting outside and the hum of Belltown traffic on Sandringham Drive. Finally Katherine said, "Really?"

Kara nodded.

"Is this a case of love at first sight?" Alexandra seemed to have forgotten the slice of apple held halfway to her mouth.

"Well…" Kara wasn't sure how to answer without revealing too much.

"Is he doing this for your sake?" Katherine didn't seem to need a reply. "I didn't think Daniel had it in him. I mean, I like and respect the guy, but this seems so…off the wall."

"Off the wall?" Kara repeated.

"Impulsive." The apple completed its journey to Alexandra's mouth, cutting off further comment.

"We're getting married on Sunday afternoon at my friend Tansho's house." Kara handed them pretty envelopes tied with gold cord. Inside each was a sheet of stationery lettered in calligraphy with the address and time. "I'd be grateful if you could come."

"Of course I'll come," Katherine said. "I'm honoured."

Alexandra tried in vain to speak through the sticky peanut butter. She nodded mutely.

"I'm afraid I won't be able to drive for the Matsubas after tomorrow," Kara said. "I believe Akio will be able to make the deliveries alone, now that he has his license. But I'd be happy to make lunches until I have the baby. I want to volunteer, since I don't have work papers."

"Are you sure it's not too hard, standing at the counter for a couple of hours a day?" Katherine asked.

"I can sit at the table part of the time," Kara pointed out. "Besides, I'd miss seeing you and the children. I want to be here."

"Then thank you. We could certainly use your help. You

know, I've interviewed a few more people for the teaching job, but there's no one I like as well as you. You're great with children, and several parents have mentioned that they'd love for their kids to begin learning Japanese."

"That would be fun," Kara said. "But it may take a while."

"Even though she gave her notice, Rona Opitz is willing to hang on until you get your immigration status sorted out," Katherine added. "Once you and Daniel are settled, I'll talk to him and see if we can't hurry up that green card."

"Thank you so much. I'd love to work for you." Not only would the job allow Kara to teach, but once the baby was born, she could bring Dorima with her.

A tap at the back door made them all turn. Kara frowned at seeing a grizzled homeless man peering through the screen. Many such lost souls frequented the tunnels beneath this part of the city. The tunnels had been formed when the streets were raised during a rebuilding following the great fire of 1889.

Elders deserved honor. However, Kara had seen enough of the city to know that many homeless people suffered from drug and alcohol abuse. Her first priority, like that of Katherine and Alexandra, was the children's safety.

"Go away!" she demanded. "You don't want us to call the police, do you?"

"Oh, that's Gary Devlin." Alexandra found her voice again. "I've sort of taken him under my wing, although he doesn't usually come right up to the house. I'm trying to find his family."

"You're sure he's not a problem?" Kara asked.

"After all the research Alexandra's done into his background, if he had a criminal record, she'd have found it," Katherine said. "Still, I agree it would be best if he stayed outside the fenced area."

"No problem." Alexandra pulled on a jacket she'd thrown over a chair. "I'm going to run out and buy him some lunch.

Besides, the more time I spend around him, the more he fascinates me. One thing I'm sure of—he wouldn't hurt a fly.''

Kara had to admit that there was a deep sadness about the man's sunken face and pale-blue eyes. Still, most likely his gaunt appearance came from heavy drinking, not from poetic thoughts.

''Why does she find him so interesting?'' she asked Katherine when the pair had left.

Her friend sighed. ''I'm not sure how much you know about Alexandra. Her parents died in a fire when she was six.''

''I heard she was an orphan,'' Kara said. ''I don't know the details.''

''She went to live with some relatives in Montana, but she never really got over her parents' deaths. No wonder—she nearly died in that fire herself. She swears this man reminds her of her father, and I have to admit, sometimes he seems to know odd details about her. But he's obviously not her father.''

''Could she have a long-lost uncle?'' Kara asked. ''Perhaps her father had a twin?''

''Not that we know of. Besides, Gary doesn't look anything like the pictures she has of her dad. I don't mind her being nice to a homeless man, but I'm afraid he's become an obsession.''

Kara's heart went out to Alexandra. ''She was young to lose her parents. She must have made up stories to herself about how they were secretly alive and would return. Even though she's grown up, perhaps deep inside she hasn't accepted that her dream can never come true.''

Katherine's dark eyes glittered. ''I never thought of it that way. It's hard to give up dreams, isn't it?''

Her wistful tone reminded Kara of their conversation at the wedding. ''Are you talking about yourself now?''

''I suppose I am,'' her friend conceded. ''I went to the sperm bank and filled in the paperwork. Before we can proceed, I've got to have a complete physical. Although I'm due to have one, anyway, I keep putting it off.''

"Are you afraid of doctors?" Kara knew several women back home who were too intimidated by them to ask personal questions. Doctors were much more authority figures in Japan than in the United States.

"Not exactly," Katherine said. "I've got this irrational hope that Mr. Right will show up and sweep me away so I won't have to go through with having a baby from a laboratory. I'd much rather do it the old-fashioned way, but who am I kidding?"

"You never know what the future will bring," Kara told her. "Look at me and Daniel!"

"That's for sure." Katherine gave her a hug. "I can't believe how many of my friends are getting married. You and Hannah and Millie, too! Maybe miracles can happen."

Akio poked his head through the back door. "Boy, they make great coffee at Hy's! You ready to go, Miss Engaged Lady? If not, I'm open for more bribes."

"No way." Kara took her leave of Katherine. The last thing she noticed as she hurried down the steps was the longing on her friend's face.

Someday, she thought, Katherine would find a man of her own. She had only to be patient—and perhaps a little daring, as well.

TAKING A FEW HOURS off on Wednesday to apply for a marriage license put Daniel behind in his work, forcing him to stay late at the office for the next two days. He was so busy that he had little time to think about anything beyond keeping his head above water.

Whenever he got a spare moment, he tried to reach his father in Chicago. Vernon's cell phone was turned off and he didn't answer his home phone or his e-mail. Although Daniel hated to call the law office, he finally did and learned that his father had gone on a fishing trip to Canada for two weeks and had left no forwarding number. Vernon hated to be disturbed on vacation.

Daniel wasn't sure whether to be relieved or disappointed. He didn't like postponing the inevitable confrontation. On the other hand, his life was complicated enough right now.

As for the Bellevue house, it remained torn up despite the contractor's assurances that the new flooring would soon be installed. On Saturday, as Daniel stowed most of his remaining possessions in the garage, he wondered if he would indeed be reclaiming them within a week or two, or whether they'd remain there indefinitely. Perhaps someday explorers from the far-distant future would discover them buried beneath the ruins of a collapsed civilization and wonder what catastrophe had forced their owner to pile them in a jumble and flee.

On Sunday, April sunshine broke through the cloud cover by noon. A little before one o'clock, wearing a dark suit, Daniel arrived at the Matsubas' modest, well-kept house in the university district.

Drew awaited him on the front porch. "You know, I was tempted to bet that you wouldn't show up," his friend told him. "Not that you're unreliable, but this whole thing seems unreal."

"You're the one who gave me the idea of marrying her," Daniel reminded him.

"That's right, I did." Drew cocked his head. "Well, my sister's delighted about it, so I guess it was a good idea."

"Does she understand the circumstances?" When he agreed to go through with a wedding ceremony, Daniel hadn't thought about the fact that it made it appear to their guests that he and Kara really were a couple. He wasn't anxious to broadcast the fact that this was a green-card arrangement of course, but neither did he want to mislead his friends.

"I'm sure she figured it out," Drew said. "She has her own ideas about things, though."

At the door, they were met by Tansho Matsuba, who wore a bright-pink dress. Only a slight paleness revealed where the cast had been removed from her wrist. Daniel was glad to see she was healing.

She gave him an approving once-over and invited him inside, along with Drew, whom she'd apparently already met. "We're out in the garden," she said. "Thank goodness the weather cooperated."

"The fates smile upon you and Kara," Drew said.

"So it seems."

The house was decorated with the simple elegance Daniel had come to associate with Japanese people. He liked the openness, the translucent room dividers and the spare, tasteful furnishings accented by a few vases of spring flowers. The house where he'd grown up in Chicago had been overstuffed with dark antiques and heavy curtains, a legacy from his father's parents. He hadn't realized at the time how oppressive it felt.

As Tansho escorted them down a hallway, the murmur of voices reached him from outside. Daniel felt a prickle of nerves. In the past few days, he'd been too bogged down to give much thought to the ceremony. For the first time, the fact that he was entering into a solemn contract began to sink in.

There were not only social and legal but also financial implications that he hadn't addressed, because a prenuptial agreement would be a dead giveaway to the feds.

If anything went wrong, however, he would be vulnerable. Since he could never admit in court that he'd perpetrated a fraud, Kara would be entitled to claim a share of his property when they divorced, particularly if they stayed married for a couple of years. Also, legally, her baby was going to be his responsibility, and he might be required to pay long-term support.

If he'd been advising one of his clients, he'd have told the man to turn tail and run. He could still take Kara aside and call the whole thing off.

Tansho led him and Drew through the kitchen and onto a patio, beyond which lay an enchanting garden. Despite its modest size, a profusion of plants pruned in round shapes that reminded Daniel of clouds screened out the rest of the world and enclosed the visitors in a timeless haven. A small, brightly painted bridge arched over a fishpond.

On the curving, stone-patterned patio, an altar and folding chairs were set up. Atop one of several tables near the back of the house perched gaily wrapped packages, some fastened with fancy bows and others with elaborately knotted red silk cords.

He spotted Katherine and Alexandra, along with Drew's wife and son. There were half-a-dozen Japanese, some wearing black kimonos, which he gathered must be formal wear. He assumed these were members of Tansho's family, as well as a couple of neighbors Kara had mentioned. Kara's friend Mr. Sakioka, the minister, stood talking with a middle-aged Japanese man in a business suit, whom Tansho introduced as her father.

Daniel, trying not to show that he was having second thoughts, exchanged bows and greetings with the men. After a moment's hesitation, Drew bowed, also.

Under other circumstances, there would have been a wedding rehearsal the previous night, but Kara hadn't mentioned one and Daniel hadn't asked. They'd barely found time yesterday to go shopping for a ring. Kara had picked out a simple gold design with graceful curves like a swallow in flight.

"What do we do now?" he asked in a low voice.

"The bride wishes us to wait here," said the minister.

"Maybe I should walk down the aisle with her. Or along the path, since there doesn't seem to be an aisle." It hadn't occurred to Daniel until now that Kara had no one to escort her to the altar.

"She'll be fine," Tansho told him. "Don't worry about it." She gestured for a young Japanese man to join them. "This is my brother Takeshi."

"I'm shooting the pictures," he said unnecessarily, since he held a camera in his hands. "This can take both still and video pictures. It's the latest digital model."

"Excellent. Thank you." Daniel's mind returned to Kara. He wondered what she was thinking right now.

She'd put a lot of work into staging this event, which was largely to impress the immigration authorities. Surely she didn't take it too seriously, did she? Maybe this hadn't been such a good idea, after all.

From a hidden part of the garden, a flash of light caught his attention. It was gone before he could look for the source. "What's that?"

"Never mind." Tansho moved to the side and knelt by a portable CD player.

Drew grinned. "I think they're signaling each other with mirrors."

"Is this an old Japanese tradition?" Daniel asked Mr. Sakioka.

"I think you have a very creative wife," said the minister.

Bell-like music floated into the air, reminiscent of wind chimes. Although Daniel knew it came from the CD player, it mingled with the gurgle of water and the whisper of the breeze as if it, too, were part of the garden.

A sigh of appreciation arose from the guests, who, following Tansho's example, gazed toward the pond. Daniel caught the swish of a bright color, and then he saw Kara emerge from a hidden part of the garden.

Her gaily patterned red-and-white dress blended East and West with its kimono-style sleeves, a princess waistline and fabric that swirled lightly around her figure. A spray of flowers anchored her dark, upswept hair, and she carried an open red-and-white fan. As she posed against the greenery, he noticed Takeshi busily shooting the scene.

Kara kept her eyes demurely lowered as she glided onto the arched bridge. She looked like a figure from a fairy tale, mysterious and magical.

Suddenly he knew what she was thinking. *She's hoping like crazy that she doesn't trip.*

What an imaginative, brave woman she was, despite look-

ing so fragile. Daniel's nerves began to settle. They were going to get through this wedding and this marriage just fine.

With measured steps in her embroidered slippers, Kara
traced the curving bridge as if floating from her country's
mythical past into her own bright future. The guests all
seemed to hold their breath. It occurred to him that he was
doing the same thing.

At last she reached him and raised her eyes shyly. When
she saw his smile, she answered with a twinkle of her own.

Daniel offered his arm. His fiancée laid her hand atop it,
and together they turned to say their wedding vows.

It was too late to back out now.

CHAPTER TEN

THIS WEDDING RECEPTION was nothing like Kara's first one, a year ago. Although that event, held at a hotel, had been lively enough, her mother-in-law's glowering had weighed down Kara's spirits and she'd felt only a mild liking for her groom.

Today, she was free to laugh with her friends, play American music on a CD player and enjoy not only her guests but the drop-ins: butterflies from the garden that fluttered through the crowd and a neighbor's cat that sat on the fence, cleaning its paws and watching the goings-on.

Most important, every time she looked at Daniel, her heart lifted. It had taken all Kara's self-control not to break into a trot when she emerged from the greenery and glimpsed him standing by Mr. Sakioka. Now that the ceremony was over, she half wished her guests would make an early departure so she could go home alone with her new husband.

She kept trying to remind herself that they were supposed to be only friends. Yet she'd never had a friend who affected her the way he did.

Yesterday, Daniel had brought some of his possessions to her apartment. After he left, she'd stored several of her own garments in a small chest, then removed his suits from the valise and arranged them in her closet. Although his clothes bore cleaning tags, his subtle scent persisted in weaving a spell around her as she worked.

Now, as happy chatter flowed past her, Kara forced her attention onto the patio and the refreshment table. The lemonade was running low, she noticed, so she went inside to fix more.

Mrs. Matsuba joined her in the kitchen. "You are a beautiful bride and your husband is very handsome. May I offer you a word of caution, however?" She shifted into Japanese so they could speak more freely.

"Of course." The older woman had welcomed Kara into her home and helped her get established in an apartment. Any advice she offered was sure to be well-intentioned.

"I saw Daniel's face when he caught sight of you at the bridge." Mrs. Matsuba removed a tray of sweet bean cakes from the refrigerator. "He lit up like the sun. I said to myself that he's very attracted to her."

Kara's heart pounded so loudly she couldn't speak. She'd had the same impression but was aware that she lacked objectivity. "Do you think so?"

"Although the reasons for your marriage are practical, he has developed an affection for you," the older woman said. "I believe you may return his feelings. My advice is to guard your heart. Men are different from women, and Americans are different from Japanese."

"What do you mean?" Kara said.

"Americans have very romantic ideas," Mrs. Matsuba said. "They are always falling in and out of love. Look at their divorce rate!"

Kara knew it was even higher than in Japan. "Even so, many people stay happily married. Once they truly decide to get married of course."

"That's so." Deft hands shifted the cakes to make a more artistic pattern. "Attraction is important. Still, when Tansho makes her choice of a husband, I hope she picks a man with a similar background and compatible habits."

Kara didn't want to argue. Nor could she accept that there was no hope for this new, precious spark between her and her husband. "Daniel has many good habits," she said.

"Of course, Mr. Adler is a responsible man, very polite,

and he works hard. I only caution you to take him at his word.''

"He only said two words," Kara joked. "'I' and 'do.'"

"You must not forget that he has promised you a temporary marriage," Mrs. Matsuba reminded her. "A woman might think that if she and her husband grow close, the rules will change, but in my observation, a man may not make that assumption. Knowing how impulsive you are, I fear you might wish for more and be severely disappointed. Unless he says so specifically, you must not believe that anything has changed."

Kara tried to breathe and found that it made her chest hurt. "You are kind to warn me."

"Daniel may care for you very much," Mrs. Matsuba continued. "That is fine and will make your time together more pleasant. But you must prepare yourself for the future. Otherwise, you and your baby will meet difficulties when the marriage ends."

To her embarrassment, tears stung the insides of Kara's eyelids. She knew the sight of them would make her friend's mother uneasy, so she busied herself mixing more lemonade. "I plan to go to work at the day-care center. Then I will be able to support myself and the baby."

"That's good." The older woman nodded. "I'm sure, with your many fine qualities, that you will succeed."

"Thank you. You have been more generous than I can ever repay." Kara bowed to her, and Mrs. Matsuba bowed back. They made a little parade out of the kitchen, Mrs. Matsuba carrying the bean cakes and Kara a pitcher of fruit drink.

How ironic, she thought, that in her union with Hiro, which she had expected to last a lifetime, she'd had no difficulty withholding her heart. With Daniel, as her friend's mother had observed, things were very different.

Daniel excited and stimulated her. She found everything about him fascinating, including his physical side. How was she going to hold back for months or years while they lived together, dined together and slept near each other? But Kara saw the wisdom of the advice she'd just received.

She must not yield to the temptation to build her life around her new husband. Whatever happened, she must always keep a clear view in mind of the open road that lay ahead, a road she and Dorima were going to have to travel on their own.

"KARA NEVER CEASES to amaze me," Katherine said, standing with Daniel and a small group of friends. "You'd think that in her condition, she'd want to do nothing but put up her feet, and here she planned a whole wedding in a few days. And a gorgeous one at that."

As they watched the bride offer lemonade to the elderly minister, Daniel felt a little uncomfortable about having involved so many people in this wedding, especially since many of the guests appeared unaware it was all for show. "She did a beautiful job."

"Speaking of which, you are footing the bill, I hope?" Drew nibbled at his plate of hors d'oeuvres.

"Of course." Daniel had insisted on paying for everything. And although the earnestness of the ceremony had made him feel slightly guilty, he had to admit this was a terrific party.

He decided to think of it as a kind of housewarming, a celebration of his new home—even though he wasn't able to move in yet—and the fact that Kara was going to be living there with him for a while. For however long this marriage lasted, the two of them needed to forge a working relationship, and there was nothing wrong in having fun with their friends.

He was glad, however, that Kara had her own dreams and goals. He didn't like to think about what it really meant to get married, and how many ways things could fall apart.

"I'm delighted that she's offered to fix lunches at the day-care center," Katherine said. "I presume you know about that."

"Yes, of course." Daniel was glad Kara had told him first. It could be awkward if one of them didn't know what the other one was doing, since they were supposed to be married. Well, actually, they *were* married, at least for the time being.

"I'm still eager to get her on staff full-time," Katherine told him. "Several of the parents became very enthusiastic when I mentioned that we might hire a teacher who speaks Japanese."

"I hope you're not in too much of a hurry," Daniel said. "For one thing, she's due to have a baby any day, and I'm sure she'll need some time afterward to recuperate."

"Some women recover quickly," she reminded him. "Surely now that you're married, we can get her a temporary work permit."

"I plan to look into it." Daniel wasn't sure why he felt such reluctance at the idea of Kara going to work full-time. After all, that had been the reason Katherine had asked him to meet her in the first place. "Right now, thank goodness, she doesn't have to worry about being snatched off the street and sent back to Japan."

"Thanks to you," Katherine said. "Don't think I don't appreciate it."

He hadn't done this for Katherine, Daniel thought. He decided not to mention that, though. He didn't know how to explain, even to himself, why he'd gone so far out on a limb for a woman who was virtually a stranger.

The music changed from a soothing background melody to a catchy tune. "I wonder if Julia would like to dance," Drew said.

"You can't ask her!" his sister objected.

"Why not? The baby's asleep." He indicated a blanket in the shade where eight-month-old Jeremy was taking a nap.

"That's not what I meant," Katherine said. "Don't you know the bride and groom get the first dance?"

Daniel had forgotten that tradition. "I've been remiss in my duty as the, er, groom. I'd better go take care of it."

"Take care of it?" Katherine repeated. "You sound like you're going to fix the radiator!"

"Give the man a break," Drew chided his sister. "For a

guy who's so straight you can use him as a plumb line, he's doing the best he can.''

"Thanks for defending me, but that's not exactly high praise," Daniel protested.

After excusing himself, he joined Kara and a group of people talking in Japanese. They immediately switched to English, including him in their discussion of the effect of Seattle's growth on the school system.

"We need more teachers," said an elderly woman. "We are lucky to have Kara here. We need many more talented individuals like her."

"Daniel, may I present my neighbor, Mrs. Yamamoto?" Kara said.

Daniel bowed at the same time as did the kindly-looking elderly woman. When they finished exchanging greetings, he said, "Kara, it seems we have an obligation to dance. No one else is allowed to take the floor before the bride and groom, and I see some toes tapping. Would you do me the honor?"

"Oh!" Her hands flew to her mouth. "Of course! How could I be so neglectful of my guests?"

"I'm sure no one has noticed," Mrs. Yamamoto said.

With another bow to her friends, Daniel drew Kara away. As soon as he touched her, he discovered how much he'd missed holding her. They'd had almost no contact since the moment he brushed a light kiss across her mouth at the behest of the minister.

"We should have done this sooner," he told her. "And I don't mean because of etiquette."

"You like dancing?" She swayed against him, both of them adjusting instinctively to her bulge. Daniel realized that he had come to accept the pregnancy as simply a part of her.

"I like holding you." The words slipped out before he could stop to examine their implications.

She relaxed in his arms. "I like it, too."

He lowered his head close to hers. A spring breeze brought hints of garden greenery to mingle with her perfume, giving Daniel the sensation of waltzing through a field of flowers.

He reasserted his grip to keep her from floating away, or perhaps to keep himself from spinning out of control.

Events had happened so quickly this week that they'd scarcely had time to sink in. Something inside had propelled him along. It was still propelling him, arousing unexpected images of Kara lying on her futon bed beside him, laughing as she peeled away her pretty dress.

Slowly Daniel became aware that people were watching them. He should have expected as much, since they were the bride and groom, but the thought had slipped from his awareness. When had he, a man notorious for his stiffness in company, become so unguarded?

He lifted his head to meet his friends' gazes. "Come on, everyone," he said. "Join us!"

"You bet!" Drew didn't wait for a second invitation. He caught Julia's hand and pulled her into the center of the patio.

When the song ended, Daniel knew it would be unwise to continue dancing with Kara. He didn't like the fact that holding her kept stirring forbidden longings. Yet it was hard to draw away, hard to release her.

His dilemma was resolved when Mr. Matsuba suggested that they sing karaoke. The name, he added, meant "empty orchestra" in Japanese.

Tansho produced a portable karaoke player that displayed the lyrics on a small screen. Daniel got the impression that using it was an accustomed part of the festivities.

"Everyone must sing," Kara announced. "That is how we let down our hair and show that we are good sports."

"This ought to be interesting," Drew said. "I want to hear Mr. Uptight Lawyer belt out a few bars of 'My Way.'"

"Does this machine come with earplugs?" Daniel asked. "I'd hate to drive our guests screaming into the street."

Kara laughed. "I'm sure they will be polite, even while they are suffering. Perhaps we should sing a duet. Then they can't hear either of us very well. Or at least we can both take responsibility for breaking their eardrums."

"Fine with me," he said, which was stretching the truth to

the breaking point. Daniel had avoided singing in public for many years for reasons he hadn't cared to think about, but they came rushing back to him now.

When he was in junior high school, his mother had encouraged him to join the school chorus. To her delight, he'd enjoyed the rehearsals and concerts, even chancing a few solos until his voice began to change. While he was struggling to regain his confidence, his mother had left. Anything connected with her became too painful to bear, for him and for his father. Daniel had given up singing so completely that he no longer even sang in the shower.

Kara's enthusiasm and the obvious anticipation of their guests, however, erased his reservations. This was going to be fun, pure and simple, and he discovered that he looked forward to singing again.

The two of them flipped through the list of available songs. Daniel tried to pick one that wasn't too sentimental, but several friends mischievously insisted on an old favorite, Don McLean's "And I Love You So."

"You always stop to listen when it comes on the radio," Drew declared.

"It's a beautiful song," Tansho said.

"Perfect for a wedding," Alexandra added.

But not for this one, Daniel thought. "It's kind of a wistful song, if you ask me. How about something more cheerful?"

"You should sing 'We've Only Just Begun,'" Katherine suggested.

"I like that," Kara said.

It was all right with Daniel, too. They *were* starting something new, after all.

Since he'd never sung karaoke before, it took a while to catch on to the timing. He started in the wrong place, then misread the lyrics. No one laughed at him, though, and he lost his awkwardness as Kara's sweet, clear soprano moved smoothly through the words. Without thinking, he looped his arm around her waist and they swayed together in instinctive harmony.

Daniel's voice had matured into a light baritone that negotiated the difficult musical intervals with ease. He relished both the surge of melody and Kara's heartfelt expression. She gave the song a bouncy, happy flair.

Close to her and surrounded by friends, Daniel felt connected in a way he'd almost forgotten was possible. Memories of a happy, loving childhood swelled in him, memories that he'd cast aside more than half his lifetime ago. This was a wonderful celebration, no matter how unlikely the events that had inspired it.

When the song ended, he stood blinking in the late-afternoon sunshine. For a moment, only the chirp of birds in the garden broke the silence, and then applause rang out.

"That was brilliant!" Drew said. "I'm impressed."

"I had no idea you sang so well," Kara told him.

"You're the one who sang well," Daniel protested. "I was just humming along."

A chorus of disagreement filled the air. "You have a beautiful voice," said Mrs. Matsuba. "You should come here often and sing karaoke."

"I made a lot of mistakes." Daniel was sure he'd gone flat on a couple of notes. "I'm not much of a singer."

"Yes, you are. I have the proof!" Tansho's brother hefted his camera. "I recorded the whole thing."

"I'm surprised I didn't break it," Daniel said. "Okay, if you insist, one of these days I'll come back and try again. But right now, it's someone else's turn."

"I'll do it," said Tansho, and soon she was belting out "I Heard It on the Grapevine," complete with sinuous body movements.

Several others followed, including a blushing but good-humored Katherine. The singers didn't seem to care if they lost track of the tune or got a few words wrong, because they were enjoying the fellowship. Inside Daniel, the warm glow persisted. He'd missed this sense of belonging.

He knew it wasn't real and wouldn't last. But right now

he just wanted to stay here among friends and his wife until the sun went down and the stars came out, and let tomorrow take care of itself.

DARKNESS FINALLY DISPELLED the gathering at the Matsubas' house. Daniel and Kara retreated to Kara's apartment with their gaily wrapped gifts, joking and trying to avoid facing the fact that two virtual strangers had committed themselves to sharing a room and possibly much more.

When she'd invited Daniel to stay in her apartment, Kara had thought only of how much she would enjoy his company and of saving him money on the hotel room he'd canceled. Now that they were alone, she became aware of how overwhelming his presence seemed and how uncertain she felt about what to do next.

"It's not exactly a honeymoon suite," Daniel said. "Maybe I should have rented a place for both of us." He stood near the kitchenette, his forehead furrowing as he regarded the spare furnishings and the compact bundle that was his not-yet-inflated mattress.

"We'll be fine. No one notices the size of the room while sleeping, and during the day you'll be at work." When she was flustered, like now, Kara tried to find something practical to do. "We should open the gifts so I can write thank-you notes."

"You're going to write thank-you notes tonight?" he asked dubiously.

"I can note the givers. I'll write to them tomorrow."

She hadn't had a chance to open any of the presents in advance. In Japan, personal gifts were sent ahead and money was given at the reception. However, there hadn't been time to stick to tradition, so today they'd received a mixture of both.

"Why are you hogging all the thank-you notes, anyway?" Daniel teased.

"What do you mean?" Kara asked in surprise.

"I can write some of them," he said, "although I don't promise to use calligraphy."

"Really?" She'd never expected such an offer.

"It's a new American tradition," Daniel explained. "It's called equality of the sexes."

"I approve of that." Kara still wanted some activity to keep them both occupied. "Let's open the gifts together, then."

"Sounds good to me."

She took a seat on a tatami mat next to the low table where they'd set the gifts. When Daniel cleared his throat, she looked up inquiringly.

"I've never had any ambition to turn myself into a pretzel," he said. "Frankly, I don't know how you sit that way in your condition, either."

"I'm used to it," Kara said. "I'm sorry. I don't have any other table where we can work."

"If you can manage, I suppose I'd better learn how, too." After removing his shoes and jacket, Daniel folded himself onto the mat opposite her. His knees, which seemed to have a will of their own, bumped the table. Both of them grabbed for the packages and envelopes barely in time to prevent them from tumbling. "Well, that wasn't a great start."

"You're doing very well adjusting to Japanese furniture." She pretended not to notice how one of his ankles rubbed lightly against her knee. It was of no importance if warmth spread through her, and certainly she didn't intend to call it to Daniel's attention. "Let's start with the biggest one."

Daniel handed it to her. The package, wrapped in red-and-white paper with a fan-shaped ornament on top, came from the Matsubas. After Kara carefully removed the decoration, she opened the box to reveal a red-lacquered tea set.

"I hope this doesn't mean I have to give up coffee," Daniel joked.

"It means that soon I can perform a tea ceremony for you," Kara said.

"A tea ceremony?" He quirked one eyebrow, as if expecting her to deliver a punch line. "That sounds like a lot of trouble for just the two of us."

"The point of the ceremony is to focus the senses," Kara explained. "It clears the mind, like a form of meditation."

"I can see I've got a lot to learn," he said. "I never knew tea could have such an uplifting effect. Is it an aromatic blend?"

"Actually, it's quite bitter," Kara replied. "You can eat a candy first to coat your mouth. It's like balancing the good and bad moments in life."

"I definitely like that part," Daniel said. "Who's keeping notes on the gifts—you or me?"

"Me." Roused to her duty, she wrote a reminder about the tea set on a pad and picked up the next present.

Several of the Japanese guests had given money, following the custom of contributing toward the couple's wedding expenses. Although Daniel appeared uncertain about accepting such contributions, Kara assured him that it was not a negative reflection on his abilities as a provider. Besides, she pointed out, it wasn't all that different from the gift certificates that Americans sometimes gave.

Other friends had selected personal items. Drew and Julia had sent a handmade quilt with a striking flower design. Katherine gave them a playpen and a yellow-and-green layette set suitable for either a boy or girl.

The last gift was a private one from Tansho, in addition to her family's present. The moment Kara saw the book inside, her cheeks warmed and she pulled the paper back over it.

"What is it?" Daniel asked.

"A personal item," she said quickly.

"What kind of personal item?"

"Female," she said.

"That's funny." He reached across the low table for it. "I could have sworn it was a book."

Distracted as she wrote on her notepad, Kara didn't realize his intent in time. He brushed away the paper and lifted the volume. "'*Sexual Frolicking for Married Couples,*'" Daniel read. "Who's this from?"

"It's Tansho's idea of a joke," she said.

To her dismay, he flipped it open and let out a whistle. "Wow. They don't pull any punches, do they?"

"It's very explicit," Kara admitted.

"You mean you've read it before?"

"No!" she said. "Only the other one."

"What other one?"

She should have weighed her words before speaking. "Tansho lent me a different book," Kara said reluctantly. "She thought it might be educational."

Daniel turned a page. "Yes, this is very educational. There are some positions here I've never even imagined."

Kara didn't want to think about the possibility that her husband had experienced some of these activities with previous girlfriends. His life before their marriage was like the mists of early morning, rapidly dissipated by sunshine. "It's nothing. We should put it away."

"I'm sorry. I didn't mean to annoy you." He handed back the book. "We agreed this would be a marriage of convenience. You don't need to worry—I plan to keep it that way. I apologize if I gave you any other impression."

His body language had changed, as if he were withdrawing. Katherine had told Kara how reserved Daniel was, but until now he'd been open with her.

She didn't want him to draw away. Tonight, she'd enjoyed the way his body had swayed against hers as they danced. Although she didn't dare go as far as those people in the book, that didn't mean she had to spend her married life never touching or holding Daniel again.

"This marriage is not convenient," she said. "Not for you."

"I'm fine, believe me," he said.

"I meant that I am the one who receives all the benefits," Kara said. "You're helping me stay in the United States and have my baby here. There should be advantages for you, as well."

"There already are." His dark eyes grew intense in the soft light from a corner lamp. "For example, I'm learning a lot about your culture. And you're going to help me decorate my house.''

Kara couldn't sit here for another moment without touching him. "Let me at least help you relax. After all, you have a long day tomorrow.''

"How do you plan to do that?''

"I'll show you.'' Pushing up from the mat, she went to kneel behind him. She had learned massage techniques a few years ago to help when her mother was recovering from surgery. She'd never tried it with Hiro. She would have felt awkward even suggesting it.

Daniel was different. To touch him was to strengthen the flow of energy between them and affirm her own vitality.

Before she could begin, Daniel's jaw tightened as if to argue. When he twisted as if to confront her, Kara made a fist and shook it with pretended anger. "You must let me do this! Consider it my wedding gift.''

"You're a feisty little thing.'' He grinned for the first time since she'd put away Tansho's book.

"You have to let me.''

"Are you sure? You don't owe me anything,'' Daniel said quietly.

"This is not payment. Giving you pleasure inspires me.'' Kara had never imagined such a thing was possible. Until she'd met this man, it hadn't been, not for her.

"Then I think I'd enjoy it.'' He settled into place, yielding. Kara braced herself and reached for him.

Her fingers probed his back, gently pressing each muscle until it released its resistance. He was large, with such broad shoulders that she had to rise on her knees to reach him better, and lean close because of her pregnancy. The contact registered at every point from her breasts to her abdomen.

Kara's breathing sped up. So, she noticed, did Daniel's.

His head sank back and she felt his heat on her nipples. They tightened, fuller than usual, like those of a fertility statue she'd seen in a museum.

As her cheek grazed his thick hair, his spicy scent spread.

through her. Firmly, Kara applied herself to kneading the taut muscles along Daniel's spine, down to his waist, where his spine disappeared beneath his belt. A mischievous impulse urged her to reach around and undo the buckle, just so she could rub him more thoroughly, although she knew that would be tempting fate. Or, more realistically, tempting her husband.

Her fingers tingled as she imagined slipping them around Daniel's waist and lowering them to his thighs. How would that part of him feel beneath her hands? She'd never had the slightest interest in doing such a thing with Hiro, but the thought of touching Daniel intimately gave her an unexpected thrill.

As if he were reading her thoughts, a moan slipped from his throat and he flexed his shoulders. Perhaps she had already gone too far to stop. Perhaps he believed it was his right to claim her and satisfy the hungers that she had aroused.

Awareness rushed over Kara of exactly how little she knew her husband and how little she understood what he expected from a woman. What if she disappointed him? Or what if they made love and she craved more of him, becoming an obsessive woman who was sure to end unhappily?

Mrs. Matsuba's warning flashed in her mind. To such an experienced man, lovemaking might be an enjoyable pastime, but it could never mean as much to him as it would to her.

Alarmed, Kara realized that while she was lost in thought, her rubbing had strayed from Daniel's lower back down to his tight buttocks. In response, he leaned back so that the crown of his head nestled between her breasts. Eagerness flamed through her. Despite her pregnancy, she couldn't help wanting to do everything that the woman in the book was doing and more.

She lifted her hands away. Scooting backward, she blurted, "Now you should be able to sleep." For a clumsy moment, she struggled to lever herself upright, and she finally managed it. "I borrowed a bicycle pump so we can inflate the mattress. Would you like me to help?"

When Daniel didn't respond, she wondered if she'd given

offense. He would be justified in growing angry after she'd tempted him like a lover.

When at last he spoke, unaccustomed gruffness shaded his voice. "I'll take care of it. Why don't you go do whatever you do before you retire for the night?"

It seemed too abrupt to leave him this way. Kara could almost hear her mother's voice instructing her to offer him something to eat or drink and to see to his comfort. However, she sensed that, in this case, it would be an error to follow her upbringing. Far from wanting to be fussed over, her husband was seeking a few minutes alone to compose himself.

"Yes, I'll take my turn in the bathroom," she said, and went to do just that.

Behind a closed door at last, she inspected herself in the mirror and saw that her skin had become flushed and her lips fuller. This was a person she didn't know, a woman standing on the brink of an exciting, but perhaps dangerous, experience. It was oddly disappointing when, as she washed and changed to her nightclothes, the heat abated and she became herself again.

By the time she emerged, Daniel had made up his inflatable bed and prepared her futon bed, as well. "I'll get ready now," he said briskly, and hurried past her.

Kara wanted to stay awake until he emerged from the bathroom. On their wedding night, something more should pass between them. A kiss, at least, or an exchange of wishes for happiness. But when she lay down, she was sucked almost instantly into the deep sleep of pregnancy.

DANIEL STUDIED the soft form on the futon bed, observing the velvety texture of Kara's skin and the dark curve of her eyelashes against her cheek. In sleep, this woman had the delicacy of a child, yet his response told him that she was a full-grown woman.

Despite his best efforts, he'd been keenly attuned to the heat of her body while she was stroking his shoulders. If that kind of massage helped Japanese men fall asleep, they must be wired very differently from American men, he thought wryly. The desire still lingered, refusing to dissipate.

It was hard to know what to make of Kara. Sometimes she seemed so innocent, even though she'd been married before and was about to become a mother. She'd blushed like crazy when she saw that risqué book, and then she'd stroked him with such passion that he'd become thoroughly aroused. Yet had she really felt any passion? Perhaps she'd been trained in how to please a man and had behaved the same way with Hiro.

He'd known when he asked Kara to marry him that there might be legal ramifications. It hadn't occurred to him that the situation would present other difficulties or, more accurately, temptations. Well, he'd been naive.

Daniel released a long breath. There was so much to learn about his new wife. He supposed he should have asked in advance what she expected from the marriage, but then, this wasn't a real marriage.

Resignedly, he lowered himself onto his mattress and pulled up the new wedding quilt. Although his bed was more comfortable than he'd expected, he felt awkward sleeping on the floor. It didn't help that masculine longings continued to cascade inside him, holding sleep at bay.

From now on, if he wanted his back rubbed, Daniel decided to book a massage at his health club. He also resolved to move as soon as possible to his house, where they'd have not only the luxury of real beds but, above all, separate rooms.

CHAPTER ELEVEN

ON MONDAY MORNING, Kara's alarm clock woke her at eight. Seeing daylight flooding through the window and under the impression that she'd overslept, she nearly leaped out of bed.

Then she remembered that she wasn't delivering fruits and vegetables any longer. She didn't have to be at Forrester Square Day Care until ten.

The only reminder of Daniel's presence was his mattress, deflated and folded in a corner with the neatly piled bedding. Kara wished she'd been awake to see him off to work and make sure he wasn't angry about last night.

She'd made a serious blunder by massaging him in a sensual manner. Where she'd intended to create harmony, she'd left only dissonance. It was important to be more careful of her husband's feelings in future.

The problem was that in some ways she felt like a wife. Well, she wasn't really one, and she had to stop thinking that way.

In the kitchen, Kara found a note with money clipped to it. In firm, if hurried, script, Daniel had written, "Please take a taxi, instead of the bus. If you like, I can lease a car for you."

Kara's eyes filled with tears at her husband's thoughtfulness. She hadn't expected him to take such an interest in her well-being. Despite his generosity, however, she tucked the money away in case she needed it later. In good weather, walking to and from the bus stop was good exercise.

When they went to live at Daniel's house, she might need a car to do the shopping, especially once she had a baby to carry with her. Still, it seemed like a lot of money for him to spend on a temporary mate.

Kara began planning the meal for tonight: spaghetti with tomato sauce, French bread and fresh Washington-grown vegetables—a truly international meal. She wanted to say thankyou with her hands, as well as with words.

She arrived at Forrester Square a few minutes early. Instead of entering through the kitchen door, she indulged herself by using the rear entrance into the main corridor, where she stood breathing in the scents of chalk and pine cleanser. From where she stood, she could hear the happy chatter of four-year-olds in the nearest classroom.

This was where she wanted to be during the day while Daniel was at work. It felt like a second home.

Stepping out of the office down the hallway, Hannah spotted her and waved eagerly. Apparently not wanting their conversation to disrupt the classes, she gestured toward the kitchen.

Glad to see her friend back from her honeymoon and looking healthily rounded with early pregnancy, Kara spoke as soon as they were alone. "Did you have a good time? Only a week! But I'm sure it was wonderful."

"We had a great time bonding as a family," Hannah said. "Laguna Beach is too cold for swimming this time of year but Adam had fun playing in the sand and we spent a great day at Disneyland. We'd have stayed longer, only Jack couldn't take any more time off." He worked as a parole officer, Kara remembered. "You're the one with the big news! I can't believe you and Daniel got married."

Kara filled her in while checking the day's menu, cleaning up and beginning preparations. The meal, although simple, was tasty and nutritious, and she enjoyed the colors and smells of the food.

After smoothing her chin-length honey-blond hair behind her ears, Hannah joined in, since one of the other part-time helpers was off sick. As they worked, they talked about their marriage ceremonies, their husbands and the babies they carried.

Hannah listened intently to Kara's explanation of why she had decided against inviting her parents to the wedding. "At least you know who they are and where they stand on things," she said. "What would you do if…" She broke off.

Realizing her friend wanted to bring up a sensitive subject, Kara gave her an encouraging smile. "Yes?"

"Suppose you found out that things weren't the way you'd always been told?" Hannah asked. "I'm talking about my parents, I guess. You know they got divorced when I was little?"

"I'd heard that," Kara murmured.

"Well, they're not… I mean, there's something wrong with…" Hannah cleared her throat. "I found out that my blood type doesn't match. They're both RH negative and I'm positive. I can't be their biological child."

"You're adopted?" Kara cut the sandwiches she'd made into triangles. The children enjoyed them more that way, and they looked nice on the plates.

"Neither of them will admit to anything," Hannah said. "They claim there must have been a mix-up at the lab, but I had my type rechecked and it's definitely positive. It makes me wonder who I really am."

"You're the same precious person you always were," Kara told her. "The woman Jack and Adam love."

"Thanks." Hannah thrust her hands into her apron pocket. "I appreciate that. I'm especially sensitive to this because of being pregnant. My children ought to know for sure who their grandparents are."

"That's important," Kara agreed.

"Speaking of grandparents, have you had any luck tracking down your grandfather's family, or doesn't that matter now that you're married?" Hannah arranged carrots on the plates.

"I haven't been lucky yet. I do still want to find them," she said. "Daniel's very kind, but I should do as much as I can to help myself. If I can find my family, he won't have to worry about me anymore.''

''Maybe he wants to worry about you.''

''I don't like to be trouble for him.'' Kara broke off as the back door opened and Alexandra breezed in from the playground, her eyes bright.

''I hope you don't mind if I slap together a sandwich for Gary Devlin,'' she said after greeting them. ''He showed up outside and he looks hungry.''

Kara had forgotten about the homeless man. ''I'm sure we have plenty of food.''

''Did you learn any more about his background while I was gone?'' Hannah asked.

''I keep hitting a blank wall,'' Alexandra said as she washed her hands. ''I thought for sure when I checked his fingerprints that I'd get to the bottom of things, but it hasn't worked out that way. I need to figure out why he seems so familiar to me.''

''If you want to dig deeper, it's time to bring in an expert,'' Hannah said. ''I told you about my friend Dylan Garrett from my college days, didn't I?''

Alexandra reached around Kara for two slices of bread. ''You mentioned that he's partners in an agency that reunites families.''

''It's called Finders Keepers, in San Antonio, Texas,'' Hannah said. ''He's the one who helped me find Adam and, of course, Jack. If you're serious about tracking down this guy's past, you should talk to Dylan.''

''Is it okay if I take a couple of slices of turkey?'' Alexandra asked.

''Of course.'' Kara handed her the package.

''Well?'' Hannah persisted.

''Well…okay,'' Alexandra said. ''Give me the guy's phone number and I'll make the call. I promise.''

Although Kara disliked intruding into the conversation, she couldn't resist. ''Do you think he might be able to find my grandfather's relatives?''

"Like I said, he's the best," Hannah replied. "Don't you remember, I suggested his company to you once before? It sent you into a panic."

When her friend had mentioned Finders Keepers previously, Kara had been terrified at the idea of notifying anyone in authority about her situation. A private agency might not be the same as a government organization, but how could she trust it? With Daniel on her side, however, she no longer lived in dread.

"I don't have much money," she said. "Do you know what they charge?"

"I'll find out when I call Dylan," Alexandra offered.

"Actually, I'd rather approach him about Kara myself," Hannah said. "She told me some details about her family earlier, and I may be able to persuade him to run them through one of his databases as a favor to me."

"Thank you!" Kara said. "I'd be very grateful."

Unexpectedly, she felt a twist of anxiety. Until she met Daniel, locating her grandfather's family had been her dream. Since then, she'd thought of them only occasionally. The much-cherished fantasy of being welcomed into a loving household had been replaced by a new friendship and new hope.

Kara wanted Hannah's friend to succeed because she knew how much it would have meant to her grandfather. Also, if her relatives took her in, it would relieve Daniel of the burden he'd so generously assumed.

It would also mean never learning how it felt to get close to him. Never again seeing his dark eyes warm at the sight of her. Never again joking with him or singing karaoke together.

She mustn't think in such a selfish way. The sooner she removed herself from the picture, the sooner she could set Daniel free.

"What, no free favors for me?" teased Alexandra.

"Your case is probably more complicated, judging by what

you've told me," Hannah said. "I can't help suspecting there's something unusual in Gary's background."

One of the playground monitors banged on the back door. "Alexandra! You'd better come quick!"

"What's going on?" Dropping the sandwich, she hurried out with Hannah and Kara right behind.

Gary Devlin, a frail, sixtyish man, sat on a bench nursing a large gash in his hand. Elongated like a string bean, he had shaggy gray hair and watery blue eyes that searched the faces of the teachers and children surrounding him as if desperate to find someone he recognized.

"What happened?" Alexandra plopped onto the bench beside the man and inspected his hand as if he were one of their charges. He glanced at her uncertainly and after a moment began to smile.

"He fell down." A little boy pointed toward the fence around the property.

"I thought he should sit," the monitor said. "You don' mind my bringing him in here, do you?"

"No, of course not," Alexandra said.

Looking at the sidewalk, Kara noticed a break in the concrete. "There?" The boy nodded.

Hannah went over to take a closer look through the fence. "That's dangerous. We'll have to see about getting it fixed. I'd hate for one of the kids or a parent to trip on the way to their car."

"He needs to see a doctor." Alexandra bent worriedly over Gary's hand.

"It's not bad," he said, trying to hide the injury under his loose shirttail.

"You need a tetanus shot," Alexandra told him. "I don' suppose you remember the last time you had one?"

Slowly and regretfully, the man shook his head.

"I can take him if you'll lend me a car," Kara said.

"That's good of you, but no thanks." Alexandra gave her a shadow of a smile. "I'm the one he knows and trusts. Be

ides, someone's going to have to pay the bill unless he qual-
fies for government aid.''

"You could ask if the doctor has any ideas about how to
ind his medical records,'' Hannah added. ''That might help
our search.''

"Good idea.''

At Alexandra's instructions, the man stood obediently and
walked with her toward her car. ''Okay, everybody,'' Hannah
aid. ''The show's over. Back to whatever you were doing!''

The children, teachers and playground monitors dispersed,
nd Kara and Hannah returned to the kitchen.

They were running late, so there was no time for discussion
s they hastened to get the food ready before the first shift in
he dining room. As she poured juice for the children, how-
ver, Kara's mind kept replaying and reviewing the events of
he past few minutes.

She hoped Alexandra was able to learn Gary Devlin's back-
round, both for her own peace of mind and for his family's.
t occurred to her that her great-uncle, who would be in his
ighties if still alive, might be in distress, as well. If so, Kara
vould do her best to help. The important thing was to find
im.

Perhaps Finders Keepers would succeed where she'd failed.
Keeping that positive thought in mind, Kara went to put food
n the tables.

ON TUESDAY EVENING, Daniel brought pizza and flowers
ome for Kara. It was his way of atoning for Monday night,
vhen he'd gone straight from work to inspect the house in
sellevue. It hadn't occurred to him that she might be prepar-
ig dinner until he arrived home much later, satisfied that the
ooring was being properly laid, only to find her fighting tears
mid the stone-cold remains of what must have been a lovely
paghetti dinner.

"I'm sorry—I'm not used to considering someone else's
lans,'' he'd told her.

She'd averted her face. ''It was my mistake.''

"I'll bring dinner tomorrow," he'd promised. "And I'm going to write more than half the thank-you notes, too." So he had, and now here he was, carrying two varieties of pizza along with salad.

As he let himself in with his duplicate key, it struck Daniel that he should have asked Kara whether she liked pizza. His worry evaporated when he saw her beaming like a kid on Christmas morning.

"Two kinds!" she said reverently, eyeing the boxes. In a loose jumper over a casual top, she looked sweet and welcoming. "You mean I get a choice?"

"You can have as much as you want of either or both," he promised.

They coiled their legs on the mats at the low table, which she'd set with flowered plates and glasses, and dug in. Daniel supposed that he might eventually get used to dining on the floor, but he intended to use an American-style table in their new home. After all, he'd be living there alone eventually.

The prospect rattled him. Sometimes he almost forgot that this marriage wasn't going to last indefinitely.

Kara ate daintily, her full lips parting with unconscious sensuality. Daniel kept thinking about how they would feel beneath his. Yesterday and today, he'd spent a lot of time imagining her soft body wriggling against him and her thighs encircling him. He needed to stop doing that.

He dragged his mind back the subject he ought to be concentrating on. "We need to get to know each other better. The feds are going to interview us one of these days, and it will look weird if I don't know little details about you. They're going to compare our stories, you know."

Rounded eyes peered at him over a slice of pepperoni pizza. "They won't interview us together?"

"I'm afraid not."

Kara set the slice down. "Everything we say has to match?"

"That's right," Daniel said. "I haven't done a lot of research yet, but I'm sure they'll ask how we met, what we did on our first date and how we fell in love. The fact that we got married within a week is going to look suspicious, not to mention your being pregnant.''

"They will ask you why you want to raise another man's child,'' she said. ''What will you tell them?''

''That I love kids,'' Daniel responded automatically. ''A child is a child, and one who looks like you is sure to be cute as a button.'' Of that, he had no doubt.

Kara smiled, then grew serious again. ''Why will you say we got married so quickly?''

''Because I couldn't wait to get you in the sack?''

''You mean in the futon!'' She wrinkled her nose. ''But I'm in no shape for such activity.''

''Some men find pregnant women unbearably sexy,'' Daniel said. Before he'd met Kara, he hadn't understood how a woman in that state could arouse a man. Now he understood, perhaps better than he wanted to.

''You must want to get me pregnant again right away,'' Kara teased.

''Oh, yes. We'll have five or six little scamps running around before you know it.'' Daniel shook his head. ''Man, they'll never buy this. We're going to have to work on our stories better.''

''We have to be creative,'' she said.

''I'd prefer to stick as close to the truth as possible,'' Daniel said. ''That way it's easier to remember.''

It would help, he mused, if he had more romantic experiences to draw on. He scarcely knew what points to address and which questions to ask Kara.

During college, he'd tried living with a woman and found her exasperating. She would invite her friends over without checking first, play the stereo too loud and demand that he take her out when he needed to study. When he'd complain, she'd accused him of being cold and self-centered. Daniel had concluded that he wasn't emotionally suited to sharing quarters with a woman, and he hadn't met anyone since then who'd changed his mind.

He had to admit, however, that he didn't mind staying here with Kara for a week. She was one of the few people he'd met who kept things neat enough for his tastes. Also, restricted though the apartment was, he liked the lightness of it. And when Kara was here, the air seemed to sparkle.

"What are you thinking?" she asked, reaching for a third slice. A string of mozzarella caught in her hair, and Daniel plucked it free. Enjoying the silkiness of the dark strands, he brushed them away from her face and tucked a wedge behind one ear.

"I was thinking how nice you look," he said.

"And how messy!" Kara spread her hands apologetically, indicating the cheese he'd wiped on a paper napkin. "The authorities will never believe you fell in love with a walking food magnet."

"We'll make sure there's nothing stuck to your face before the interview," Daniel assured her. "Now, let's see. We'll have to tell the truth about you coming to see me for a visa problem, because they might ask Katherine for her version. I'll say that the moment I saw you, you knocked me off my feet."

"Because I'm so clumsy," she joked.

"Because you're so alive," Daniel said. "You open new vistas for me, like introducing me to karaoke. And I'm looking forward to visiting Japan with you."

"You are?" Kara regarded him uncertainly. "Or is that something you're making up for the interview?"

"I mean it," he said truthfully, although he'd never pictured himself visiting Japan until now. "I don't know much about it other than what I learned in high school. What's your favorite thing about your country?"

"I feel safe there," Kara said promptly. "I can leave my door open and nothing gets stolen. My friends and I could go out at night without worrying."

"That sounds good," Daniel said. "Not that I've had any problems in Seattle."

"Also, I miss the heated toilet seats."

"They have heated toilet seats?"

She nodded vigorously. "The heat level is adjustable."

Daniel whistled. "We've got to get one of those. Now I want to visit Japan more than ever!"

"To experience the toilet seats?" Kara asked.

"To experience a lot of things," he said. "I'm also curious to meet your parents."

"My father's very stern." Kara pulled a long face. "He looks like it hurts him to laugh. Ho, ho, ho!" She shook her shoulders and mimed a shocked expression.

"He sounds like my dad," Daniel admitted. "When my mom left, all the joy went out of his life. He never seemed to take pleasure from much of anything except going fishing."

"He was happy around her?" Kara asked.

Daniel tried to remember. He'd been too young to see his parents as individuals separate from their roles as his mom and dad. "He was always pretty strict, but he smiled more back then. When she left, she really did a number on him."

"And on you," Kara said.

Remembering an e-mail he'd received, Daniel scowled. "She had the nerve to message me today. She invited me to a gathering her family holds every July. This year it's in St. George, Utah."

"The whole family meets every year?" Kara asked. "That sounds like fun."

"It used to be." He'd accompanied his mother each summer when he was young. His father had gone a few times, although he hadn't always been able to take time off. There'd been picnics and parties at varying locales. Many of the relatives brought RVs and some stayed at hotels, so there was always room for more.

After his mom left, the uncles and aunts and cousins had faded from Daniel's mind. He'd made no effort to keep track of them, perhaps because it had been too hurtful to think of anything connected with his mother.

"She must miss you," Kara said.

"She has a daughter now," he answered.

"One child can never replace another." Kara waggled her fingers apologetically. "I'm sorry. I've made you frown."

"It's not your fault," Daniel said. "It's her e-mail that annoyed me. She said she wants to reestablish ties after all these years. Well, it's too late. She can't have her cake and eat it, too."

"Are you going to tell her about me?" Kara asked.

"I haven't been able to reach my father yet," Daniel said. "I'm certainly not going to fill her in before I tell him."

Without answering, Kara arose and began clearing away the dirty dishes. He jumped up to help her. Something in her averted face and subdued manner told him he'd touched a nerve.

How strange, he thought. He'd been told so many times that he was insensitive to others' feelings that he'd come to assume it was part of his nature. Yet with Kara, picking up clues from her body language was sometimes as easy as deciphering the intent of a clause in a contract. "What's wrong?"

"It's not my place to interfere in your family business." She removed the leftover pizza from its carton and slid it onto a piece of aluminum foil.

"For the time being, you qualify as part of my family," he said. "Feel free to make any comments you wish." He knew she would never criticize unkindly, nor would she try to manipulate or control him. With Kara, it was safe to talk openly.

"You've told me a lot about your mother," she said, "and yet, very little. I think there is more to her story. It might be useful to let her tell it to you."

The simple honesty of the observation appealed to him. "Maybe I will," Daniel said. "After I talk to Dad."

"Of course. Your first loyalty must be to him," she agreed. They finished cleaning up in reflective silence, until she said, "Would you like me to prepare the tea as I promised?"

Daniel dragged his thoughts away from wondering how his

father would react. "You said it helps focus the mind. That sounds like exactly what I need."

She smiled. "It will take a few minutes for me to get ready. Also, I must change clothing."

"Change clothing?" he asked.

"I want to wear the traditional dress." Kara cleared her throat. "The bathroom is too small for me to put on my kimono. It might drag in the sink."

"I won't look, I promise."

"Thank you."

Daniel took out some briefs and busied himself reading. He avoided looking up as rustling noises announced that she was dressing. Trying in vain to concentrate on work, he listened to the fabric whisper across her skin. Her fragrance sent a tingle running through him, as if she were drawing the silk across his bare flesh.

At last she stood before him, lovely in her green kimono. "You look beautiful," Daniel said.

"Thank you." A flicker of eye contact told him that, during the whole process, she'd been as keenly aware of him as he'd been of her. "I will start now."

He set aside the brief. "I don't want to miss any part of this. Can I help?"

"You can watch," Kara said.

"That sounds good."

In the kitchenette, he leaned against the wall, enjoying the sight of her putting on water to boil. In the kimono, with her hair brushed back simply, she had a directness and lack of vanity. Those qualities, coupled with her womanly shape and the subliminal awareness of approaching motherhood, gave her the air of being completely at home with herself.

"The tea ceremony can take as long as four hours if it includes a meal," she said. "Someday we should go to a real Japanese teahouse so you can experience it."

"I'd rather have you fix my tea," Daniel said.

"I'm afraid I don't have the skill to do it properly," Kara said as she set out their new teacups on a tray alongside the matching pot. The red-lacquered set bore black Japanese lettering. He supposed the characters must have some meaning, but the shapes contained a beauty of their own. "In my classes, I was always a slow student."

"You took classes in how to perform this tea business?"

She glanced at him guiltily. "Not as often as my mother wanted me to."

"How hard can it be to make tea?" Daniel asked, although he was beginning to suspect that doing anything Japanese-style required a subtle intricacy beyond what might be apparent to a Westerner.

Kara retrieved some candies and a container of tea from a cabinet. "Brewing tea isn't the hard part. It's the mental preparation. To present the tea ceremony properly, you must appreciate everything from poetry to flower arrangement. You must enter into a state of mind and body that fine-tunes all your senses."

"You're scaring me," Daniel joked. "You sound like some guru from the sixties."

"Guru?" she asked.

"Wise man."

She laughed. "I'm hardly wise. To truly master the tea ceremony would be like becoming a concert pianist. Anyone can tap out a simple melody on the keys, but a true artist understands music and history. She knows the piano and how it is made. She practices for hundreds of hours. She reads the mind of the composer."

"The only mind I want to read right now is yours." Although a little surprised to hear himself speaking so frankly, Daniel was in earnest.

"Reading my mind is easy," Kara assured him. "I hide nothing from you."

He wanted to believe that. In his family, however, very little had been discussed. He suspected that in every relationship there were secrets, although sometimes unintentional ones. "That isn't possible."

"It is," she assured him. "I cannot imagine deceiving you."

Tension he hadn't even been aware of eased from Daniel's muscles. "I'm glad at least you try your best to be open. I promise to do the same. After all, we could be sharing quarters for a long time."

"Now you must set aside your self-consciousness and concentrate on the tea ceremony," Kara told him. "Otherwise you won't receive the full enjoyment."

"Point taken," Daniel said.

During the next half hour, he focused on her gentle movements and the details of the tea ceremony. The green tea, which she mixed from a powder, was called *matcha*. There was a lot of bowing, and the promised piece of candy to sweeten the mouth, and a ritual that involved turning the teacup in the hand before drinking. As she'd warned, the brew was bitter, and yet its contrast to the sweetness made Daniel keenly aware of what a gift it was to be able to taste.

They talked only about the ceremony itself and the beauty of the tea set the Matsubas had given them. After a while, Daniel shed his random concerns. He channeled the serenity of this moment.

Kara had underestimated herself, he thought. If the tea ceremony was intended to restore harmony, she had mastered it beautifully.

Inside Daniel, walls began to crumble that had been erected so long ago they'd become a part of his internal landscape. For the first time, he could see over them to glimpse the green freshness of the future. Kara had done this. She hadn't so much torn the walls down as dissolved them.

It occurred to him as they finished the ceremony that it might not be so hard, after all, to convince the government that they had married for love. He was almost ready to believe it himself.

CHAPTER TWELVE

AS SHE APPROACHED the kitchen door to Forrester Square Day Care on Thursday, Kara spotted two boys of about four years old crouching together near the corner of the house, partially out of view of their teachers. Although it wasn't her duty to supervise the youngsters, she recognized potential trouble when she saw it.

"What are you doing?" She marched toward them in her most commanding manner.

"Just playing," one of the boys said.

"You should stay out in the open," she told them. "Come on."

"We're not doing anything." The other turned away. His movement revealed what he'd been trying to hide: a crumpled piece of paper erupting in flame.

"Get away from there right now!" As she shooed them off, Kara saw more wads of paper catch fire on the ground. She snatched a cigarette lighter from one boy's hand and reached for a nearby hose. She never took fire lightly, having grown up in a country with many wooden houses.

There was no immediate danger to the sandstone brick structure or to any of the children playing in the yard, thank goodness. As she turned on the faucet, Kara gestured to Alexandra, who had just come out the back door. "Look what those boys did! Don't worry. I'll put it out." The co-owner of the day care turned so white Kara feared she might faint. "Are you all right?" she asked as water sent the flames hissing into oblivion.

Alexandra took a deep breath. "It's nothing."

"You are distressed," Kara said worriedly. "Look, it's all gone." After dispersing the blackened remains of paper with her shoe, she held out the lighter. "Can you believe this? One of those boys must have stolen it from his parents."

Alexandra quivered as if intending to reach for it, but stopped short. "I'm sorry. You wouldn't think it would still bother me after all these years, but I'm terrified of fire."

She'd narrowly escaped the fire that killed her parents, Kara remembered. "I'm sorry. I'll give it to someone else."

"We'd better send a reminder to parents not to leave dangerous materials where their kids can get them," Alexandra said. "Thanks for catching this in time, Kara." Her color slowly returning, she inspected the ashes. "It's dead, all right. We'd better go tell Katherine. Do you know which boys were involved?"

"Yes. Just a minute." Kara went to the playground and after pointing out the boys to one of the teachers, returned with their names.

Alexandra still appeared shaken as they traversed the hallway toward the office at the front of the building. To distract her, Kara asked, "How is Gary Devlin? Is his wound healing all right?"

Her friend nodded. "He'll be fine. At least, his hand will be."

Kara saw that although her friend was no longer panicky, the question had troubled her. "Is there another problem?"

"Can you believe it? He looks like he's only in his sixties, but the doctor said he's already showing signs of Alzheimer's disease. They'd have to do a complete workup to confirm the diagnosis, because there are other kinds of dementia, but the doctor wasn't optimistic."

"You haven't been able to find his medical records?"

"I'm afraid not."

Kara knew Alexandra had called Finders Keepers on Tuesday. If they hadn't been able to track down Gary's records, perhaps they couldn't find Franklin Loesser, either.

She almost wished they wouldn't. She had an obligation to

free Daniel of the burden he'd assumed on her behalf, yet it hurt to think of leaving him. According to Japanese tradition, a married woman belonged to her husband's family, but this wasn't a real marriage. Kara had to do what was right, and that meant sparing Daniel from an unnecessary obligation.

He'd been putting in long hours the past few days, spending most of his spare time in Bellevue. She hadn't seen the new house, which was so torn up that he didn't want her to risk walking through it. They planned to visit on Saturday, when, if the contractor honored his schedule, the place should be ready for occupancy.

Even in the brief times they'd spent together, however, Kara had felt a new ease between them. When Daniel came home last night, he'd given her a gentle hug and sat beside her on the futon. As he talked, his low voice had rumbled through her like a melody.

The sensations he aroused went beyond her physical response. Together, they were like cherry blossoms in springtime, emerging from winter stillness into the sunshine.

But she must not forget Mrs. Matsuba's warning. However tender Daniel might seem, he had promised her the protection of his name only until she could secure the proper papers.

In her office, Katherine listened to the account of the fire and wrote down the boys' names. "Do you think I should call the fire department, just to make sure it's completely extinguished?"

"It might frighten the parents if they arrive and see a fire truck," Alexandra said. "If there were the slightest danger, I'd urge you to do it, but after watching Kara kick the ashes apart, I'm sure there isn't. And believe me, I don't take fires lightly."

"I know." Katherine locked the lighter inside a drawer. "By the way, I sent Hannah home for the day. She was a little under the weather, and at this point in the pregnancy, I didn't want to take any chances."

"Absolutely not," Alexandra agreed.

"I'd better go start fixing lunch." Kara had seen two part-time workers in the kitchen as they passed, but she wanted to do her share.

"Oh, my gosh! Wait a minute. I nearly forgot something important." Katherine dug through the papers on her desk. "Hannah asked me to give you this. Her friend Dylan faxed it to her. I think it must be about your family." She handed over a folded sheet of paper.

Kara was almost afraid to look at it. Realizing she didn't want to face the news, good or bad, in front of anyone, she tucked it in her pocket. "Thank you."

"Aren't you going to read it?" Alexandra demanded.

"Not right now."

"Give the girl a little privacy," Katherine chided her partner. "Believe me, only my high ideals and moral upbringing prevented me from peeking, but I stood fast against temptation."

"Quit showing off," said Alexandra. "I wasn't trying to read it without permission."

"She'll tell us in her own good time," Katherine said.

Kara barely heard her. With a mumbled apology, she hurried into the hall.

The fax burned in her pocket. Here might be the news she'd sought for months. Or perhaps this might confirm that Franklin Loesser was nowhere to be found.

Seeking a place where she wouldn't be disturbed, Kara pushed open the arched front door and exited. Traffic was slight on Sandringham Drive at this hour, and except for a couple disappearing into Caffeine Hy's next door, she didn't see anyone around who might interrupt her solitude.

Kara descended the steps between two wrought-iron lamps, each supporting a basket of colorful flowers. She found this small bit of nature comforting as she sank onto one of the twin park benches that flanked the bottom of the stairs and drew the paper from her pocket.

The fax bore the official-looking letterhead of Finders Keepers, with a San Antonio address. Her heart thumping against her ribs, she began to read.

Dear Hannah:

Your friend's timing is excellent. I found a database entry dated about six weeks ago seeking a Mr. Albert Loesser or any of his descendants, possibly in Japan. It cites the name Franklin Loesser as his brother.

The contact is listed as Leila Loesser. I've attached her address and phone number.

I'm always happy to be of service. Congratulations again on your marriage. I'll always feel privileged that I was able to help bring you and Jack together again.

Sincerely,

Dylan Garrett

At the bottom of the page, he'd listed Leila Loesser's address and phone number in Los Angeles. Judging by her name, obviously she was a relative, although the information didn't hint at her age. Could she be a great-aunt, an aunt or even a cousin?

Kara could pick up a phone and dial her anytime. She could learn whether her great-uncle still lived, and perhaps find the refuge she'd been seeking.

She sat motionless, scarcely noticing the cool April breeze on her face. Down the street, a well-dressed woman emerged from an antique shop and clicked along the sidewalk. A bus wheezed to a halt at the corner. All around, the world whirred on as if nothing had changed.

But it had, fundamentally and irrevocably. She'd found her grandfather's family and not only an aged great-uncle but a woman named Leila who'd cared enough to enter the information in a database.

That didn't mean that she would be willing to sponsor Kara for a green card. Perhaps this Leila sought to obtain medical information or was compiling a family scrapbook. Yet suddenly the dream Kara had nurtured for so long verged on coming true.

She knew she ought to be strong, and that a strong woman would not hesitate to call the number. But during the past week and a half since Daniel proposed, the tenor of her imagined future had changed. She wanted to see the home in Bellevue where she had pictured Dorima taking her first toddler steps. She wanted to hold Daniel again and experience that pulsing inner demand, even if it could never be fulfilled.

It wasn't time to let go yet. Kara's spirit needed to absorb this latest twist and integrate it into her inner reality.

She wasn't ready to talk to Leila. Until she did, there was no point in mentioning this discovery to Daniel, since its implications remained unclear. Kara didn't want to give the impression that he would soon be free when that might not be the case.

I won't wait too long, she silently promised the Daniel who lived in her mind. Then, tucking the paper into her pocket, she went inside.

BELLEVUE, KARA LEARNED when they drove there on Saturday, lay a short distance east of Seattle across Lake Washington. They took one of the two floating highway bridges that connected the sprawling community to the metropolis.

A wheat-colored fisherman sweater molded itself to Daniel's husky upper body, in contrast to his dark hair. As he drove, he was more animated than usual, no doubt because the contractor had assured him that the work was finished at last.

"If it's all right with you, we can pack tonight and move in tomorrow," he said, glancing at her and then back to the road. "I've corralled Drew to help with the heavy lifting. It's lucky we don't have much furniture."

"The Matsubas said for us to take whatever we like of my furnishings." Kara had eaten lunch with Tansho on Friday. In addition to talking about the move, she had found it a relief to share the news about Leila Loesser.

"She's probably not prepared for a pregnant cousin to descend on her lock, stock and diapers," Tansho had agreed. "You're wise to take your time."

Today, as they flashed above the blue waters of the lake,

Kara felt as if she had all the time in the world. Only this moment existed, captured in the flow of forever like a photograph. Dorima would always lie snug in her belly and Daniel would always sit beside her, describing Bellevue, a place with award-winning schools and an array of parks. And in this snapshot, she would always be happy.

The area had its own shops and restaurants, Kara noticed, once they reached land. Near a supermarket, they passed a pair of young mothers chatting while they pushed strollers. Her chest swelled almost painfully with the wish that she belonged here as completely as they did.

"There are some new developments, but the older homes have bigger lots, which is what I wanted," Daniel said. "One of these days I intend to take up gardening. I'm not planning to put in anything as elaborate as the Matsubas have, but I'd like to grow vegetables and flowers."

A garden would be wonderful, Kara thought. She only hoped she was here to enjoy it. "That sounds lovely."

The house, when they reached it, was nestled in a stand of trees. "It's exquisite." As Daniel parked in the circular driveway, Kara studied the modern brick structure with its white paint and blue trim. "From the way you talk about the place, I believe your soul has embraced this house."

"I knew it was right for me the minute I saw it," he said. "I'm glad you like it, too."

Daniel swung out of the car and came around to assist Kara. When she emerged, he caught her hand and pulled her along the front walkway.

Inside, she removed her shoes, not only from custom but also out of respect for the new, cream-colored carpets stretching through the rooms. The architecture and low-key color scheme reflected a sensitivity to the natural setting that put her immediately at ease.

"How do you like the kitchen?" Daniel showed her an updated expanse of granite counters and gleaming appliances. Without waiting for a reply, he tugged her into the adjacent family room. ''We could put a karaoke player in here. What do you think?''

Kara couldn't tell whether he was joking or simply bursting with good humor. ''That would be fun.''

In the hallway, he indicated a sun-brightened chamber. ''That will be the nursery. You can fix it however you like.''

''It's perfect.'' Any baby would feel welcomed in such a room. ''I can sleep in here, too.'' According to tradition, the baby should sleep in bed with her mother, although Kara had heard a nurse at the clinic advise against that practice. She hadn't made up her mind yet.

Daniel indicated the room opposite it. ''I'm going to set up a home office there.''

''That's a good choice,'' Kara said. ''It's not as sunny, so you'll have less glare on the computer screen.''

In the master bedroom, the amount of space amazed her. Almost the size of her whole apartment, it opened onto a private rear patio. Visible through a glass door, the dappled lawn resembled a glade among the spring-green trees. ''It's like a secret retreat in a forest.''

''Secret is right,'' Daniel said. ''The real-estate agent assured me the neighbors can't see into the yard.'' Casually, he ran his hand up her arm. Wine replaced the blood in Kara's veins. ''I haven't decided yet where I want to put the bed.''

She examined the room. ''Which way is north?''

''That way.'' Daniel pointed toward the front of the house. ''Why?''

''The bed should be oriented north-south.''

He studied her with a bemused expression. ''Why on earth?''

She shrugged. ''For luck, I think.'' She stretched, trying to ease a mild backache from the strain of carrying the baby.

''Is that part of *feng shui?*''

''I don't know,'' Kara admitted. ''My mother told me when I married Hiro that it was very important, the first time we made love, for the bed to lie north and south.'' She felt herself coloring brightly. ''I didn't mean anything by that.''

Moving behind her, Daniel massaged her back lightly. The power in his hands hinted of even greater power in his arms. His nearness made Kara's knees feel weak, but she struggled not to show it. "If the bed was north-south, but you lie on it crossways, would that be bad luck?"

"Who would lie in bed that way?" Torn between laughter and a growing urge to touch him back, Kara waved her hands vaguely. "Of course we lie north-south."

Close to her ear, Daniel said, "If it were me, you wouldn't remember which direction we were lying because we'd be all over the bed."

Kara's heart sped up at the implication. "We don't have a bed yet," she said in one last attempt to conclude the dangerous discussion. "Besides, we will be sleeping separately."

"I keep trying to remind myself of that." A low groan escaped from his throat.

"We should go and...and plan where to put things." Realizing that her words could be taken more than one way, she said quickly, "I mean the furniture."

"I know what you mean." His voice sounded ragged, but he didn't move away. "You're right." Instead of letting go, however, he bent to nuzzle her hair, his breath caressing her neck like a warm breeze.

Since the first time she'd touched him—no, since the day they'd met—Kara had wondered at some level what it would be like to connect intimately with Daniel. Now she could only lean back against him and wish he was really her husband. Already he seemed more of a husband than Hiro had been.

As if he couldn't stop himself, Daniel drew both hands across her belly, ruffling the loose fabric of her jumper. Slowly, a little afraid of how he might react, Kara turned and lifted her face to his.

There was a moment's hesitation, a darkness in his gaze, and then he brushed her lips with a kiss across her lips that made her forget that they shouldn't be doing this. As they moved together, her arms wound around his neck.

They shifted in unison, inventing their own private dance.

His body buffed hers and then swiveled to play against her from another angle, while his lips traced her temple.

Kara couldn't think straight through the roaring in her ears. Was this hot-blooded lover really the arrow-straight man who'd seemed so unbending when she first met him? The strangest part was her own eager response. When she was in his arms, all her sensible thoughts turned into hummingbirds and darted away.

As a plant unfurls in the sunshine, she opened herself to Daniel. She explored his neck with the tip of her nose and inhaled a scent as rich as freshly mown grass. Wondering, she raised her eyes to meet his.

His hands cupped her pregnancy-enlarged breasts and he kissed her again so sweetly that time seemed to stand still. If she had expected him to call a halt, Kara understood now that he wasn't going to. Perhaps he couldn't. And neither could she.

Whether she stopped now or whether she threw herself into Daniel's embrace, her longing for him would last for the rest of her life. If only this once, she wanted to know him absolutely. Among all the truths that Kara had learned, the one that came to her now was that life was a journey, not a destination. She intended to share this part of the journey with Daniel, and she would never allow herself to regret it.

"Yes," she whispered.

"I didn't ask you anything," he murmured.

"You don't have to."

His hands still containing her breasts, he ran his tongue lightly around the shell of her ear. Kara lost herself in the intimacy of his mouth. She lifted herself to get closer, wanting to blend right into him, but her bulge held them apart.

Silently, she urged Dorima to snuggle tighter. As if in response, she felt a sudden squirming.

"There seem to be three of us here," Daniel said. She couldn't tell if he was joking.

"She's trying to get out of the way."

He smiled a bit crookedly. "That's cooperative of her."

"She can't move far enough," Kara admitted, her spirits heavy with disappointment. "I don't think it's possible to make love at this point."

"There are other ways of giving pleasure." Daniel eased her down onto the carpet. "Is this comfortable for you?"

"Yes, except that we're not close enough."

"I can fix that." He stretched alongside her and offered his arm as a pillow. When she relaxed, he resumed stroking her breasts, careful of their sensitivity.

Curious to know him better, Kara reached out to trace the line of Daniel's thigh beneath his charcoal slacks. Finding his muscles firm, she dared probe upward to where the belt ran along his hip. His body tightened as if urging her onward.

Impatient with the clumsiness of her position, Kara sat up so she could explore under the sweater to the smoothness of Daniel's T-shirt. Beneath that lay the expanse of his chest, where she discovered his heart's rapid thrumming.

"Touch me," he said. At first, Kara didn't understand, because she was already in contact. He took her hand and adjusted it downward, beneath the belt and the fabric, until she found his hardness. A gasp tore from him.

Kara supposed she should have been dismayed. Never would she have imagined doing such a thing with Hiro. With Daniel, however, she took pleasure in fingering his erection, getting to know his shape. The best part was when the contraction of his muscles and his quickened breathing gave her a sense of his vulnerability.

Just when she thought he might lose control entirely, he removed her hand. "Let me do something for you," he said.

"For me?" Kara didn't understand.

"As long as we're playing with fire, I want you to feel the heat, too." He lowered her beside him and trailed a kiss from her lips down her breasts. It tickled her stomach, and then traveled lower.

Kara could scarcely breathe. She wanted something she didn't dare name, but was she ready for it?

Daniel slid the underclothing from beneath her dress and

pulled it free, revealing her. A moment of self-consciousness passed as the heel of his hand massaged her private flower.

Petals of ecstasy unfolded inside Kara. She cried out, her body arching against him, and gave herself to the exquisite sensations. He caressed her with growing intensity until, with a cry, she rose into a sunburst of unexpected splendor.

"You're incredibly responsive." Daniel fondled her a moment longer before removing his hand and cuddling her against him.

The brilliance settled into a glow. "I never felt that way before." Kara hadn't even known it was possible. "Is that why those people in the book do such odd things?"

His smile answered her. "I'm glad you're figuring it out."

"They look so awkward," she recalled.

A chuckle rolled from Daniel and vibrated into her. "I suppose they do."

"I want to do this for you," Kara told him.

"That isn't necessary."

"My satisfaction won't be complete until I make you joyful, also," she said. When he'd made the sun explode inside her, she'd known nothing else in the universe but him. She wanted to mean that much to Daniel, too. Then, no matter what happened afterward, a little part of him would always belong to her.

"Thank you," he said. "I'll tell you what to do."

Kara sat up and, following his directions, slowly removed his clothing. She relished his growing excitement as she manipulated his masculinity. Gradually, her boldness increased until she no longer needed instructions and he became too lost in sensation to give any. When she impulsively took him in her mouth, he writhed beneath her.

It thrilled her to hold Daniel this way. She only wished she could give him more, but it was not possible in her condition. Not yet. Would it ever be possible? Or would he come to regret letting her so close? She couldn't stop to think about that now.

Below her, Daniel began to move. Kara didn't think she

could ever get tired of giving him pleasure. When he released his ecstasy with a shout of joy, she felt her spirit fly with him.

On the carpet, she lay beside him. Happiness grew around them like a bright patch of spring greenery. This moment was perfect, Kara thought. One perfect thing in a lifetime might be as much as anyone could ask. But for the first time, she began to hope for more.

CHAPTER THIRTEEN

DANIEL WAS GLAD he'd left a couple of towels in the master bathroom, assuming he might need them while moving in. He'd been eager to try out the oversize bathtub, for one thing. He'd certainly never expected to be cleaning up after becoming intimate with Kara, who'd already used the bathroom and was checking out the kitchen at her leisure.

The room whispered of her roselike fragrance, which also lingered on his skin. Daniel almost hated to wash it off.

He closed his eyes and enjoyed the sensations drifting through his body. Who would have expected such fearlessness from such an apparently shy woman? He could feel Kara's hand cupping him, and then her mouth... He'd better stop thinking this way, because he was getting hard again.

Daniel splashed cold water on his face. Kara had evidently enjoyed herself, and yet he knew they shouldn't have gone this far. They'd crossed a bridge without looking ahead to see what lay on the other side.

Pulling a comb from his pocket, he smoothed his unruly hair into place. The man staring back at him in the mirror had a wild glint in his eye that would have amazed the partners at Stephenson & Avenida. It would have amazed Daniel, too, before he met Kara.

He struggled to figure out what had gotten into him today. From the moment he'd brought Kara into this house, he must have known at some level that he wouldn't be able to resist taking her in his arms and kissing her senseless. He certainly hadn't planned on going as far as they had, however.

He grew very still as he examined his feelings, something

he didn't normally care to do. By becoming so close, he and Kara had torn away more of the wall that he'd long ago built around himself. This wasn't simply a marriage of convenience anymore. But what was it?

Fundamentally, he still knew very little about her. Not only did she come from a different culture, but she'd been married before. She'd been a dutiful wife to Hiro and even carried his baby, yet it appeared that she'd never truly loved the man. Daniel's instincts told him that he meant more than that to her, but he couldn't be sure.

As for him, there was no doubt he enjoyed this spirited young woman and her unexpected responses. That wasn't enough to build a real marriage on, however. People needed to have compatible goals and worldviews. They needed to work out their differences before they took a leap into space. And they had to be the right sort of person to make a marriage succeed, which he very much doubted he could ever be.

Sooner or later, Kara was going to leave. He couldn't ask more of her, or of himself, than they'd agreed to.

Never mind the regret twisting inside him. He'd promised to let her go, and when the time came, that was what he intended to do. He couldn't help being glad that it wouldn't be for months, though, or maybe longer.

After straightening his sweater, Daniel walked out of the bathroom and the bedroom and headed slowly down the hallway. When he reached the family room, he stopped where he could see Kara in the kitchen, facing away from him as she opened each cabinet in turn. She was deciding where to put things, he supposed.

He watched her inspect the interior of the refrigerator, which he'd bought from the previous owner. Frowning, she removed one of the adjustable shelves and raised it a notch, no doubt planning where she would place each type of food.

The first time he'd looked inside the small fridge in her apartment, he'd been surprised to see each item stored in clean packaging and sitting on a paper doily. The jars and bottles in the side shelves had been tiered in order of size. In the storage bins, the washed and trimmed vegetables were each placed separately in a nest of colored tissue paper.

Kara treated every moment and object as if it were special, even the contents of her refrigerator. From her, Daniel had learned to celebrate each occasion, no matter how small. He'd changed since meeting her, in ways he was only beginning to appreciate. It was hard to believe that two weeks ago, he hadn't had a clue she existed.

He would never be sorry he'd met her or offered to take her under his protection. He only hoped he wouldn't hurt her and perhaps himself in the process.

Right now, they needed to return to Seattle and pack for their moving day tomorrow, Daniel thought, and went to collect his wife.

AT DANIEL'S INSISTENCE, Kara merely observed on Sunday while he and Drew handled the heavy lifting. She couldn't argue. Although there was no sign of true labor, she'd experienced a few brief episodes of muscle tightening, called Braxton Hicks contractions, which she'd been told about at the clinic.

While staying out of the men's way, she did her best to prepare the place so the two of them would be comfortable here tonight. A box marked "linens" provided the essentials, enabling Kara to make the bed—aligned north-south as she'd suggested—and hang fresh towels in the master bathroom. Now that they had become close, it seemed natural for them to share a room.

In late afternoon, she decided to unpack her books and organize them on a small set of shelves in the bedroom. While removing them one by one, she found herself lingering over a scrapbook from Japan.

Each photo, carefully chosen and arranged, brought to life the people and events she'd left behind. Kara gazed fondly at a portrait of herself with her brother, Enoki, and their parents in a park in Sapporo. Her mother was squinting a little in the sunlight, and her father wore an impersonally polite expression as if at his job as a tour-company executive. Another picture caught her eye, of herself and Tansho in their high-school uniforms. How young they looked!

Flipping another page, Kara came to a portrait of herself and her preschool students, also in uniforms. Such adorable little faces! She remembered each personality clearly.

Suddenly she couldn't wait to start teaching at Forrester Square Day Care, especially since they'd finally found more permanent kitchen help and didn't need her to volunteer any longer. Her mind filled with games the children would enjoy and ways to introduce new words of Japanese each day to help them pick up the language, as their parents wished. She knew she'd awake each morning eager for the day's challenges, just as she'd done back home.

Daniel poked his head in the door. He looked rumpled and appealing in a gray sweatsuit with black racing stripes, which he usually wore only to the gym. "How are you doing? When I don't see you for a while, I get concerned that you might have gone into labor."

Kara shook her head in pretended dismay. "I'm not so delicate!" She held up the scrapbook. "This was me with my students. I'm going to add the photos that Tansho's brother took of our wedding, and soon I'll have a portrait of my new class at Forrester Square."

"Your new class?" Daniel said.

"I know the visa situation isn't resolved," she said, "but Katherine seems to think I can start soon."

"You don't need a job, Kara." He frowned. "I can support you, and you'll have plenty to keep you busy with the baby. I thought we'd agreed on that."

"Did we?" She remembered him saying only that he was worried about her straining herself during pregnancy. Still, it seemed selfish and perhaps insulting to point out that he had no right to interfere with her deep-seated need to teach. "The day-care center is counting on me."

"There are plenty of teachers in Seattle," Daniel said. "None as charming as you, but I'm sure Katherine can find someone else. I don't want you rushing off to work. It's hard on a family when the mom isn't around. I thought Dorima was your first priority."

Kara's heart sank. She wanted to be happy here with Daniel and the baby, but how was that possible if she were isolated? "I love teaching and I'd miss my friends."

"I don't mean forever," he said. "Just while we're adjusting to our situation and to the baby. Otherwise, we'll both be rushing off in the morning and coming home tired, picking up take-out food on the way and collapsing in front of the TV set in the evening. That hardly seems fair to you or to the baby."

He did have a point, but she couldn't give up her career that easily. "I might have more energy than you think."

"If you stay home, you'll have a chance to really get to know Dorima," Daniel said. "It's a chance that may never come again. Surely you'd enjoy taking a break after how hard you've struggled."

Kara wasn't sure how to react. Perhaps he understood better than she did the demands that lay ahead. In any case, since a decision didn't have to be reached immediately, there was no point in arguing and creating friction between them. "I'm lucky to have such a considerate husband."

"I'm glad we're in agreement." After a smile that bathed her in sunshine, Daniel returned to his labors.

Kara closed the scrapbook and shelved it, uneasy questions playing through her thoughts. Would there still be a teaching job available when Daniel decided it was okay for her to go back? What would she do if their marriage ended sooner than expected, leaving her out of work?

It made no sense to torment herself with doubts when he was offering her respite and a safe haven, Kara thought. She shouldn't be so ungrateful.

Determinedly, she returned to her self-imposed chore. At the bottom of the box, she found the book Tansho had given them. In light of her experience with Daniel yesterday, she examined it with new eyes.

Kara tried to imagine each position from the point of view of the participants. What fun they must be having! Surely they'd giggled as they tried to fold themselves into such funny shapes.

She set the book atop the shelves and went to see how the two movers were getting along. She came across them in the kitchen, installing Daniel's table and chairs. Unopened boxes covered much of the floor space.

"Looks like we're about finished." Drew told her. "You guys bought a fantastic house. And even better, it's close to Julia and me."

"This place is not exactly a mansion, but it's right for us," Daniel said.

"Well, if we're done, I'm outta here," his friend said. "Julia promised me a back rub, and I can't wait!"

"You've been a great help." Kara couldn't resist bowing.

"It was a pleasure." He sketched a bow in return, one arm in front European-style. "See you guys soon."

Daniel walked him to his car. When he returned, he said, "Hungry? We can send for pizza."

"I packed sandwiches." Kara indicated a cooler stowed to one side. "I thought you might be too tired to go anywhere." She clapped her hands. "I have an idea!"

He regarded her with appreciation. "What is it?"

"Let's move my low table to the bedroom." They'd left it in the living room to serve as a coffee table. "We can eat there while we gaze at the beautiful backyard. It will be like having a picnic, only less itchy."

When Daniel hesitated, she realized that sitting on the floor might be uncomfortable for him, with his muscles stiff from the day's work. But he rallied quickly. "Let's try it. I'm game for a bit of adventure."

They arranged the small table in front of the glass patio door, giving them a view of their private park. When they sat down, Kara enjoyed the casual intimacy with which their legs entwined.

"I want you to promise not to wear yourself out unpacking

tomorrow,'' Daniel said as they unwrapped the sandwiches. ''There's no law that requires you to put everything away in a day. I don't mind a little mess.''

''You don't? Wonderful!'' she teased. ''Every time you want coffee, you can dig your cup out of one box and your spoon out of another. You can hunt every morning for your shoes and every evening for your DVDs. I'm sure you'll love that.''

Daniel's mouth twisted wryly. ''Okay, I admit, I'm a bit of a neatness freak. I still don't want you wearing yourself out.''

''I'll try not to.'' Kara knew, however, that she wouldn't be able to stop herself from bringing harmony to her new home as quickly as possible. She wanted to get the work done before Dorima was born.

After they finished, Daniel cleared their paper plates into a plastic bag. ''Thanks for the food. It was great.''

''You're welcome.''

When he stood, something atop the shelves caught his eye. ''What's this?''

Remembering that she'd left Tansho's gift there, Kara felt her cheeks heating. ''I was putting it away.''

Daniel reached for the book. Just the idea of him running his hands across the binding sent quivers down her spine.

''You'd have to be a gymnast to get into some of these positions.'' He flipped through the pages, his dark eyes crinkling in amusement. As he read, his hips shifted and he ruffled his hair with one hand as if subconsciously reacting to the book's message.

Kara wanted to feel his hands running through *her* hair and his hips moving against hers. ''I'll bet it's not that hard.'' She lifted the book from his hands and studied the picture. ''They're just twisted around a little.''

''I mean, in your condition, we couldn't…'' Daniel stopped himself. ''Let me rephrase that. We can't risk repeating what happened yesterday.''

Disappointment arrowed through her. "You mean until after the baby's born?"

"I mean, ever." He released a ragged breath. "We had an agreement."

It was just as Mrs. Matsuba had warned her. To Kara's chagrin, her eyes misted over. She turned away to hide her emotions. "Yes, of course."

"I didn't mean to upset you." Daniel drew her into his arms. "Yesterday was special. I can't tell you how much it meant to me."

"To me, too." She couldn't bear to think of spending a lifetime without ever again experiencing the pleasures they'd shared. If only he understood that she didn't mean to make any claims on him! "Do you remember the tea ceremony?"

"Of course," he said, still holding her as if he didn't want to let go.

"Remember how we thought and talked of nothing except what was happening right then?" Kara asked.

"Yes. It was very relaxing."

"It focused our spirits," she said. "Well, that is how I want to spend our time together—playing and feeling free, not worrying about what will happen tomorrow. When it is over, I promise to honor our agreement, Daniel."

He lifted his head. Warmth suffused his face. "Exactly what sort of playing did you have in mind?"

Mischievously, Kara indicated the book. "I just want to see whether we really could get into this position. With our clothes on, of course."

His breath tickled her ear. "You mean as a scientific experiment?"

"Purely in the interests of research," she agreed.

Indecisively, he glanced from her to the illustration and back. "Just for a minute. And definitely with our clothes on."

The bed was softer than the carpet, Kara noted as they lay down. Holding the book, she posed on her side with one knee up. "You have to prop yourself on one elbow," she instructed.

"Like this?" He threw one leg across her, enclosing her next to his heat.

"A little more on top of me." She tried to keep her voice steady. It wasn't easy, with tongues of flame licking across her most sensitive points. The faint masculine aroma of perspiration from a day's hard work only added to Daniel's desirability.

He released a sharp breath. "I know we shouldn't do this. When I'm around you, I can't think straight."

"You're not supposed to think straight. You're supposed to think like a pretzel."

He started to laugh, but it ended in a groan. They were wrapped around each other, held apart only by a thin layer of clothing and Kara's enlarged abdomen. "If you ask me, we're way beyond whatever those people are doing in the book."

"That's because those models are pretending," she said.

"And we aren't?"

"No," she whispered. "We aren't."

Because of the bulge, she couldn't squeeze any closer to Daniel, so she coiled alongside him while his mouth shifted from her earlobe to the vulnerable point where her jaw met her throat. After a moment's hesitation, his palms closed over her breasts and he lowered his mouth to the fabric.

Kara felt her own control slipping away. She moved rhythmically against Daniel, and he caressed her until she didn't believe she could bear any more. Gently, he removed her panties and, as her pelvis rotated instinctively, lowered his head.

Uncontrollable pleasure rolled through Kara. She thrashed beneath Daniel's ministrations, cresting wave after wave until at last the raging storm inside her began to abate.

She lay breathing hard, scarcely believing the response he'd woken in her. It surpassed even what she'd felt their first time.

Once she recovered, she began kissing Daniel, casually at first and then with rising intensity. Raising herself on one elbow, she ran her fingers across his scalp, smoothing the hair away from his face until his eyes closed and he gave himself over to her.

At last it was Kara's turn to enjoy her husband's body. She relished the hints of roughness on his cheeks and the hollow of his stomach when her hand reached down. Lower, she found him ready for action.

Her palm seemed to know what to do, and then her mouth. It gave her joy to draw him into wild ecstasy. Every moan and thrust stimulated her as if she held him inside her.

His thigh pressed insistently between her legs, lifting her to an exquisite plane. The points of her breasts throbbed and her skin prickled. This bliss had no end, Kara thought as her molten center bloomed again in a fiery explosion like a thousand suns. Her cries of ecstasy matched Daniel's until they vibrated in synch, sharing a perfect climax.

When it was over, they lay with her head on his chest and his arm curled around her. They dozed, later managing to strip off what remained of their clothing and slide beneath the covers to sleep in each other's arms. It was, Kara thought, the perfect way to spend their first night in their new home.

She only wished that this was really her home, where she could stay forever.

ON MONDAY MORNING, she put the house in order. During his lunch break, Daniel swung by with a car he'd leased for her. "I don't want you to feel like I'm locking you up in a castle," he said. "You can come and go as you please."

Kara flung her arms around him. Had any woman ever had a more considerate husband? She fixed him lunch and then, after dropping him at his office, she went to clean her old apartment so the Matsubas could rent it again.

While she was there, she visited some of her former neighbors. Mrs. Yamamoto gladly accompanied her back to the house and went through it, making suggestions for good *feng shui*. Later, when Daniel came home to accompany Kara to a doctor's appointment he'd made for late afternoon, she told him what her friend had said.

He agreed that they should buy extra lamps to improve the lighting and remove some of the trees blocking the flow of energy in front of the house. "This *feng shui* business makes sense," Daniel said. "The place could use more light, and the trees are definitely too thick."

The doctor, a local obstetrician recommended by someone at Daniel's office, gave Kara a checkup, reviewed her records from the clinic and pronounced everything in order. To her question about the fact that Dorima had been kicking less often lately, he said it was common for a baby to grow quiet in the final days before birth.

"There's not much room to move around," he explained.

"Are you sure she's all right?"

"The heartbeat's strong," he told her. "I wish you'd had more complete prenatal care, but everything looks fine, Mrs. Adler. You're both very lucky people to be having such a healthy baby."

Daniel avoided the man's eyes. It was awkward, the way people assumed him to be Dorima's father. Kara only hoped that he'd soon come to accept her daughter and cherish her for as long as they stayed together.

That night, she fixed a meal of "fusion food," a new type of cuisine Tansho had described that mixed Eastern and Western tastes. It was gratifying the way Daniel lingered over his filet mignon with Chinese steak sauce and rice topped with black sesame seeds. Afterward, they watched TV in the family room and then went to bed, exhausted. Although she would have enjoyed a repeat of the past two nights' activities, Kara was content to fall asleep with her husband stroking her hair.

Tuesday, she used her new car and the credit card Daniel had given her to buy two lamps and several sacks of groceries. She decided to leave shopping for baby furniture until the two of them could choose things together. She wanted to do everything possible to encourage Daniel to feel comfortable with Dorima.

She still hadn't told Katherine that she wasn't going to be taking the job at Forrester Square. It was too much to ask her to hold the position much longer, Kara knew, especially when she couldn't give a definite date for starting.

Disappointment dimmed her happiness as she put away the groceries. But surely she would find joy with such a wonderful man as Daniel. He seemed eager to share his home, and his attitude toward her job made it clear he was in no hurry to send her away.

Kara returned to the car and lugged a lamp into the family room. She set it on the end table next to the couch.

With a start, she saw Daniel's cell phone sitting on one of the couch cushions. It must have slipped out of his pocket last night, and he'd taken off for work without it. Since she had her own cell phone, Kara didn't think he'd left it intentionally for her to use.

She took the phone into the kitchen and set it on the counter. "There, now he'll see you when he comes home," she told it, and went to pour herself a glass of milk.

Sitting at the table, she gazed through the window into the yard. New canes thrust upward from the tangle of rosebushes showing a few early buds. Elsewhere, low clumps of green protruded from neglected beds. She wondered how many were weeds and how many volunteer flowers or vegetables sprung from the seeds of some long-ago garden.

Kara would have liked to bring order to the mess, but in her condition, she couldn't bend far enough to do any weeding or planting. So she sat here in unaccustomed idleness dreaming of profusions of flowers, until her thoughts turned to the fax she'd left in a drawer.

She still hadn't called Leila Loesser and she didn't intend to, at least not for a while. Matters were too delicate between her and Daniel right now to broach the subject of her relatives.

Once she'd had the baby and could make love without restriction, they would draw closer. Then they could share everything.

She didn't want to dwell on the risk that he might resent Dorima because she was another man's child. So far, she couldn't read Daniel's reaction to the baby, and perhaps he didn't truly know how he felt himself.

The whirring of his phone broke into her reverie. She hesitated before answering what was likely to be a business call. Since Daniel had left one of his business cards for her, she supposed it would be all right to give out his work number so the caller could reach him right away.

Cautiously, Kara flipped open the phone. It took several rings for her to spot the right button.

"Yes?" she said after pressing it

There was a brief pause, as if the caller wasn't certain whether to proceed. Then a man's nasal voice said, "I'm trying to reach Daniel Adler. Do I have the right number?"

Kara's first, unsettling thought was that this might be his father, but the man didn't sound very old. "This is his wife," she said. "He left his cell phone at home today."

"I didn't realize he was married."

The perplexed but casual tone definitely didn't sound like a father. "We've only been married a week," Kara said. "May I ask who this is?"

"My name's Ed Riley. I'm an immigration attorney and I wanted to give him a little more information."

"Oh, that's for me!" she said. "He was asking for my sake."

Another silence stretched so long that she wondered if they'd been cut off. At last the man said, "I hope this isn't what I think it is."

Kara nearly forgot to breathe. Had she made a terrible blunder by speaking so frankly? Mr. Riley was an attorney, though, not an agent of the government. "What do you mean?" she managed to say.

"You're the immigrant he was asking about?" the man said. "How long have you known Daniel?"

A chill ran through her at his line of questioning. "Not very long."

He cleared his throat. "I know this is none of my business, but people tell me I'm a real buttinsky."

"A what?" Kara asked.

"A person who butts into other people's business," Mr. Riley said. "So forgive me for butting into yours, but this isn't a green-card marriage, is it?"

She didn't know what to say. The idea of lying offended her, yet she could hardly blurt out a truth that she and Daniel were going to such pains to hide. "Not exactly," she temporized.

"'Not exactly' as in you don't want to admit it?" asked Mr. Riley. "I don't blame you. I'm sure you're a nice person or Daniel wouldn't have gone out on a limb for you. But I hope you appreciate exactly how much of a risk he's running."

"He could get into trouble, I suppose," Kara said in a small voice.

"A lawyer who commits fraud can be disbarred," the voice persisted. "That means he'd lose his license to practice law. Look, I'm not going to go into all the ramifications of what you've done, or the fact that you have to leave the country to get a visa in any case. It's just that, being in the immigration business, I see people try this kind of thing all the time and it almost always ends badly. I'm sorry Daniel let himself get sucked into this."

"I wasn't trying to hurt him." Kara's abdomen tightened, becoming rock hard. Since she'd been experiencing occasional contractions, she ignored it.

"I probably shouldn't tell you this, but being a buttinsky, I'm going to do it, anyway," the man said. "Get an annulment and let him off the hook. Go home, or go to some other country like Canada and get a visa. From what Daniel told me, you've got an employer who might be willing to sponsor you."

"I can't," Kara said. "I'm going to have a baby any day."

"Yeah, that's really going to play great with the feds," the lawyer remarked sarcastically. "Daniel fell head over heels for a woman who's nine months pregnant. You don't expect them to believe that, do you?"

"Why are you being so mean?" Kara asked.

"Because I learned a long time ago that it's no favor to soft-pedal the truth to my clients," he said. "I tell it like I see it."

"Well, I'm not your client!" She wanted to add that nobody had asked for his advice, but that wasn't exactly true. Instead, she said, "You're just jealous that we fell in love, because you're so cruel you probably hate the whole world!"

Without waiting for a response, she pressed the disconnect button and sat there shaking. How dare he talk to her that way! He'd made her feel about three inches tall.

Kara knew she shouldn't have insulted Mr. Riley that way. What she'd said might not even be accurate. In his private life, perhaps he was the most romantic man in the world. No, a man with such a nasal voice could never be romantic, she thought. And he hadn't cared about her feelings at all. She was glad she'd told him what she thought of him.

All the same, it scared her what he'd said about Daniel. From the beginning, she'd suspected her husband might be courting danger, but he hadn't made an issue of it and she'd let it slip from her mind.

Suppose she couldn't make a convincing case to the immigration people? It was unthinkable that Daniel's kindness might deprive him of his career or even land him in jail. Yet, while Ed Riley might toss off advice about an annulment as if it meant nothing, it would rip out Kara's heart to leave Daniel.

She had foolishly ignored Mrs. Matsuba's advice and fallen in love with her husband. Closing her eyes, she found she could still sense the daytime brightness through the window, but she was lost in darkness, just as she would be without him.

When had this happened? She'd believed she was guarding her emotions by reminding herself that the marriage was only short-term. But somewhere along the line, she'd given her heart.

Again, Kara's abdomen tightened. Dorima was reminding her of her obligations.

You must prepare yourself for the future. Otherwise, you and your baby will meet difficulties when the marriage ends. Perhaps it wasn't too late to heed the wisdom of Mrs. Matsuba's words.

Dragging herself from her seat, Kara went to get Leila Loesser's phone number.

At least she could gather information and give Daniel a choice. She knew already that he would never abandon her, but releasing her to stay with relatives would save face for everyone, and it might spare him the trouble she'd caused.

CHAPTER FOURTEEN

KARA'S HANDS felt damp as she took out her own cell phone. Who was Leila Loesser, anyway? A woman her mother's or grandmother's age? Someone putting together a family genealogy?

She hoped the woman wouldn't be disappointed to learn of Kara's awkward circumstances. A pregnant relative involved in a green-card marriage was a lot to absorb.

After punching in the number, she sat on the couch listening to the phone ring. If there were no answer, she wasn't sure she would ever find the nerve to call again.

"Hi, this is me."

The young, upbeat voice sounded so much like a recording that Kara sat waiting for it to add, "Please leave a message."

"Hello?" the woman said. "Is someone there?"

"Oh!" To her humiliation, Kara realized she was being rude. What a terrible beginning! "I'm so sorry."

"Who are you calling?"

"I'm trying to reach Leila Loesser," Kara said.

"That's me."

"You sound so young," she blurted.

A chuckle greeted this response. "Yeah, I get that a lot. I mean, I'm twenty-six, but lots of people assume I'm in high school. What can I do for you?"

"I'm Kara Tamaki." No, that wasn't right. "I mean, Adler. No, wait. I can't think." Dorima was squeezing her again.

"Whoa," Leila said. "Tamaki is a Japanese name, right? Don't tell me you're calling about Albert Loesser!"

"He was my grandfather." This young woman must be a descendant of her grandfather's brother Franklin.

"Unbelievable!" came the response. "Are you for real? This isn't one of my friends playing a trick on me, is it?"

"I assure you, I'm real." Of all the reactions Kara had imagined, she'd never thought of this one. "In which way are you related to Franklin?"

"I'm his granddaughter," Leila said. "I guess that makes us cousins. Are you calling all the way from Japan?"

"Seattle," Kara said. "I live here now."

"That's fantastic! I'm in Southern California. We're practically neighbors."

"More or less." Having studied maps of the United States, Kara knew that, although both on the West Coast, the areas were about a thousand miles apart.

"I can't believe this! I only input the information in the database last month." Leila was silent a moment, then said, "Hey, I've got an idea. Are you near a computer?"

"Yes." Daniel had installed one in the bedroom last night. He'd invited Kara to use it any time she wanted.

"I'm going to e-mail you a photo of myself. I'm working on my computer right now, as a matter of fact. Hold on."

Within a few minutes, the photo arrived. It showed a young woman with long, straight blond hair and a narrow face enlivened by a friendly smile. In the meantime, Leila filled in the blanks about her grandfather's life and why he'd never contacted his brother.

It seemed that at the time of Albert and Umeko's wedding, Albert's father—Kara's and Leila's mutual great-grandfather—had been suffering from a heart condition. To avoid upsetting him, Great-uncle Franklin had taken his side against his brother. Later, he'd tried to find Bert through a servicemen's organization and, eventually, via the Internet, but never had any luck.

Franklin had moved from Ohio to Southern California, lived into his eighties and died a few years ago. He'd told his son Bill, Leila's father, about Bert and his once-scandalous marriage.

Knowing of the connection, Bill and his children, Leila and Bill Junior, had developed a strong interest in Japan. Leila had spent a year studying near Tokyo, and although her Japanese wasn't as good as Kara's English, she enjoyed using it a bit on the phone.

A few months earlier, Leila explained, she'd taken a programming job with a computer company and gained access to a database for locating family members and friends. She'd decided to make one more effort to find Albert Loesser's family.

Today, she was working from home, which was why she'd been on hand to receive the call. The company allowed her to telecommute several days a week from her apartment, she explained.

"It's amazing that you're in Seattle," she said. "How did you happen to move there?"

Kara hesitated. "It's a complicated story."

"I can't wait to hear it!"

Shyly at first, then with growing confidence in the face of her cousin's sympathy, Kara told of her two marriages, her pregnancy and the offer of a job at Forrester Square Day Care, omitting only the details of her blossoming relationship with Daniel. As she talked, her abdomen tightened again. Never before had the contractions come this close together, but she was too fascinated by the conversation to worry about it.

"A green-card marriage—what a hoot!" her cousin said. "And you're pregnant, too. That's incredible. We've absolutely got to meet."

"I would like that," Kara said.

"My parents will be thrilled," Leila went on. "My brother and his wife, too. They've been telling my niece and nephew about our Japanese connection for years. We all live in the L.A. area, so you can meet us en masse. You know, there's no need to stay in this marriage of convenience if you don't want to. I've got an extra room in my apartment, and I love babies.''

It was exactly what Kara had hoped to hear. It would free Daniel, just as they'd planned. If only her heart didn't ache at the thought of leaving him, but that couldn't be helped.

''I'd like that,'' she said. ''I have to talk to my husband before I make any plans, though.''

''He must be a heck of a nice guy to help you out this way.'' She could picture her blond cousin smiling as she spoke. ''But now that I've found you, we're not going to let you go.''

''You're very kind. I'm glad you—'' Kara felt suddenly as if a vise was squeezing the breath out of her.

''Is something wrong?''

At first, she couldn't answer.

''Kara? Don't tell me you're sick!''

''I think the baby has decided to come,'' she said.

''Now?'' Leila let out a whoop. ''This is a good sign, you know. We start talking and the newest member of the Loesser family decides to make an appearance.''

''I suppose I *am* a Loesser, aren't I?'' Kara paused at the threat of another squeeze, but it was only a twinge from her muscles, reacting to their unaccustomed exertion. ''I have to call Daniel.''

''What hospital are you going to?'' Leila asked. ''I need to know so I can send flowers.''

Kara gave her the name of the nearby facility where her new doctor worked. In the brochure, it looked large and modern.

Over the phone came the tapping of computer keys as Leila noted the name. ''Great!''

''I'll talk to you later. I'm glad we've found each other.''

''You and me both!''

Kara barely managed to click off before the pressure seized her again. How long had it been since the last contraction? She dialed Daniel's office.

He promised to come immediately. Kara packed an overnight bag and notified the Matsubas. With a few minutes to spare, she fixed herself a large snack. A midwife she'd consulted in Japan when she first learned of her pregnancy had said that a large meal during labor provided energy for pushing.

Kara wished she could use a midwife here, but that wasn't the custom in America. Although physicians attended most births in Japanese hospitals, certified nurse midwives staffed the delivery rooms and massaged their patients. They must be doing something right, because she'd heard that Japan had the world's lowest rate of infant mortality.

When Daniel arrived, he was so nervous he stumbled on their way out the door and had trouble putting the car in gear. Kara would have laughed, except that she was having another contraction.

"Dorima is eager to join us," she gasped when she was able to speak again.

Daniel paused in backing the car and slanted Kara a tender, worried look. "It's a good thing we have excellent medical care available."

"Nature is the best doctor," she told him as they pulled onto the street and headed toward the hospital.

"I hope you're not saying you'd like to give birth in the woods!"

His question reminded her of the name of a hospital she'd always found intriguing. "Only if the woods are the Cedars of Sinai!"

"That's more like it." Daniel reached over to brush back a strand of her hair before returning his full attention to the road.

Would he be distressed or pleased to learn of her plan to move in with Leila Loesser? Kara was in no mood to find out right now. She wanted to cling, at least a little longer, to the man whose strength renewed her courage.

Their physical closeness had made her feel as if they belonged to each other, even though she knew that some men and women did such things with virtual strangers. Daniel's scent and his laugh had imprinted themselves on her. How could she bear for them to be separated, yet how could she be so greedy as to go on endangering his future when it was no longer necessary? And when she knew that, sooner or later, this was all going to end, anyway?

At the hospital, the staff admitted her while Daniel filled out paperwork. By now, the contractions were coming closer together and her muscles were starting to complain.

"I'm ready to have the baby now," Kara told a nurse.

"I'll bet it feels that way," came the reply. "Did you and your husband take classes?"

"I already speak English," Kara said.

"I meant preparation-for-childbirth classes."

"What a silly idea," Kara said. "Nature prepares us for childbirth."

"Excuse me?"

"She's Japanese," said a passing orderly, who looked Asian himself. "They take a different approach than Americans."

"This ought to be interesting." The nurse sighed. "Let's get you to Labor and Delivery."

After a discussion with one of the staff doctors, Daniel was allowed to join her. "I gather they're displeased that I didn't earn an advanced degree in synchronized breathing and ice-chip technology," he joked.

"Just hold my hand," Kara said. Unfortunately, as he obeyed, Dorima exerted her full force, inspiring Kara to grip so hard that his face went white.

When she let go, Daniel extracted his hand gingerly. "If what you did to me is anything like what's happening to your body, you're one heck of a trouper."

The nursing staff proved sympathetic and efficient. Urged by Daniel, they tried to persuade Kara to accept some medication when the pains strengthened, but she refused.

"I must not give in to pain." She had heard this advice from both her mother and her mother-in-law. "It would bring shame on my husband's family."

"My family won't mind," Daniel assured her. "I certainly don't."

"I mind for your sake," Kara said. "Also, I will appreciate my baby more if I endure a great deal for her."

"I don't believe that for one minute!"

"It's true." Although she was willing to accommodate most American customs, Kara had heard childbirth lore from the time she was young. "A cousin of my mother's used a lot of medication and she neglected her son." It had been so shameful, her mother had spoken about it only in whispers.

Daniel gave up arguing. Kara hated to distress him, but she knew she must endure this trial to prove herself worthy as a mother.

Daniel didn't approve of her attitude, she could tell. But he would learn that, although she might look weak, she was strong like bamboo, strong enough to endure whatever might come.

Or at least she hoped so.

IN THE DELIVERY ROOM, Daniel was keenly aware of his lack of preparation. He didn't know how to help Kara and he couldn't avoid showing his anxiety. Perhaps his wife, who was clearly suffering despite the brave front she put on, would be more comfortable if he went to a waiting room, he thought.

It didn't matter. He simply couldn't leave her, even if he didn't believe he provided much help.

After a labor that seemed to stretch forever, but in fact lasted only a few hours, the baby came in a rush. The medical personnel worked intently but calmly while Kara's cries of pain tore at Daniel's soul. At last the warmly wrapped newborn was laid in her mother's arms and Kara rested, spent but satisfied.

The baby was an incredible little girl, with a shock of black hair and dark eyes and the world's cutest nose. She had tiny, perfect fingers, too.

At the sight of her, a hard knot formed inside Daniel. She was so delicate, he couldn't even bring himself to touch her.

And so precious. Would he ever have a child of his own, and if he did, could he possibly love her any more?

The thought startled him. He wasn't prepared to be a father, or a husband, either. How could he even think along those lines?

"Do you have a name picked out?" the doctor asked.

"Dorima," Kara whispered. "My dream." She looked exhausted, and no wonder, after what she'd been through.

"She's your husband's dream, too, I should think," the man said jovially.

Daniel didn't know what to reply. He hadn't told anyone at the hospital about their circumstances, since there was no medical reason the doctor needed to know. "Thanks," he said at last, then added gamely, "If they give medals for bravery in childbirth, I'm sure my wife deserves one."

Kara closed her eyes. Tears sparkled on her lashes. Seeing no reason for her to be upset, he supposed she was simply on emotional overload.

Later that evening, the Matsubas came to see the baby, but insisted they didn't want to interrupt Kara's rest by visiting her. When Daniel suggested they drop by in a few days after she was home, Mrs. Matsuba was horrified.

"In Japan, a mother stays in the hospital for at least seven days," she said. "She will be much too tired to go home so quickly."

"Did you stay in the hospital that long?" asked Tansho's brother, Takeshi.

"No, but my mother-in-law came to take care of the house and my babies for a few weeks each time," his mother said.

"I'm afraid my mother isn't likely to do that, but perhaps we could hire a nurse," Daniel said. Privately, though, he doubted that Kara would allow anyone else to care for her baby.

"In any case, I'll bet she won't follow the old tradition of not bathing or washing her hair for a week," Tansho teased.

"That is not necessary," her mother agreed. "I'm sure it

dates from old times when women became chilled and fell ill. Today we have antibiotics.''

"She wouldn't refuse to take those, would she?'' Daniel asked, thinking of Kara's refusal to accept medication during the delivery.

"Japanese people respect modern medicine,'' Mrs. Matsuba said. "We also try to stay in balance with nature. If antibiotics are necessary, I'm sure Kara will accept them. Childbirth is a different matter.''

"I'll make sure she gets plenty of sleep when she comes home." After Kara's phone call, Daniel had arranged to spend a few days away from the office on the condition that he work from home so none of his clients would be left dangling. Since he'd left in such a hurry today, he had to go in tomorrow morning to collect his case files.

"We know she's in good hands," Tansho said.

"If you need anything, call us," added her mother.

A short while after the Matsubas left, Katherine and Alexandra came by, explaining that Tansho had called them. They oohed and aahed over the infant, but also declined to visit Kara so soon after the birth. Hannah, they said, sent her best wishes, but was under doctor's orders to rest. She'd insisted on handling the day-care center's bookkeeping from home.

Daniel wondered if Kara had mentioned that she wasn't going to take the teaching job. Surely Katherine would say something if that was the case. He decided this wasn't the proper time to bring it up.

He wasn't sure why the prospect of Kara's taking on work obligations bothered him so much. After all, this wasn't a real marriage. Yet it was beginning to feel more and more like one.

For years, he'd resisted any relationship that threatened to become serious. Always he'd found problems that he couldn't or didn't want to resolve. He'd persuaded himself that he simply wasn't cut out to spend his life with someone else.

Yet with Kara, he hadn't put up the same resistance because

he'd been so certain it was temporary. Then today, in the delivery room, emotions had nearly overwhelmed him. Love for that miraculous baby. And another kind of love he didn't know what to do with, a sweeping emotion that made him want to dare everything for one smile from Kara.

He didn't know how he felt or what he wanted. Which meant he shouldn't say or do anything until he figured it out.

When the visitors had gone, Daniel grabbed a bite at the hospital cafeteria and then, almost reluctantly, went upstairs to visit Kara, who currently had a double room to herself. She lay beneath the covers wearing a red kimono-style bed jacket. With her dark hair spilling across the pillow, she looked so fragile he wished he could take all her pain onto himself. Afraid he might hurt her if he even touched her after what she'd endured, he quietly took a seat beside the bed.

Daniel related what her visitors had said about the custom of staying in the hospital for a week. ''I can understand why Japanese women are even more exhausted than American women, since they refuse to take pain medication.''

''It's better this way,'' Kara insisted.

An argument would only exhaust her further. ''Perhaps you're right.'' After a moment, he added, ''I'm sorry we didn't have time to buy baby furniture.''

''There's no hurry,'' she said. ''Dorima can sleep with me.''

''Is that safe?'' he asked.

''It's traditional in Japan. I'm sure we can manage for a while.'' She glanced at him uncertainly. ''Perhaps we should talk about...well, about our arrangement. I mean, we did agree that it's only temporary.''

Was this the time to tell her he was having second thoughts about giving her up? Once he mentioned the subject, there'd be no going back. She might expect him to make a commitment right away, and he wasn't ready to do that.

Every time he considered the possibility of trusting Kara with his heart and soul, a kind of panic filled him. It was as if, deep down, he couldn't trust her. Or fate. Or himself.

It didn't make sense. At the moment, nothing did.

"I don't think this is a good time to discuss it," he said. "You've been through one heck of a lot today."

On the edge of the bed, Kara's hand cupped his. Her nails were trimmed into ovals and buffed like pearls, he noticed. "I don't want to make your life difficult," she said.

"You don't make it difficult." How could she even think that, when she brought him such joy?

"This marriage could get you in trouble."

"Let me worry about that," he said. "Besides, it's a bit late to bring it up now, don't you think?"

Before she could answer, an attendant wheeled in a clear plastic bassinet. Inside, Dorima gave a yawn. "Your milk probably hasn't come in yet, but you should let the baby try to nurse," the woman said.

Kara glanced at Daniel uncertainly. He decided to take the hint. "I'd better leave you to handle this nursing business. I'll see you in the morning."

"Isn't she beautiful?" Kara asked.

"Of course!" he said. "Any baby of yours is bound to be beautiful." *And I love her, though I have no right.* Just as he had no right to love Kara when he couldn't bring himself to offer her a real, permanent home.

The attendant set the baby in Kara's arms, creating a picture that filled Daniel with a fierce, protective joy. In a way, though, he felt like an intruder, because these two had bonded long before he entered the picture.

And they'll be together long after I'm gone.

He tried to picture Dorima growing up, taking toddler steps on chubby legs, gazing trustingly at someone holding her hand. A father, that was who ought to be there. A man who knew how to be part of a family. Why couldn't he do that?

"You're frowning," Kara said.

"I feel like a stranger," he admitted. "I mean, I don't know anything about babies. Or being a father. I guess that's pretty obvious."

"You could learn," Kara said, "if you wanted to."

He didn't think a man could learn to do something like that. It had to come naturally, as it had for Drew, even though he wasn't a biological father, either. "Maybe so." When in doubt, he knew enough to change the subject. "Is there anything I can get you? A warmer robe or a teddy bear for the baby?"

"No, thank you. Now go, go." With her free hand, Kara made a shooing gesture. "You are the one who needs to sleep. I can be lazy tomorrow."

"I can stay," he offered.

"No, please. I will see you in the morning." She kept her gaze fixed on Dorima.

Reluctantly, Daniel departed. He sensed that in some way he'd disappointed Kara. There was a gap between them he didn't know how to bridge. Until now, he'd assumed they could simply continue being friends and casual lovers indefinitely. Apparently, he'd been wrong.

On the way home, he swung by a bookstore he'd spotted earlier and saw that it was ablaze with lights. Although he'd had a long day, curiosity got the better of him, and he decided to take a look.

Inside, on a rack labeled Parenting, he found more books than he'd expected on what ought to be a common-sense subject. There were personal accounts and tips from doctors and advice for adoptive and foster parents. He found checklists of what to shop for and numerous illustrated volumes about the stages of child development. New moms and dads apparently needed an advanced degree to undertake what the previous generations had done by instinct and tradition, Daniel mused.

Although he wasn't sure what to make of the new tension between him and Kara, he obviously was going to be sharing his home with a baby for the foreseeable future, and he didn't like being ignorant. Besides, he really wanted to know more about this mysterious and fascinating little creature named Dorima.

He paged through a couple of volumes about fatherhood, most of which dealt with the emotions that the authors had experienced after the births of their children. None touched on the situation of a man who found himself thrust unexpectedly into being a parent. Daniel supposed that situation didn't happen often.

It had happened to his father, though, in a way. When his mother, Renée, left abruptly, workaholic Vernon had had to adjust to being the sole parent of an adolescent boy. He'd been moody and critical at first, but he'd also had enough sensitivity to notice when Daniel became withdrawn. After that, Vern had begun spending more time taking him to ball games and movies and helping with his homework, and gradually they'd developed a relationship that served them both well.

After picking out a practical volume about infant development and care, Daniel made his purchase at the front counter and returned to his car.

It was time to make another effort to track down his father. Come to think of it, Vern ought to be back in Chicago by now. Daniel checked his watch. It was too late to call tonight, given the two-hour time difference.

He wasn't sure what kind of advice his father would give or how helpful it might be. But it was long past time to get in touch with him.

KARA WAS GRATEFUL for a lot of things. She was grateful when the attendant went away, grateful that she didn't have a roommate, and grateful that no one but Dorima saw the tears sliding down her cheeks. She was ashamed, even though she'd heard new mothers were often emotional. Perhaps sometimes they overreacted, but she was certain she wasn't overreacting now.

She should have known better than to get her hopes up. Today, when Daniel had stayed by her side through the delivery, she'd clung to his hand like an anchor in a storm-tossed sea. Even when the contractions made her so cranky she could scarcely bear to be touched, she'd held on to him.

Each time the hospital staff referred to him as her husband, her joy had briefly eclipsed her pain.

Then the doctor had made that remark about Dorima being *his* dream, as well as hers. From Daniel's mumbled response, she could tell how troubled he'd been.

This evening, she'd tried to tell him about her cousin and the possibility that she would be moving to Los Angeles. She'd hoped he might beg her to stay. Although he'd tried to dismiss the subject of their temporary arrangement, she'd intended to bring it up again a little later.

Until Dorima arrived. That was when she'd noticed Daniel grow tense and pull away from them both. Although he'd offered to retrieve anything she needed, it was clear he hadn't wanted to hold the little one.

Without realizing it, she'd been assuming that once Dorima arrived, the three of them would begin to feel like a family, at least for a while. She'd pictured Daniel's house as a safe shelter for the little girl during her first months or perhaps even years. What a foolish fantasy that had been!

Daniel's withdrawal had been subtle but obvious, at least to Kara, who had grown up in a society attuned to shades of mood and expression. In her upbringing, a polite hint was not only preferable to brash confrontation but also more effective. As a result, she found herself hypersensitive to the reactions of people she cared about, and there was no one she'd ever cared about as much as Daniel.

Except, perhaps, her daughter.

His remark about feeling like a stranger conveyed a whole universe of meaning to a person who knew how to interpret it. What he was really saying was that he couldn't love another man's child. Dorima would never truly be welcome in his home.

Kara supposed she should have expected such a reaction. Even an enlightened modern man couldn't control his basic impulse to reject another man's offspring. And Daniel had never misled her. From the beginning, he'd made it clear he was only helping her out of a difficult situation.

Not really becoming her husband. Certainly not becoming Dorima's father.

The tears stopped. This pain was much too deep for that.

Cradling the baby against her heart, Kara wondered where to go from here. She loved Daniel more than she would have believed possible and she wanted to stay with him. But how could she?

Every sacrifice she'd made these past months was for the sake of her daughter. She'd even been willing to accept Daniel's decision that she turn down the job at Forrester Square Day Care, although she longed to teach and to see her friends every day. But how could she bear his indifference to Dorima?

Lost in misery, she lay back against the pillow with the baby in her arms. She'd held her own in the delivery room today. This was no time to yield to weakness.

She was grateful that she'd found Leila, even though leaving Seattle would feel like going into exile. Daniel had left her no other choice.

CHAPTER FIFTEEN

THE CELL PHONE Daniel had accidentally left behind was ringing when he got home. Hoping there wasn't an emergency at the hospital, he raced through the house to answer it.

"Adler here," he said.

"Adler here, too," came his father's voice, raspy from cigarette smoking even though he'd quit several years ago. It summoned to mind an image of Vernon from last Christmas, his skin creased and weathered, but his hair still black with only touches of silver.

"Dad! I figured it was too late to call you tonight." Daniel leaned against the kitchen counter.

"What's going on?" his father asked. "No one was answering your phone this afternoon."

"I left it at home by mistake," Daniel told him.

"Right," his father said. "Then there's the other matter."

"What other matter?"

"When I tried your office, the secretary mentioned something about your wife having a baby."

In his usual understated manner, Vernon didn't pepper his son with questions. He simply let the silence speak for itself.

"I tried to reach you," Daniel said. "You went fishing."

"I don't recall being gone for nine months," his father said dryly.

"It's a long story." Daniel hardly knew where to start. If only he'd had a chance to prepare himself for this call.

"I've got plenty of time."

Daniel decided to take it from the top. "About two weeks o, I met a woman...." As tersely as possible, he spilled the story of meeting Kara, trying to resolve her difficulties and marrying her. Through it all, his father made a few inquiries but otherwise gave no sign of his reaction.

He hardly needed to. Daniel knew where his father stood on any kind of underhand behavior. This time, his father refrained from giving him a lecture, but his reaction was pointed nonetheless.

"I don't suppose I need to tell you that this woman could take you to the cleaners financially if she chooses, and she probably will."

"Money isn't the issue, Dad," Daniel said.

"I know I sound cynical, but it usually boils down to that."

"Did it with Mom?" The moment the words were out of his mouth, he regretted them. "I'm sorry," he said. "That was uncalled-for."

"There's no comparison." Vernon, much like Daniel, rarely wasted time worrying over inconsequentials. "Your mother and I were married for sixteen years. It was a real union, even if it didn't last. What you've entered into is a legal fiction, not a marriage."

"That might change," Daniel said, and then wondered what he meant.

"You're telling me this woman's got her hooks into you?"

"There are no hooks!" he flared. "And she isn't 'this woman,' she's Kara."

"You don't sound like yourself," his father said.

"I guess not," Daniel conceded. "Half the time I don't even understand what's happening to me."

"I can't tell you how to run your life," Vernon said. "I'll give you credit for having enough intelligence not to fall in with some scheme, so let's assume this woman…Kara is sincerely seeking a way out of her difficulties. What makes you think she has feelings for you?"

"A lot of small signs," Daniel told him. "Of course I'm no expert on women."

"If you were, you could make a million dollars advising

other men. I could have used some expert advice when Renée left.''

This was a new twist. "What do you mean?''

Vernon cleared his throat. "Let's just say that what went wrong wasn't entirely your mother's fault. That doesn't mean she was justified. Running out on her family the way she did was wrong. But a man can't hold on to a woman when she wants to go.''

"Kara doesn't want to leave,'' Daniel said.

"I don't suppose so, under the circumstances,'' growled his father. "Just let me give you a bit of advice.''

"Sure.''

"Watch your back, son.''

The comment was so typical of his father that Daniel chuckled in recognition. "I'll do that.'' Remembering his intention to ask about parenting, he added, "By the way, I'm not sure how to relate to the baby. Got any tips?''

"I'm no expert in that department. I just kind of stumbled through it myself. For the record, though, when it comes to grandchildren, I wouldn't mind having one. And as far as I'm concerned, a grandchild's a grandchild, regardless of how he or she comes into the family.''

"Thanks,'' Daniel said.

His father took down his new address and said an affectionate goodbye before clicking off.

Daniel wasn't sure whether he'd learned anything that would help him with Dorima. He hoped that, like Vernon, he'd be able to stumble through and somehow figure out what to do next.

In any case, he had plenty of time to sort out his emotions. Kara and Dorima weren't going anywhere.

WEDNESDAY MORNING, Kara's muscles screamed as if she'd run a marathon the previous day and then performed as a contortionist. She'd never imagined she could hurt in so many ~ces.

~hen a nurse arrived to show her how to feed Dorima,

Kara thought that was ridiculous. Women had been nursing infants for thousands or maybe millions of years without anyone instructing them. The problem, she soon discovered, was that although she'd spent a lot of time with toddlers and preschoolers, she had practically no experience in handling newborns. It took a considerable amount of angling and shifting to get the baby's mouth and her breast in the right position.

After Dorima was returned to the nursery, Kara lay back with a profound sense of relief. She was almost grateful that Daniel, who'd phoned earlier, had to drive into the city this morning to pick up his case files. She was almost afraid to see him because she knew she was going to disgrace herself by bursting into tears.

Her eyelids drifted downward. Half dreams stole across her mental landscape. Babies and children, the day-care center, the garden behind Daniel's house…

"Oh, my gosh. I can't believe it's really you!"

Her eyes flew open. She was staring into a huge bouquet of flowers that appeared to possess the power of speech. "Excuse me?" Kara said.

"It's me!" Blond hair swung out from behind the flowers, followed by an animated face that, after a startled moment, she realized must belong to Leila Loesser. "Surprise!"

It took a lifetime of etiquette training for Kara to overcome her impulse to simply stare in shock. "It's…it's an unexpected honor to meet you in person."

"I couldn't resist flying to Seattle." Leila rearranged the bedside table to make room for the mass of flowers. "I realized I forgot to get your phone number and address. Of course, you gave me your e-mail address, but people change those all the time. So I figured I'd zip up here while I still know where to find you."

"How sweet," Kara said, staggered by the onslaught of words. She'd been eager to meet her cousin, but now that she was here, Kara didn't quite know how to deal with such a dynamo.

"I told Mom and Dad about your call, and they can't wait

to meet you.'' Leila pulled up a chair. "Listen, I've been figuring this whole thing out. There's plenty of room at my place, and Mom will be thrilled to help with the baby. That way, if you want to go to work, you won't have to worry about day care.''

It was the answer to her prayers, wasn't it? Kara would be able to live with relatives, and by getting an annulment, she'd spare Daniel from possible serious legal problems. She could also go back to teaching whenever she wished, although unfortunately not at Forrester Square.

The only thing wrong with this neat solution was that she would have to give up the man she loved. Once she went away, she might never see him again. But if he couldn't accept Dorima as his daughter, what choice did she have?

One thin hope remained. When he learned of the plan, Daniel might refuse to give her up. Maybe he would declare that he couldn't live without Kara and the baby, that he adored them both and that they belonged with him forever.

And maybe she was a silly girl with a head full of impossible fantasies.

Snapping out of her daze, Kara realized her cousin had gone on chattering. "I've got so many plans," she was saying. "Oh, never mind me! Mom says I tend to ride roughshod over people. How was your labor?"

"Well worth it." Kara wondered how to explain to this enthusiastic cousin how conflicted she felt. She didn't want to discourage Leila's generous offer of help, however, until she learned where Daniel stood.

A hospital volunteer arrived with two large floral arrangements, one from the Matsubas and the other from Forrester Square Day Care. "Where would you like these?"

"I don't know." Other than the unoccupied second bed, which was obviously off-limits, Kara didn't see a free surface.

"I'll take care of them." Leila hopped to her feet. "I'm an expert at organizing things."

"You might try the windowsill," said the volunteer.

"Good idea!" Leila applied herself to the task.

The volunteer left. Scarcely a minute later, a nurse came into the room. "Hi!" Leila said. "It sure is busy around here."

"We don't want anyone to get too much sleep," the nurse joked. To Kara, she said, "It's time to get up for your walk."

Kara stared at her in dismay at the prospect of moving her aching body. "I've already been to the bathroom."

"You need to walk a lot farther than that," said the no-nonsense RN, whose name tag read Edith. "Let's get you moving. You need to be in shape for tomorrow."

"What happens tomorrow?" Kara asked warily.

"Most likely you'll be released."

"So soon?" Despite what Daniel had said, she hadn't believed that the hospital would be that cruel. In his stories of America, never had her grandfather warned that the hospitals tortured new mothers. "I want to stay here and let people take care of me."

"And wake you up every five minutes?" Edith asked. "You've noticed we're good at that."

"You have a point." Longingly, Kara pictured the bed in Daniel's room. Perhaps American mothers chose to hurry home because they knew that was where they could sleep undisturbed.

But she wouldn't be going home to Daniel's house. At best, she'd probably stop by to pack a few suitcases. She would never see the flowers and vegetables in his garden. The baby would have no chance to enjoy the lovely room they'd designated as hers. And someday, another woman would come to receive the good luck of the north-south bed and the *feng shui* lighting.

Kara didn't dare think about that, not with Leila and the nurse standing here watching her. Stiffly, she sat up and swung her legs over the edge of the bed. Although she felt extremely sore, she refused to show it. With the nurse's help and Leila fluttering around trying to assist, she managed to stand and slide her feet into her slippers.

"Do you want me to come?" Leila asked. "We could visit the nursery. I'd love to see Dorima."

Kara decided to limit her exposure to her gung-ho relative until she felt less light-headed. "I need your help with the flowers."

"Oh, right!" Leila gave a little wave. "Go on, then. I'll have everything fixed up by the time you get back."

Leaning on the nurse's arm, Kara set out for the corridor. There would be time enough when she got back to make arrangements for moving to Los Angeles.

INSTEAD OF FLOWERS, Daniel purchased a bouquet of silk butterflies at a Seattle market. That way, he decided, Kara could bring them home and enjoy them for a long time.

His visit to the office had taken longer than he'd intended. Several clients had called while he was there, and one of the senior partners had numerous questions about a case. Not until nearly noon, when he finished work and got back in the car, was Daniel free to try to figure out what he wanted to say to the woman he'd married.

The funny thing was that he kept thinking of their wedding as if it had been real and not merely a demonstration to convince the authorities. Last night after talking to his father, he'd sat in bed reading the book on child development and imagined himself sharing the childhood landmarks with Dorima as if she were his own child.

This was all wrong. Daniel hadn't meant it to turn out this way. But he no longer remembered why it was wrong.

He'd always been in control of himself. Now something had happened that he couldn't control: he'd fallen in love with Kara. Every time he pictured her, he wanted her so much it hurt.

What he hoped for, Daniel reflected, was a miracle. What he feared was that he was about to make a huge fool of himself and embarrass Kara so much they would never be comfortable around each other again.

the hospital, he parked and took the elevator to the maternity ward. Forcing himself not to hurry, he strolled into her room expecting to find her resting or perhaps sitting up against a plumped pillow.

There was no sign of her. The only person in the room was a young blond woman in jeans and a striped T-shirt. Judging by the flowers she was fussing with on the windowsill, he guessed she might be a volunteer from the gift shop. If so, someone ought to instruct her how to dress properly

"Excuse me," he said. "Where's Mrs. Adler?"

"Mrs. Who? Oh, you mean Kara! She's taking a walk with the nurse." The woman scrutinized him as if trying to decide whether to make a purchase. "You must be Daniel."

"That's right." Put off by this stranger's take-charge attitude, he waited to see what she would do next.

"I'm Leila Loesser." She thrust out her hand. He shook it. "I'm Kara's cousin from Los Angeles."

This was news. "I didn't know she had a cousin from L.A."

"I guess she didn't have a chance to tell you," the woman said.

He recalled some mention of her grandfather having relatives in the U.S. "Are you the people she was looking for?"

"Yes! We just connected. Isn't it terrific?" Leila didn't wait for an answer before plunging ahead. "She's coming to live with me."

"There must be some misunderstanding," Daniel said. "She's my wife."

"Oh, yes, she told me about the marriage-of-convenience thing. That was really nice of you. But we've been looking for my great-uncle's family for a long time, and when Kara called me, everything fell into place. We'll figure out how to keep her in the country, don't you worry."

"Kara called you?" This was unsettling news. "When?"

"Yesterday morning," she said.

Daniel tried to make sense of this information. After they'd made love and moved into the new house together, Kara had called this woman asking for help? It felt like a betrayal. "I don't follow you."

"I know this is sudden," Leila said. "But Kara doesn't want to depend on you. I've got plenty of room in my apartment and my mom can help with the baby."

He didn't want to believe that Kara was so eager to leave. When they made love—or the next best thing—he'd assumed that it filled her with happiness the way it did him. Even though he hadn't come to terms with it until last night, Daniel had believed at some level that she was falling in love with him, too. Was it possible she'd simply been trying to please him as she'd done with Hiro?

Every marriage is a business arrangement, she'd told him when they met. What else had she said? Oh, yes. *I don't have romantic fantasies.* At least she'd been honest. He ought to be thankful for that. But he wasn't.

It especially bothered him that she'd called her cousin without informing him and hadn't said a word about it since. When had she planned to tell him? The day she got out of the hospital and waved sayonara as she left for L.A.?

Well, Daniel wasn't ready to take this stranger's word about Kara. "Let's wait and see what my wife has to say."

"Of course." Cheerfully, Leila swiped the butterflies from his arm. "I'll figure out where to put these. This place is overflowing with bouquets, isn't it? She's sure a popular girl."

"She certainly is." Daniel struggled to maintain a polite front when what he really wanted to do was hustle this interfering cousin out the door. "I'll go find her."

"I don't know which direction she went," Leila said. "I'm sure they won't be long."

He was about to conduct a search, anyway, when Kara shuffled in alongside a nurse. "You should let us give you some pain medication," the woman was saying. "There's no need to tough it out."

"I prefer to do things my way," said the young woman se angelic looks hid a will of iron.

The statement thudded heavily into Daniel's sensibility. Yes, Kara definitely did things her way. She'd lived in the moment with him for as long as it suited her, and now she was moving on to something that suited her better.

His father's advice rang in his mind. *Watch your back, son.*

When she spotted him, Kara flushed. She must realize that he'd met her cousin and learned of their plans. Was a trace of awkwardness all she felt?

A wave of anger rolled through Daniel. Even though he knew it wasn't Kara's fault that he'd misjudged her, it hurt that he'd finally fallen for a woman only to discover that she intended to leave him.

Grimly, he forced himself to stay calm and wait to hear what she had to say for herself.

KARA FELT THE STILLNESS in Daniel and knew Leila must have told him about her plans. Was he angry because she was leaving, or simply annoyed that he'd learned about it from a stranger?

If he asked her to stay, should she? Deeply as she loved him and keenly as she would always long for his smile and his touch, she knew it might be impossible for them to spend their lives together. First, she must learn how he felt about her baby.

She didn't expect him to say anything in front of others, because he risked losing face that way. Kara only wished he would give her a clue as to how to proceed. Right now, her usual skill at reading moods failed her completely.

"Let's get you into bed." Oblivious to the undercurrents in the room, the nurse eased her into place. "You're one tough little cookie. I wish you'd reconsider about taking pain medication."

"I'm fine, thank you."

No one else spoke until the woman left. Kara wished her brain weren't distracted by throbbing muscles.

"I went ahead and introduced myself," Leila said. "Aren't these butterflies cute? Daniel brought them."

"They're beautiful." Kara smiled at him hopefully. He didn't smile back.

"How are we going to handle this?" her cousin asked. "I don't suppose you'll want to get on a plane right away. I can book a flight for later in the week."

Daniel's jaw tightened. Kara wished her cousin would stop chattering and go away, but she didn't want to offend her. "I haven't thought about it."

"Are you sure you want to do this?" Daniel asked.

No! I want to stay here with you! If only there weren't other voices speaking in Kara's head: her mother's, warning her to be careful of others' feelings; her mother-in-law's, telling her that such a stupid girl and her baby were sure to be a burden; and, most of all, Ed Riley's, scolding her for endangering Daniel's career.

"I want to do what's best for everyone," she said.

"It makes no difference to you personally whether you stay with me or go to L.A.?" he asked.

"I want to do what's best for Dorima," Kara clarified. "She needs to be with...family."

Daniel scowled. She quailed at this sign of his dislike for her baby. If he couldn't accept her daughter as part of his family, how could they shape a future together?

"Thank you for giving me a straight answer." For a moment, she thought he might add something more. Then, with a nod to her and Leila, he strode out of the room.

Leila gave a low whistle. "Boy, is he uptight! I can see why you want to get away."

"I never said that." Kara hoped her cousin wasn't going to make a habit of putting words in her mouth.

"Whatever. You look tired." Leila adjusted the window blinds to reduce the light. "Get some sleep."

"Thank you for coming." Kara knew she should be glad her cousin was here, but all she could think about was how upset Daniel had appeared.

She was glad when the nursery attendant brought Dorima. lding the baby close and tending to her soothed some o

Kara's anxiety. A child, however, was no substitute for a man she could talk to and share her heart with. To her sorrow, it appeared that she couldn't have both.

HE SHOULD HAVE KNOWN better. In spite of all the warning signs, in spite of his own well-developed sense of logic, Daniel had allowed wishful thinking to get the better of him.

He didn't blame Kara. She'd never made any secret of the fact that her daughter's well-being was her first concern and that she'd married him because of it. He'd simply allowed himself to get distracted by matters that obviously meant more to him than to her.

Such as how good it felt to be with her. Such as the fact that, for the first time since he was a child, his heart lifted the moment he stepped through the door of his home.

Now, when he entered from the garage into the side hallway by the kitchen, all he found was echoing emptiness. No, that wasn't quite true. This was much worse than emptiness, Daniel discovered as he carried his briefcase into the kitchen.

Everywhere, little touches reminded him of Kara: a small framed print of Mount Fuji on the wall, freshly pressed place mats on the kitchen table, and the tea set displayed on the counter, a stinging reminder of the illusory happiness of their wedding.

All along, he'd believed Kara was the vulnerable one. He'd misinterpreted her penchant for creating beauty as revealing a special tenderness toward him where none existed. He hadn't recognized how thoroughly she'd bypassed his defenses until it was too late.

No, not too late. His defenses had sprung back full force. Daniel doubted they would ever come down again.

He spent the next few hours trying to work on contracts and achieving very little because of his agitated state of mind. By the time six o'clock rolled around, he was starving and more than a little frustrated.

He yanked open the refrigerator door. Great. It was full of

vegetables, sushi and seafood. Kara must have intended to prepare these for him, and he'd have relished every mouthful.

Now he couldn't bring himself to touch any of it. It was a relief when he came across a pizza in the freezer. Daniel ripped off the packaging and stuck the thing in the microwave oven.

When the doorbell rang, he nearly didn't answer, since it had to be a salesman or someone seeking the former owner. A second, insistent ring changed his mind, and grumpily he went to see who was pestering him.

A thin, red-haired man in a suit gazed at him expectantly from the porch. After a beat, Daniel's memory clicked into place. He'd met Ed Riley twice at bar-association meetings, in addition to having talked to him on the phone about Kara.

"Hello." He struggled to marshal his social skills and mask his inner turmoil. "What brings you here?"

"I tried to reach you at the office, but they told me you were working from home," Ed said. "I live in the area, so dropped by."

"Come in." With an effort at courtesy, Daniel stepped back to usher him inside, although he was in no mood for conversation. "What's up?"

"I tried to call you yesterday and got hold of your wife instead." Ed shifted by him, his quick gaze taking in the nearly empty living room. "I'm glad to see you folks don't believe in clutter."

"Japanese people appreciate simplicity." So did Daniel. Of course, he wasn't going to be living with a Japanese woman any longer, so it hardly mattered, he reminded himself. "Whatever you and Kara discussed, she didn't have time to tell me. She gave birth yesterday."

"Congratulations, if that's appropriate." The immigration attorney wasted no further time on pleasantries. "The reason I'm here, frankly, is that I owe you and your wife an apology."

"Why is that?" Daniel was still having a hard time being more than minimally polite.

The man gave an embarrassed shrug. "I figured out you had a green-card marriage and I read your wife the riot act."

A glimmer of light shone in the darkness. Here might be a clue to Kara's decision to go behind his back and arrange to live with her cousin. Was it possible she hadn't been so indifferent to his feelings after all? "What exactly did you say?"

"Pretty much what I told you when we talked earlier. That she has to leave the country to get a visa."

"She already knows that." Daniel had mentioned it himself.

"I also told her she was likely to ruin your career and that she ought to give you an annulment and let you off the hook," Ed admitted.

The brutality of the man's approach took Daniel aback. His words must have hit Kara like a slap in the face. "You had no right to say that."

"I agree," the other attorney said. "It was none of my business. Furthermore, my timing was lousy. A woman about to give birth is in no shape to make that kind of decision. I hope I haven't caused any problems."

Daniel frowned. "She decided she should move in with her cousin from Los Angeles. Maybe she believes she's doing me a favor."

"Really?" Ed looked uneasy. "I'm afraid I might be to blame, though at the time, I didn't think she was buying it."

"Why not? What did she say?" Afraid he might be grasping at straws, Daniel was determined to get all the facts before reaching a conclusion.

Ed grimaced. "She accused me of being jealous of your happiness. Also, as I recall, she said I was mean and was picking on her because I hated the whole world. Or words to that effect."

Daniel grinned. "You must have really ticked her off."

"I have to say, she's got guts. I can understand what you see in her."

"You mean you're not offended at being accused of out-grinching the Grinch?" Daniel asked.

"She's not the first woman to mention that I might be a touch insensitive." The other man ducked his head. "Usually, I don't own up to it, but the way she lit into me shook me up a little. I hope she's not still angry."

"I'm sure she'll get over it." *Although I'm not sure I will,* Daniel mused, uncertain what to make of this new information.

"Please extend my apologies," Ed told him. "If there's any way I can help with the visa thing, I'd be glad to."

"I appreciate that, and I'll let her know." Daniel extended his hand.

Ed shook it heartily. "Welcome to the neighborhood."

"Thanks."

After his visitor left, Daniel remembered the pizza. In the microwave, the crust didn't get crisp, but otherwise it might have tasted all right if he'd had more of an appetite.

At least he'd found a possible motivation for Kara's decision to summon her gung-ho cousin. Of course, just because Ed had jump-started her departure didn't mean she hadn't been planning to leave, anyway. Daniel was reluctant to go running back to the hospital until he'd deliberated further.

Was a real marriage even possible between two people from such different backgrounds, who'd married only for pragmatic reasons? It especially troubled him that Kara had made the decision to leave without consulting him.

It reminded him of his mother's betrayal. He didn't want to have to live with the anxiety that his wife, too, might be capable of running out on him at any time.

One thing Daniel knew: if he couldn't trust Kara's loyalty absolutely, he was better off saying goodbye to her now.

CHAPTER SIXTEEN

HOPING HIS INNER CONFLICT would resolve itself while he worked, Daniel unloaded a box of CDs and DVDs and alphabetized them on racks in the family room. When that was done, he positioned his speakers and tested them from all angles.

He reconsidered his discussion with Ed but drew no new conclusions. When last night's conversation with his father resurfaced, however, a line jumped out at him. *A man can't hold on to a woman if she really wants to go.* That was a concession, since Vernon had always contended that he could have persuaded Renée to stick around if she'd only given him a chance.

She'd packed her bags and sneaked away while her husband was working and her son was at school, leaving a note for each of them. Daniel had never kidded himself that he might have changed her mind, despite her written apology and assurances that she loved him. Her protestations had rung hollow to him then and still did.

She'd wanted to go, all right. He was glad that at least his father had come to terms with that. But what had Vernon meant by his other startling remark? *Let's just say that what went wrong wasn't entirely your mother's fault.*

The comment had gone right by Daniel earlier, but now it stood out as if his father had shouted it. Vernon had never before had anything positive to say about his mother, certainly nothing that would justify her actions.

If her departure hadn't been entirely her fault, that must

mean Vernon believed he'd contributed to the problem. But how? For some reason, it seemed important to find out.

It was nearly seven o'clock, which made it not quite nine in Chicago. Daniel sat down and dialed the number.

When his father answered, he didn't sound surprised to hear his son's voice. "I figured you might be curious about some of the things I said, once they had a chance to sink in."

"You seem to have a new attitude toward Mom," Daniel said. "Has something changed?"

"I'm not excusing what she did," his father warned.

"Understood," Daniel said. "Now, what's going on?"

"About a year ago, I started dating a woman I met through friends," his father said. "She's a high-school principal, a lot more assertive than Renée ever was. I guess she opened my eyes to a few things."

"Such as?" Daniel settled onto the couch. Over the years, his father had occasionally mentioned that he dated, but until now, none of the women had made a strong impression as far as Daniel knew.

His father made a humphing noise, which meant he was addressing a difficult topic. "I don't know if you recall, but at one point your mother wanted to start a catering business."

"She mentioned it a few times and then she dropped it."

"She didn't drop it. I insisted that she give it up." Vernon cleared his throat again. "I told her it would reflect badly on me to have my wife serving other people. The truth was, I wanted her world to revolve around me. It's what my friend Mary would call a control issue."

"You couldn't force her to stay home," Daniel pointed out.

"No, but she wasn't an aggressive person," Vernon said. "She didn't like fighting and I wasn't about to back down. I assumed it was my right to boss my family around because I was earning the money."

"I thought she left because of...you know." His mother's second husband had been a forbidden subject for so long that even now, Daniel hated to bring it up.

"She did run off with you-know, all right," his father said.

She moved to Denver with him and started a catering busi-
ess there. After what I've learned from Mary, I'm beginning
o think Renée left me less for another man than so she could
ve her own life.''

Daniel couldn't dismiss years of pain and resentment so
asily. ''Why didn't she try to get custody of me? Why didn't
he visit more?''

His father sighed. ''Son, I was pretty darn vindictive. You
elonged to me and I believed she belonged to me, too. I'd
ever have raised a hand against her, but that doesn't mean I
ouldn't have done everything I could to make her look bad
a court. Don't forget that we lawyers have an advantage
hen it comes to getting a divorce.''

Instinctively, Daniel knew that Kara would never give up
er child that easily. She would fight to her dying breath with
passion he deeply admired. But his mother wasn't as strong,
nd he supposed she'd probably paid almost as heavy a price
or that as he had.

''Mom wants me to visit her more often,'' he said. ''I've
een avoiding it. I figure it's too late to make up for lost time,
nd I guess I never got over the way she ran out on me.''

''Mind you, I'm not taking all the blame on myself,'' Ver-
on replied. ''Renée hurt you and me both. She was too pas-
ve, and I suppose that's something she's had to deal with
ver the years. Try not to hold grudges, son. It poisons the
ell. If I'd let go of my anger sooner, I might have remarried
ears ago.''

Daniel considered mentioning his difficulties with Kara, but
ecided there was no point involving his father. He could
olve his own problems.

''Thanks for leveling with me,'' he said. ''I know it doesn't
ome easily.''

''Don't expect this to be a regular thing,'' Vernon warned.
I'm not going to turn all touchy-feely just because I have a
rlfriend.''

''When do I get to meet her?'' Daniel asked.

''I'll get back to you on that one,'' his father promised.

"One thing I've learned is not to make commitments for Mary without consulting her first."

"Point taken."

After they rang off, Daniel reread his mother's last e-mail. Having recently celebrated her fifty-fifth birthday and watched her daughter enter high school, she'd become increasingly aware of how fast life was going by. She knew she couldn't undo what she'd done, but she hoped he'd be willing to meet her halfway.

Into Daniel's mind came the faces of aunts and uncles and cousins he'd never forgotten. He would really enjoy seeing them again this summer.

It would be even more fun if he had a wife and daughter to introduce to them. Especially if that wife was Kara.

He couldn't answer his mother yet, because he didn't know what to say. One thing he did know: relationships were a lot more complicated than he'd realized.

Maybe, like his parents, he and Kara had both made mistakes. Gazing from the family room into the kitchen, Daniel remembered how much he'd enjoyed the sight of Kara settling into their home. He could swear she'd been happy, too.

After talking to Ed, he no longer believed she'd simply tired of him and decided to move on. Her motive might have been to protect him.

As for himself, Daniel could see that he'd been afraid all along of losing her the way he'd lost his mother. He hadn't understood why the prospect of Kara working made him so uncomfortable, but now he did. For her to teach at Forrester Square meant that she would have a world that belonged to her, apart from the one she shared with him. It meant letting go of her every morning and trusting that she would always choose to return.

Daniel pictured her as she'd crossed the bridge in the Matsubas' garden, looking so charming and fresh he'd wanted to run to her. He remembered with a visceral tightening how joyously she'd joined into their lovemaking.

At the age of fourteen, he'd learned that love could hurt

worse than anything. At the age of thirty, he was beginning to understand that love was worth the risk.

Now he had to figure out what to do about it.

THURSDAY MORNING, the nurse told Kara she was going to be discharged by noon. The only response Kara could give was a silent nod.

When she left Japan, she hadn't worried too much about what lay ahead because of the certainty that she belonged in her grandfather's homeland. At every step, she'd let her instincts guide her, and until now they'd served her well.

Suddenly she didn't know which way to turn. She loved Daniel. The emotion had caught her off guard, so powerful and life-changing that she couldn't imagine living without it.

Yet her first duty, and a part of her soul that refused to be denied, belonged to her daughter. And close behind that came her obligation to avoid bringing disgrace and suffering on the man who'd extended himself to help her. For both those reasons, she had to leave.

It was a relief when Leila phoned to say she wouldn't be arriving for another hour. Due to an emergency at work, she was telecommuting from the hotel room via her laptop.

"No hurry," Kara said.

"Is Daniel taking you back to his place when they discharge you?" Leila asked. "I talked to the doctor yesterday and he recommended you wait a few days before flying with the baby."

"I guess so." If she couldn't join Daniel, Kara supposed she could stay with the Matsubas once again, although she already owed them more than she could ever repay.

Her mind kept replaying the same themes. If only Daniel understood how important it was for him to accept Dorima! And surely he knew as well as Ed Riley the dangers their marriage posed for him. Yet he'd seemed angry yesterday when he'd learned she was going to live in L.A.

Kara had hinted as strongly as possible that she was only

trying to do what was right. If Daniel were Japanese, he'd have read between the lines. Perhaps he hadn't wanted to.

Or perhaps he didn't know how.

She rolled her head on the pillow and gazed toward the mass of flowers adorning her windowsill. A Japanese arrangement would be spare, with each delicate branch suggesting a world of meaning. Westerners did things differently. If they had something to say, they poured it out. Their words, like their bouquets, overflowed.

If she hoped to learn what was in Daniel's heart, she had to tell him directly what was wrong. The prospect made her breath squeeze in her chest. It was terrifying to contemplate standing up to Daniel. She might anger him and drive him away forever.

But if she didn't try, she had no chance of making a new beginning. And that was what they needed: to start over not as attorney and client, but as man and woman.

Kara closed her eyes and prayed for courage.

DANIEL STEELED HIMSELF before entering the hospital room. He wasn't looking forward to ousting Leila. Mercifully, when he stepped inside, there was no sign of her.

Kara lay as if sleeping, but he knew her well enough by now to note the tension around her mouth. She must be aware of his presence, yet for some reason she didn't acknowledge him.

Was she really so eager to leave? A boyish voice deep inside, the one still healing from his mother's betrayal, warned that if she cared for him so little, there was no hope of reconciliation.

Daniel brushed it aside. He wasn't an adolescent, he was Kara's husband. If there was a way to win her over, he intended to find it.

"Good morning," he said.

Her eyelids fluttered upward and her face tilted toward him. In her expression, he read both wariness and resolve. The question was, what was she resolved to do?

Daniel sat on the edge of the bed. "I've been turning a lot of things over in my mind," he said.

"Me, too." She folded her arms across her chest.

"Do you want to go first?" Absently, he reached for her hand and traced the birdlike curves on her gold ring and wished he'd bought a matching one for himself. Perhaps he would do that, if things worked out.

"You can start," Kara said.

"This is hard," he said. "I'm not good at conveying my feelings."

"You're a lawyer," she said. "Pretend you're arguing a case in court."

"I don't usually go to court." Daniel hated to admit it, since he suspected Kara nursed a romantic image of his profession from the movies. "I'm not the theatrical type. That's part of the reason I chose corporate law."

"You don't point your finger at people and tell them they're criminals?" Kara asked.

"Definitely not."

"And you wouldn't do it to me, either?"

"Of course not!" What in heaven's name was running through her mind? Daniel wondered.

"Good!" Scooting into a sitting position, Kara clasped her knees. "At least I can be sure my husband isn't going to prosecute me."

"What would I prosecute you for?" he asked, puzzled.

She averted her eyes. "I'll tell you later. You go first."

Daniel took a deep breath. He'd rehearsed what to say next, and it was simple. *I love you and I want you to be my wife for real.* Now that he sat facing her, however, the words refused to come. Old hurts ran too deep. He had to lead up to it gradually.

"How did you find Leila?" he asked. "It seems like she appeared out of nowhere."

"Hannah told me about the detective who helped unite her and Jack," she said. "She offered to have him search his database for me."

"When did he find her?" Daniel asked.

"A week ago."

"You didn't say anything to me." He tried to keep an accusing note from his voice. He'd promised he wasn't going to cross-examine Kara.

"I wasn't sure I wanted to call her." She bit her lip.

"But eventually you did. Why?"

"I…" She shot him an anguished look. It dawned on him that she was struggling as hard as he was, maybe harder, to put her feelings into words. Suddenly Daniel found it easier to talk.

"It wouldn't have something to do with a know-it-all named Ed Riley, would it?" he asked.

She sighed. "Yes. How did you know?"

A weight lifted from Daniel's spirits. Kara hadn't simply grown tired of him and found an opportunity that suited her better. "He came by the house yesterday to apologize. He knew he was out of line with you."

"But he was right!" Kara said. "You risked your future for me. I can't let you lose your law license."

Quietly, Daniel said, "I won't lose my license if we follow my plan." He cupped her hand in his. "My plan is that we make it a real marriage."

Kara blinked at him for several seconds. "A real marriage?" she repeated.

"The kind we don't have to pretend is real, because it is," he said.

"How would we do that?" She appeared to be having trouble grasping what he meant.

"It might take a while to accomplish." Daniel lifted her palm to his cheek. "We ought to get started right away. Let's see. When you get home, we could cook dinner together and talk about all the things we enjoy."

"We've done that," Kara said.

"The next step would be to move into a house and organize it together," he went on, determined to weave his fondest memories into this make-believe plan.

"But we already—"

"I think we ought to position the bed north-south for good luck, don't you? Then we should make love on it. Several times, if possible."

"We did that, too." A line formed on Kara's forehead.

"Did I mention having a tea ceremony and consulting a friend about good *feng shui?*"

"You're making fun!" She pulled her hand free.

"No," he said. "Kara, I know our marriage was supposed to be in name only, but it changed, little by little and day by day. Without our recognizing it, it turned into the permanent, forever-and-a-day kind of marriage. That means you don't have to worry about hurting my career, because we're not pretending."

She stared at him. Daniel wished she would throw her arms around him and shout her approval.

"I don't know," she said after a pause.

He reminded himself not to push her. Either she came to him of her own free will or there was no hope. "What don't you know?"

"I don't understand this thing. Love." Kara said the word as if it stung.

"You mean you don't know how you feel about me?" Daniel asked, his throat tightening. Maybe he'd hoped for too much.

She closed one fist over her heart. "I know I love you. But it's sharp. It's like there's a rock stuck in here."

She loved him. That was what mattered. He was no longer afraid to pour out what he felt.

"Love is supposed to be like a rock," Daniel said. "A rock that lasts forever, a rock you can hang on to when the rest of your life turns into a raging torrent."

"Do you feel this way, too?" she asked shyly.

"All the time. In my whole body." Daniel reached for her hand again, and this time she didn't pull away. "It's so much a part of me that I can't imagine how I ever lived without it."

"Me, too," Kara murmured. "No. No, I can't stay with you. I can't."

Too stunned to react, he let the silence lengthen. He couldn't simply leave things this way, though, not after she'd said she loved him. Although the words stalled in his throat, he forced them out. "Tell me why not."

"Dorima." The name emerged in a whisper.

This was unexpected. "What about her?"

"I see how you feel." Tears sparkled in Kara's eyes. "You don't want to hold her. You don't like her, because she reminds you that I was married to Hiro." She stared toward the flowers, as if looking at him hurt too much.

"I knew when we met that you were pregnant," Daniel said, trying to sort out exactly what was wrong.

"We weren't married then," she said. "Now I'm your wife and I have a daughter, but you don't want to be her father."

"Yes, I do," he protested.

"You don't act like it."

"I don't know how a father acts," Daniel confessed. "I've never been around a tiny infant like that. Maybe I don't have the right instincts."

"Because she's not your child," Kara said sadly. "Because she's Hiro's. You're angry with me because I was married to another man before and because I had his baby, instead of yours."

"Is that what you mean by me prosecuting you?" he asked. "You think I want to punish you because of Hiro?"

She gave a couple of tight nods.

No wonder she'd withdrawn from him! "I respect the memory of your late husband," Daniel told her. "I'm glad that a part of him lives on. Otherwise, as far as I'm concerned, Dorima belongs only to herself."

"She needs more than that," Kara said. "She needs for you to love her. Maybe that isn't possible."

Daniel hoped desperately that she was wrong. "I think it is. It's just that I don't know anything about babies. I don't even know which end the diaper goes on."

"Everybody knows that!" A smile flashed and disappeared.

"Dorima's not only your baby, she's mine, too," he said. "You may have to be patient and teach me what to do, but I promise to be a good student. I even bought a book about parenting last night."

"Really?" The smile returned, and stayed.

"Really. I read the whole first section. But I'm still going to need a gifted teacher."

"It appears we are about to start the lesson." Kara nodded toward the hallway, from which issued the murmur of wheels gliding over the floor. "They're bringing the babies to the rooms."

Although the prospect of picking up Dorima made Daniel want to squirm, he squared his shoulders. He was going to hold this baby and make a fuss over her for Kara's sake And, he supposed, for his own.

Moments later, a nursery attendant wheeled in the bassinet and positioned it next to the bed. After checking Kara's wristband to make sure the IDs matched, she went about her duties.

Daniel studied the infant. With her straight black hair and ebony eyes, Dorima resembled an animated doll. She was every bit as cute as he'd thought yesterday, but a lot more intimidating now that he had to actually take charge of the situation.

"How do I hold her?" he asked.

"Make sure to support her head. Her neck muscles aren't strong yet." Perching on the edge of the bed, Kara demonstrated by picking up her daughter.

Gingerly, Daniel reached toward the infant. "What if she doesn't like me?"

"She'll spit acid in your eye and you'll die a horrible death," Kara joked.

Grinning, he slipped one hand behind Dorima's head and, cradling her in the crook of his other arm, hefted her against his chest. She seemed to weigh almost nothing.

The infant whimpered uncertainly. "She can tell I'm an amateur," he said.

"She can tell that you're ill at ease," Kara said. "Let her warm up to you. All little girls love their daddies."

It helped to think of Dorima as a little girl, not just a bundle of vulnerabilities. As he watched her blink sleepily, Daniel began to picture the future. Having spent almost no time with children, he had only the vaguest idea of what was to come—crooning lullabies, holding hands at the playground, a child clapping her hands at the sight of a Christmas tree—but he knew suddenly that he was going to enjoy having a daughter.

He bent and touched his nose to her downy cheek. The scents of powder and newness filled him. How was it possible that this perfectly formed, intelligent creature had lived all this time, unseen, inside Kara? And now here she lay, trusting him to protect and guide her as she grew.

It was a miracle.

The baby cooed softly. "She's not scared of me anymore," Daniel said wonderingly.

"She's a better teacher than I am," Kara said. "She's taught you all you need to know without a single word."

When he raised his head, he was startled to find a haze of moisture over his eyes. "I guess we're going to have to teach each other a lot of things over the years."

Dorima let out a wail. Daniel's heart constricted. "I thought we were getting along so well. What's wrong?"

"She's hungry. That's one department you can't handle right now." Kara reached out. Reluctantly, he eased the baby into her arms.

She rearranged her clothing and held Dorima to her breast. Fascinated, Daniel watched a process both age-old and, to him, brand-new.

"I really do love you," he told Kara as she nursed the infant. "You know, I asked you to stay and be my real wife, but you haven't given me an answer. Is there anything else bothering you?"

"No," she said. "Yes."

He opened his mouth to guess at the problem. Despite having Dorima balanced in her arms, Kara managed to wave one hand at him. "What?" he said.

"Let me do this."

"Do what?"

"The hard part," she said. "Spilling it out."

It touched him to discover that she was willing to work at this relationship as hard as he was. "Go ahead."

Kara's chest rose and fell as she breathed. Dorima snuggled contentedly against her. "There is something I want to do that you won't like."

"Try me." Daniel had a good idea what it was, but his wife had a right to speak for herself.

"Teach." The word slipped out under Kara's breath. She stopped in alarm, as if she'd said something incendiary. "It's not important. I want to do what makes you happy."

"Kara!"

"What?"

"We need some new ground rules," Daniel said. "You don't have to tiptoe around to avoid offending me. No more trying to second-guess each other. From now on, we say what we mean, the way you just did."

Kara's chin lifted. "I like those ground rules."

"Tell me again, only you don't have to whisper," he said.

"Teach," she repeated more forcefully.

"Teach where?"

"You know where!"

"I'm not going to fill in the blanks for you. That falls under the category of second-guessing."

"I want to teach at Forrester Square Day Care," Kara told him. "Yes? No?"

"You have the right to do what you want with your time," Daniel said. "Of course you can teach."

"If we both insist on doing whatever we want, it might hurt our marriage," she warned. "We are no longer two separate people."

"That's true." Leaning forward, Daniel encircled her and

Dorima in a hug. "We're a family. A family joins together to make major decisions. Fortunately, we both agree on this one."

"You don't mind if I teach?"

"I'd be very proud of you," he said. "I'm sorry I gave you a hard time. You know something funny? I was afraid of losing you, that's all."

Kara planted a kiss on the corner of his mouth. "You won't lose me. Not ever."

"You're sure?" he couldn't help asking.

"Very sure." She leaned her head on his shoulder. "You know the rock in my chest? It's glowing like a warm coal."

Inside him, the walls that had guarded his emotions crumbled into dust. Beyond them, he glimpsed an emerald vista of tomorrows spent with the woman he loved.

Kara's shoulder bumped something in his jacket pocket. "What's that?"

He'd almost forgotten. "I brought you a gift," Daniel said.

"You don't have to do that." Despite her demurral, she sounded pleased.

From his pocket, he retrieved a jeweler's box. He was glad now that he'd taken the time to stop at the store this morning, despite his eagerness to reach the hospital.

Since Kara was holding the baby, he helped her open the velvet box. "Oh! It's beautiful!" she said.

Daniel lifted the slender gold necklace from its silken nest. When he fastened the chain around his wife's neck, two golden flying birds, their shapes reminiscent of her wedding ring, soared against her throat. "The jeweler said they were swallows, but I think they're cranes. Aren't those supposed to be lucky?"

"Very lucky." After easing the baby into the bassinet, Kara touched the necklace lovingly. "In Japan, cranes bond for life."

"Just like us," Daniel said.

"Just like us," his wife repeated. Then she flung her arms around him and nearly knocked him off the bed. When Leila

entered a few minutes later, she stared at the pair's embrace
and then, smiling, beat a hasty retreat.

For once, apparently, no words were necessary, not even
for Kara's talkative cousin.

CHAPTER SEVENTEEN

AS SOON AS the doctor declared Kara and Dorima fit to fly, Daniel bought three airline tickets and took them to Japan. The law partners were gracious about this delayed honeymoon, especially when he explained his wife's need to secure a visa.

He was dazzled by the almost overwhelming crowds and vitality of Tokyo, where they spent a few days, and impressed with the beauties of Hokkaido. Outside Sapporo spread a wilderness of the sort he associated more with North America than Japan—forests of pine, birch and oak, wild rivers and towering mountains. Kara's father, an executive with a tour company, escorted them around the countryside.

When a pair of cranes launched themselves into the sky right in front of them, Kara clasped Daniel's hand while her free hand closed around the pendant at her throat. "A lucky sign," she told him earnestly.

At home, Kara's parents, brother and sister-in-law made him welcome and proclaimed that they were thrilled with the gifts Daniel and Kara had brought, bowls and vases made by some of the best-known Seattle artists. He wished he could speak Japanese, instead of relying on Kara's translations and her father's and brother's business-oriented English, but even so, Daniel could see that her family wasn't given to heart-to-heart discussions.

"I don't feel like I really know them," he whispered to Kara one night when they were alone. "How long does it take before they relax with me?"

She simply shook her head. "You have to learn to read between the lines."

"At this point, I can't even read the lines, let alone what lies between them," he said. "At least I'm becoming an expert on bowing." He'd discovered that the Japanese bowed at almost every occasion.

"You bow well for such a tall person," Kara said. "Fortunately, as an attorney, you are an important person, so you don't have to bow very low."

"Is that a polite way of saying my technique still needs work?"

"See?" she teased. "You *are* good at reading between the lines!"

Everyone made a fuss over Dorima, and no one referred to the unusual circumstances of her birth in a foreign land. The baby basked in the attention, or so it seemed to Daniel, who could read his daughter's moods much more easily than those of his in-laws.

The most mystifying part of the trip to him, but perhaps the most satisfying to Kara, was their obligatory visit to Hiro Tamaki's mother. Judging by what Kara had said about her, Daniel didn't know what sort of reception to expect.

"She used to tell me I was stupid," his wife explained on the drive over. Although Mrs. Tamaki lived only a few miles from Kara's parents, apparently the families had almost no contact. "She expected me to wait on her and her friends like a servant and then go sit in the kitchen by myself. To her, everything I did was clumsy. She even told me my baby would be worthless, just like me."

It was hard to reconcile this unpleasant image with the smiling, bowing woman who welcomed them to her home. She plied them with refreshments and exclaimed happily over the baby. When she learned that Kara was to be a teacher in America, she beamed with pride, although it quickly became clear that she was mostly happy for her granddaughter's sake, because she was part of a prestigious family.

Afterward, Kara grinned all the way back to her parents'

house. "Of course she couldn't show her true emotions in
your presence," she told Daniel. "But I think she is also a
little impressed with my daughter. We're not so worthless,
after all!"

Best of all, Kara was able to secure a proper visa. It would
still be a while before the two of them could prove to the
immigration authorities that their marriage was genuine, but
in the meantime, Kara could reenter the United States without
problems, and Katherine had promised to help her obtain a
work permit.

By the time they left Japan, Daniel felt both admiration
toward his wife's homeland and relief that they had accomplished their mission. Now their life together could begin on
a fresh footing.

He had developed an appreciation for her favorite Japanese
word, *wa,* or harmony. He understood that before he met
Kara, his life had lacked that quality.

Now he had it in abundance, he reflected as the plane
droned its way across the skies above the Pacific Ocean. One
glance at his wife and daughter, and Daniel's spirits took wing
like a pair of cranes.

"I'M GOING THROUGH with it," Katherine said. "I've made
the appointment."

She sat opposite Kara in the Forrester Square Day Care
nurse's room, which was otherwise unoccupied at the moment. Kara was feeding Dorima while, across the hall, Alexandra kept an eye on Kara's seven little charges during
naptime.

For Kara's first day as a teacher, everything had gone remarkably well. Already, the faces of her seven toddlers were
each engraved on her heart. One little boy, Doug Jessup, had
delighted in acting as her helper all morning, perhaps because,
as she'd learned from reading his file, his mother had died
two years earlier. Kara had so much love to give him and the
others that she scarcely felt tired from keeping up with the
energetic youngsters.

"You mean with the sperm bank?" She'd been so busy these past few weeks that she'd scarcely given any thought to Katherine's plans to conceive a baby, she realized guiltily.

Her friend nodded. "I keep reminding myself that I'm almost thirty. If Mr. Right wanted to show up, he should have done it by now."

"You never know. He might appear out of nowhere when you least expect it."

Katherine shook her head ruefully. "Men appear out of nowhere, all right, but it doesn't mean anything."

The implication fascinated Kara. "Are you talking about someone in particular?"

Katherine's cheeks flushed. "A guy caught my attention the other day, mostly because he looked so out of place around here. A rugged-looking man with a beard. He's big, about six-four with dark hair parted in the middle. Sound familiar?"

"I'm afraid not. Do you think he might be dangerous?"

"I doubt it." Her friend gave her an embarrassed smile. "He's handsome, in an outdoorsy way. Not my type, though." The day-care owner reached over to pat Dorima's shoulder as the baby gurgled.

"Oh, my goodness! She has air in her tummy." Gently, Kara laid the baby across her lap, where she'd placed a towel, and patted her until she burped. "Well, a baby is a blessing, no matter what you have to go through to get one. Speaking of babies, how's Hannah?" She'd been concerned to learn when she arrived at work this morning that her friend was still staying home.

"She's fine, except for some morning sickness." Katherine tactfully averted her eyes as Kara lifted Dorima to her other breast. "She's decided to play it safe and stay home a little longer, though. I think mostly she wants to spend more time with Adam before the baby comes."

"It's lucky that she can do the bookkeeping at home," Kara said.

The two friends chatted until the baby finished nursing.

Then Kara returned Dorima to the infants' room, under Julia's watchful eye, and reclaimed her own classroom.

The children kept her hopping for the rest of the day. Before she knew it, it was time to return them to their parents, claim her own daughter and go outside to meet Daniel. He'd promised to pick her up so they could talk on the way home.

The instant she saw him at the wheel of the car, Kara felt as if she were already home. From the light in his eyes when he spotted her, she could tell he felt the same way.

It pleased her that evening when he cooked dinner on a barbecue he'd bought for the patio. The air filled with a mouthwatering aroma as he prepared everything from vegetables to chicken right on the grill. To her amusement, Daniel wore a white apron and chef's hat that his mother had sent along with a set of barbecue utensils.

Renée had been thrilled to learn of their marriage and of Dorima's birth, and overjoyed when Daniel promised that they would join her this summer for the annual family reunion. After he talked to his mother on the phone, Kara had noticed a new lightness to his stride. She was glad these two had reconciled.

They were going to be surrounded by plenty of relatives in the months to come, she thought with pleasure. Her Los Angeles cousins would be flying up for a weekend next month, while Daniel's father was arriving a few weeks after that. He'd explained apologetically that he wished he could come sooner, but after his recent fishing expedition, he couldn't take more time off for a while. Also, he preferred to wait until school ended so his lady friend could accompany him.

Dinner, when Daniel transferred it onto a platter and carried it inside, was delicious. Despite the warming weather, he and Kara hadn't had time to buy patio furniture yet, so they ate in the kitchen. Their conversation felt easy and natural, reminding her that, even in a short time, the two of them had developed a shared history of experiences.

He's really my husband, she thought as she drank in the sight of Daniel's animated face and dark, melting eyes. *And he loves me.* The realization soothed away the slight soreness she experienced from lifting children several times a day.

After dinner, when she'd finished nursing Dorima, Daniel rocked the baby in his arms and crooned to her. She went right to sleep and didn't budge when he laid her in the bassinet they'd bought. Although Dorima would occasionally sleep with them, they'd agreed it was important that they have time together as a couple, too.

"How tired are you?" Daniel murmured as they stood gazing at their daughter.

A tickling sensation ran up her spine. "Not tired at all," she whispered back.

"That's too bad."

She frowned at him. "What do you mean, it's too bad?"

"If you were tired, we might relax in a hot bath," Daniel said.

Kara remembered the oversize tub in the master bathroom. Since they moved in, she'd been so busy she'd only taken showers in the adjacent stall. "I was being polite. The truth is, I'm so worn-out we'll probably have to soak for hours."

A slowly spreading grin warmed her inside and out. "Let's get started."

To her surprise, he produced candles and turned off the bathroom light. While the tub filled with hot water, they stood barefoot on the fluffy rug and undressed each other. Enjoying the play of shadow and light over Daniel's muscular torso, Kara stroked his masculinity with her hand until he strained against her.

"Let's not go too fast." Arms around her, Daniel breathed deeply against her hair. "I want to enjoy you."

Kara experienced a moment of self-consciousness when he held her away from him and examined her naked body. Being viewed without the familiar bulge gave her a sense of incompleteness.

"You're lovely," Daniel said. "Absolutely perfect."

Her breasts, enlarged from nursing, seemed to swell beneath his gaze. When he knelt and blew lightly over her skin, it was as if he were lighting candles inside her.

"I think we should go fast," Kara said. "Otherwise I might burst."

He turned off the running water. "We'll see."

In the tub, after he got in, Kara half floated above him, braced by her arms. As their legs tangled, he probed her mouth with his. Lost in the kiss, she let the water carry her against his chest.

Impressions drifted through her: the flickering light, the sweet indulgence of skin against skin, the anticipation reflected in her husband's face. With her stomach flat, they shaped themselves to each other with new ease.

When Kara slid onto his shaft, she could feel Daniel's joy almost as intensely as her own. Every groan, every twist resonated. She moved rhythmically and lost herself in the pleasurable increase of tension.

Catching her hips, Daniel thrust into her. Kara soared outside herself on an eruption of sheer bliss. Their cries merged, and for a flash she believed they had become one pure, shimmering entity.

She came back to herself lying against his chest, letting the water rinse away their heat. "What just happened?"

"I think we entered another dimension," Daniel said. "I vote we go there often."

"As often as possible," she agreed.

When the water began to cool, they emerged and dried each other with soft towels. Kara wished she could put her emotions into words, but the best she could manage was, "I love you."

"I love you, too." Her husband enfolded her in his arms.

In bed, as drowsiness crept over her, Kara realized something. Although she'd always known she belonged in America, until now she hadn't understood that it was because this was the land of the man she had been destined to love.

She wanted to tell Daniel, but she knew from his regular breathing that it was too late to disturb him tonight. It didn't matter. They would be waking up together tomorrow morning and every morning after that.

She would have plenty of time to share with him all the beautiful things that had come to dwell in her heart.

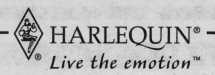
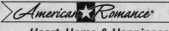

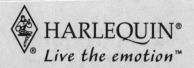

HARLEQUIN®
INTRIGUE®

BREATHTAKING ROMANTIC SUSPENSE

Shared dangers and passions lead to electrifying romance and heart-stopping suspense!

Every month, you'll meet six new heroes who are guaranteed to make your spine tingle and your pulse pound. With them you'll enter into the exciting world of Harlequin Intrigue— where your life is on the line and so is your heart!

THAT'S INTRIGUE— ROMANTIC SUSPENSE AT ITS BEST!

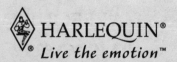

HARLEQUIN®
Live the emotion™

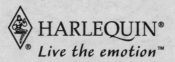

Harlequin® Historical
Historical Romantic Adventure!

Imagine a time of chivalrous knights and unconventional ladies, roguish rakes and impetuous heiresses, rugged cowboys and spirited frontierswomen— these rich and vivid tales will capture your imagination!

Harlequin Historical... they're too good to miss!